THE PINK

MARSHALL THORNTON

Published by Kenmore Books

Edited by Joan Martinelli

Cover design by Marshall Thornton

Images by 123rf stock

ISBN: 978-1-965306-12-3

First Edition

✾ Formatted with Vellum

ACKNOWLEDGMENTS

A big thank you to: Joan Martinelli, John Adams, Tina Greene Bevington, Danielle Wolff, Lemise Rory, Jennie Evenson, and Ben Thompson.

CHAPTER 1

*H*azy light cut through the elevated tracks and sliced the dust-thick air. The streets smelled of soot and horse manure, so much so that I had a habit of keeping a scented handkerchief in my pocket to hold below by nose. Breezes came off the lake attempting to freshen the air but were too weak to succeed.

Chicago was different then, on that morning, sometime in April. 1913. I have a clear memory of slouching unhappily beneath the Elevated on the corner of Fifth Avenue and Monroe. No one remembers Fifth Avenue; it's Wells Street now. In any case, that's where I was slouching. My mother always complained of my posture, telling me to straighten my back. I don't know why I slouched. I wasn't overly tall, so that wouldn't explain it. I might have felt that life was a dangerous thing and I ought to be ready to duck. That would have been wise, I suppose.

After a bit, I stood up straighter and stared anxiously at the entrance to a narrow, nine-story building wedged between two wider, taller brick siblings. The Pinkerton office. I had absolutely no desire to enter. And yet, I knew I was about to.

I'd caught glimpses of the upper portions of the building as I'd walked down the stairs from Quincy Station. The building's facade was a gray stone, and each floor had two or three windows in varying shapes. At the top, where I was expected, the windows were large half circles divided into pie-shaped panes. I took my watch out of my vest pocket and flipped it open. It was nine thirty-eight, though the watch ran a minute or two slow—or perhaps fast, I could never remember. Either way, I was nearly twenty minutes early.

The Elevated clattered by overhead and shook dust onto my shoulders. I brushed it off while thinking of the rumors I'd heard that the various lines were about to be consolidated into one. The El, as we've come to call it, had been under construction since I was a child, with different companies building new lines every few years. But then they would falter and fail and be combined. Finally, it was becoming one. It was a frustrating process, especially for those who rode it daily.

It might have been a Tuesday, a full week after my twenty-second birthday. I liked to think of myself as looking older than I was, assuming people mistook me for a mature householder, however, unless photographs lie, I looked younger than my age. My hair was blond, parted in the middle and oiled down neatly beneath my derby; my features even and appealing; my eyes nearly gray. In those same photographs, I must admit, I look uncomfortable, as though my skin was not tailored as well as my suit.

Coal black automobiles were parked at the curb, and a new one seemed to sputter along, coughing exhaust, every few minutes. Except for delivery wagons—which came and went as they pleased—horse-drawn carriages had been eclipsed in the Loop.

A newsboy called out headlines: "Connecticut ratifies Seventeenth Amendment! Wilson supports tariff!" But I barely paid attention. I had business to attend and a plan to concoct.

At the time, I lived with my mother in Hyde Park. Before they married, my father built her a two-story, clapboard house on Ellis Avenue below 54th Street. There was an apartment on both floors. Mother and I lived upstairs, while she rented out the first floor to an elderly brother and sister who augmented their small inheritance with piano lessons and embroidery, respectively. When you walked through the front door, you climbed a narrow, spiral staircase up to a small landing and our apartment, which had six miserly rooms filled with large, clumsy mahogany furniture: a parlor, a dining room, kitchen and three small bedrooms.

Angelica Wait, my mother, was in her late forties then and favored stiff, white shirtwaists with unfashionably full black skirts. Every day she wore her fading blonde hair in a severe chignon du cou, managing to never have a single hair out of place even during the dog days of summer. Most days she closed her starched collar with an amethyst broach. Her father had been in trade, operating a popular leather goods store on Lake Street. He had raised an attractive dowry, hoping to marry her off to one of the prominent families, a distant connection of the Palmers or an errant Nickerson. She, however, had other ideas.

In the summer of eighty-five, she met my father on a grip car. Aloysius Wait was a Pinkerton agent, employed at that time by the Calumet line to chase off pickpockets. When I could get her to tell the story, which was seldom, Mother said, "I thought your father was the rudest man I'd ever encountered. The way he stared at me. And derelict. He spent so much time staring at me, thieves could have made off with every last purse on that car."

Before she disembarked she gave him a piece of her mind, which made my father laugh—something that only infuriated her further. Though she wasn't so infuriated it prevented her from returning to the very same car the next day—even though she had no business downtown. They married a year later, against my grandfather's wishes. And without the dowry.

At the time, Pinkerton agents were paid well, and my father had lived frugally, so he was able to build the house on Ellis Avenue proving he would be able to take care of my mother without help. In fact, my grandfather withheld the increasingly large sum of money until my father and my older brother died of Russian flu in ninety-three when I was two years old. After that, my grandfather lavished money on my mother, though she barely noticed. Six months later, he died of consumption and Mother inherited his entire fortune, which she entrusted to a stockbroker somewhere on LaSalle Street.

We had just finished an elaborate birthday dinner, which she and the Polish girl, who came in during the week, had spent the day preparing. Mother, or rather the Polish girl, served me beef bouillon, veal roast with stuffing, mashed potatoes, succotash, creamed corn, cabbage salad and lemon sponge cake with whipped cream. All my favorites, Mother said, though they weren't. The menu had been featured in the *Chicago Examiner* just the week before.

"Well, darling, another year older. Now, I know you're waiting for your present, but I'm afraid we need to have a serious conversation first."

I did not relish those words. Mother tended toward serious conversations about temperance and suffrage; subjects I already knew far too much about. I nodded, wiping a tiny bit of whipped cream off my lip.

She hesitated, seeming almost embarrassed by what she

was about to say. Embarrassment was so far out of Mother's character that I was afraid for a moment. What terrible news was she about to impart on my birthday?

"If you've read the financial pages, I'm sure you've seen that the country is in unfortunate financial straits."

"The country *was* in unfortunate financial straits, Mother. Things have turned around."

"I suppose that's true, but *my* financial straits have not improved. In fact, they've somewhat deteriorated." She paused. I had the feeling she was waiting for me to say something, but I chose not to. "You see, Lewis, I'm afraid it's time you found employment."

Suddenly, the small room seemed smaller, and the hulking mahogany furniture appeared menacing.

"Employment? Are you teasing me?"

"I'm deadly serious." She frowned. A frown much harsher than anything she could say. "And if the idea of employment is that foreign—"

"But Mother, I have my studies to complete. After I'm finished, I'm sure I'll obtain an appropriate…"

"You'll have to postpone your studies. Perhaps in a year or two my situation will improve and you can continue. In the meantime, you need to contribute to the household expenses."

I was speechless. She reached out and covered my hand with hers. Hers was cold and dry.

"You've already earned a degree. Why can't one be enough?"

"I was invited to do research with Professor Everett."

"Yes, the young man who studies bumps."

"Mother, you're thinking of Phrenology. We're studying Physiognomy, which is similar, I grant you, but also quite different. I know people disregard its significance, which is the very reason to study it: to ascertain through rigorous scientific method if there's any truth to the idea that how we're shaped, how we look, determines or is determined by our characters. Specifically, and I think importantly, Josiah studies criminals attempting to confirm whether—"

"Yes, yes, you've told me this before."

I gave her a hard look. "What kind of position would you like me to get? Dry goods clerk? Chimneysweep? Stable boy?"

"Really Lewis, you're being overly dramatic. I've arranged an interview for you at the Pinkerton office downtown. You're to meet with John Cuthbert. He knew your father."

"How absurd," I said simply. "You want me to be a Pinkerton? Is that what you're saying? It barely makes sense."

"Well, if you have a better idea, I am happy to hear it."

"I'll talk to Josiah—er, Professor Everett. I might be able to secure a teaching position. There might not be anything until fall, but..."

"That won't do. Not at all. I wouldn't like to see you become like Professor Everett."

That sent a chill down my spine, but I was brave enough to ask, "What is wrong with Professor Everett?"

"He's bloodless and effete." A moment later, she said, "Posture, Lewis."

Utterly humiliated, I sat up straighter. It was then that she changed the subject by bringing out my birthday gift.

In a small, blue velvet box sat a gold signet ring. The letter W was carved in the center circle and on the sides were a wishbone, a four-leaf clover and a horseshoe all entwined. It was an extravagant gift and at odds with the conversation we'd just had.

"It's for luck," she said quietly. I glared at her until she added, "I picked it out before my difficulties became apparent."

I didn't believe her. Something had changed, but I

doubted she was having financial troubles. Josiah had come for dinner the week before. Mother had been gracious and charming... and false. I could see that now.

But it wasn't just Josiah she turned against... it was a life in academia. Inexplicably she'd snatched that away and was condemning me...

A Pinkerton! Her ideas of what that meant, mostly having to do with a romanticized idea of my father's time with them, were as misguided as her ideas of Josiah and my life in a world of thought.

She viewed the Pinkertons as heroic, though I couldn't see that a band of thugs and strikebreakers did anything remotely heroic. I knew she didn't believe in unions, but I was somewhat surprised that she was ready to sacrifice me to guard the wealth of some bloated robber baron.

I imagine she would have liked to see me put the ring on, but I simply closed the box and thanked her. I made my excuses and went to bed. That night, I slept poorly, too busy plotting ways to sabotage the interview so that Mother would be forced to support me until I could secure a teaching position.

But how could I accomplish it? Should I pose as an idiot? Or would it be better to play the lunatic? I could be rude, I supposed, but would that be enough? Of course, I wouldn't want Mr. Cuthbert to tell Mother I'd been stupid or mad or abrasive. It would be best for him to tell her that I was unfit by no fault of my own. That was the challenge. One I was sure I was up to.

Another glance at my watch told me it was now nine-fifty. Entering the Pinkerton building, I crossed the lobby and went straight to the elevator.

Even then I didn't care for elevators. I'd read too many stories of people falling down shafts or being cut in half when stepping out at precisely the wrong moment. I've never trusted them.

It seems to me illogical to enter what was basically a fancy crate on one floor and arrive moments later on another. I understood the engineering behind them, of course, the pulleys and the weights and all of that. Logically I know it's safe. For the most part.

Still, I avoided them whenever possible. But that morning I had no choice. I was hardly going to climb nine floors and arrive in a sweat. Politely, I asked the operator to take me to the ninth floor. He closed the brass gate and pushed the lever forward.

As we slowly creaked our way to the ninth floor, I attempted to collect my thoughts. I had decided to play the fool. I would present myself as dimwitted. Well, perhaps not completely dimwitted, just not smart enough to be a Pinkerton. I nearly laughed. How smart did you really need to be a Pinkerton roughneck? Perhaps I *would* need to play the dimwit.

When we reached the ninth floor, the attendant expertly brought the car to a stop. He opened the gate for me and, as I wished the man a good day, I stepped out onto the floor. A small area surrounded by a wooden banister acted as a sort of open lobby, while just beyond six young women clattered away at typewriters. They were all fashionably dressed in elaborate shirtwaists and long, tight skirts. Within the fenced-in area was a small desk, behind which sat a waifish girl of about seventeen. I told her I was there to see Mr. Cuthbert. She asked me to have a seat, then jumped up and made her way across the floor to the large office at the far end. Moments later, she was back to lead me there.

The office spanned the width of the floor and was dominated by the large crescent windows I'd looked up at just twenty minutes before. On one side of the room was an over-sized walnut desk with a matching credenza. In the center of the room sat a leather sofa and two chairs. Tucked against the far wall was a small desk where Mr. John Cuthbert sat reading what looked to be a report of some kind.

The girl said, "Mr. Lewis Wait," then left the room, closing the door behind her. I took off my derby and held it loosely in my hand, a little annoyed since the girl should have offered to take it.

After a moment, Mr. Cuthbert looked up from his report, rose, and stuck out his hand. "Mr. Wait. Your mother speaks highly of you."

As I shook his hand, which was smooth and warm, I said, "Mothers are expected to speak highly of their sons."

"True, but your mother is not a woman who does the expected."

The remark, which was insightful, made me wonder how well Mr. Cuthbert knew my mother. He was a small man with very pink skin and white tuffs of hair over his ears; otherwise, he was quite bald. He wore a pair of wire-rimmed glasses, which must not have been terribly effective as he squinted behind them. I heard the Elevated shuffle by several stories below us; it was a muffled sound, unexpectedly reassuring.

"Take a seat," he instructed, waving a hand in the direction of the sofa and chairs. I sat in the chair closest to the windows, while Mr. Cuthbert sat in the chair across from me. Neither of us wanted to be on the casual footing that sitting on the leather sofa would have suggested. I waited for him to say something.

"You've studied sociology with an emphasis on the criminal?"

"Yes, sir." It seemed unwise to say more than that. I also realized my plan had an obvious flaw: How was I to play a college-educated dimwit?

"That is, my undergraduate study was more general. My post-graduate study has been largely focused on the criminal."

"Physiognomy?"

I waited for him to add a derisive remark, but he didn't make one.

"Yes, physiognomy."

"You must be excited by the prospect of putting all you've learned into practice."

"Well, yes, yes that would be exciting."

To say otherwise would have been to lie outright and lying had not been part of my plan. Or rather, lying stupidly. I could not deny that applying my education would be exciting. I simply doubted I'd be able to do that with the Pinkerton Agency.

"Our company was founded in 1850 by Allan Pinkerton. In our time, we've guarded presidents, banks, railroads, all kinds of important individuals and objects. If it weren't for Allan Pinkerton and men like your father, the streets of Chicago wouldn't be safe for decent people."

I nodded. This was not new information. The praises of the Pinkertons had often been sung in my home, while their excesses scrupulously overlooked.

"William Pinkerton keeps his office here but travels extensively. His nephew has taken over the New York office, and that necessitates…" He reconsidered what he was saying. "None of that's important right now. Lewis—I may call you Lewis, mayn't I?"

"Yes, of course," I said. Even though he was a stranger to me, he was, oddly, a friend of the family.

"Well, Lewis, a Pinkerton man cannot be addicted to drink, smoking, card playing or slang. A Pinkerton detective does not accept bribes or rewards nor cases that might result in a scandal for our clients. Are you the sort of man who can live by these rules?"

I wanted to say I was not, that I was a thoroughly scurrilous individual unqualified to join his marvelous company, but not only would that be an obvious lie I would also have to face my mother's ire if I even hinted that I might drink or smoke to excess.

"Yes, I can live by those rules," I said with a dry mouth. I hoped there was some kind of entrance exam I could do poorly on, otherwise I was well on my way to becoming a Pinkerton.

"I knew your father," he said. "Good man."

"Yes, thank you. Mother said you knew him."

"Tragic business. He was a very brave man."

"I was a small child. I remember very little."

"You should be proud."

I was a confused. It didn't seem all that brave to die of the influenza. But then I decided Cuthbert must be referring to my father's behavior before he passed, his work with the Pinkertons. The exact nature of which I'd not been told.

"And now I have a test for you," he said, and I relaxed. A test was something I could fail without hesitation. I hoped it was long and had many, many questions.

He continued, "As I said, this is Mr. Pinkerton's office. I want you to go over to his desk and choose one item, and then I want you to tell me about its owner."

"But I don't know Mr. Pinkerton," I couldn't help saying. "What you're asking, that would be telepathy."

"No, it would be deduction. You have read Arthur Conan Doyle, haven't you?"

Of course, I'd read Conan Doyle. As a child, I was quite taken by the books. Of course, I hadn't bothered with the later stories as I considered myself a sophisticated adult and enjoyed more challenging writers. Novelists like Winston Churchill (the American, not the Brit) and E.M. Forster who write about social dilemmas. I smiled weakly hoping my feigned disinterest in the famed mystery writer would count against me. I stood and took a step toward William Pinkerton's gigantic desk.

"I'm to choose an item and then deduce from it?"

"If you would."

I studied the items on the desk. There was a telephone in one corner—it looked like a handle hanging over a box, quite different from my mother's candlestick. Two wooden trays sat upon the desktop for incoming mail (quite full) and outgoing mail (quite empty), as well as an ink-stained blotter, a safety pen, a paperweight shaped like a horse's head, and a rather delicate teacup. The teacup seemed out of place and was, I thought, the item I was most likely to be wrong about. I picked it up and showed it to Mr. Cuthbert.

"Excellent choice."

I sincerely hoped it was not. The cup was a man's cup. Though delicate, it was larger and not as dainty as cups intended for ladies. Across one side of the cup was a kind of porcelain bridge with a half-circle cut into for the tea to flow through. A mustache cup.

"Mr. Pinkerton has a mustache," I said. "One that he's quite proud of."

The first was obvious given the type of cup. The second, his pride, was evidenced by the mere fact of the cup. If he were loosely attached to his moustache and might shave it off at any point, then there would be no need for a special cup.

My second deduction was, "It was a gift."

It did not fit with the other items on his desk and, though they too might have been gifts, the fact that it didn't fit swayed me. The gilt on the handle and the rim was fading and there was a chip on the rim.

"It was given to him quite some time ago… by a woman who loved him. A woman who is no longer in his life."

It was a personal gift, a feminine gift. If the woman were still in his life she'd have seen the chip and replaced the cup. Each side of the cup had a young couple painted onto it. They wore clothes of the eighteenth century: knickers and stockings for the two men, and powdered wigs for the women. The couples seemed to be in poses of courtship.

"The cup was possibly given by a bride to her groom."

I glanced up at Mr. Cuthbert hoping to see him frowning at my disastrous performance. My deductions were given on the thinnest evidence possible. His face though was composed, placid almost. I could only hope I was doing poorly, and he was politely hiding the fact.

Turning the cup, I looked inside to see that it was heavily stained. I suspected that the owner drank both tea and coffee out of the cup. I sniffed the cup to see if I could determine which. Instantly I smelled the sweet, forbidden smell of alcohol. That was perfect. It very likely wasn't William Pinkerton's cup at all. A man who insists his employees not be addicted to drink would not drink in the office. That would be rank hypocrisy. Even suggesting that William Pinkerton drank in the office should be enough to ensure I would not be hired regardless of whether it was true or not.

"He drinks. Quite a bit," I said with absolute certainty. "Possibly to forget about the wife he lost."

I set the cup down onto the desk, certain I had failed the interview. But then Mr. Cuthbert smiled at me and said, "That was excellent. Be here in the morning."

"In the morning?"

"Yes, to begin work."

"But—are you saying I was right?"

"That would be indiscrete. I'm saying that you have a job."

I tried to smile but failed.

"Mother will be so pleased."

CHAPTER 2

My interest in the criminal is often assumed to have something to do with my father and his chosen profession. It's what my mother believed, it's what my professors believed when they learned of my parentage, and I imagine it's what Mr. Cuthbert believed when he hired me as a Pink. They were, of course, entirely wrong. My interest in the criminal had to do with my own nature, my own criminal nature.

It had been my hope for some time to build a life in academia, a life of books and research, measurements and charts. Quiet evenings spent reading by a fire. I wished to be hidden, safe from my felonious instincts. Even my interest in physiognomy was tied to my secret. I didn't want to learn if you could look at a person and determine their guilt or innocence. I wanted to know if others could look at me and determine mine.

The afternoon of my interview, I left the building and went immediately in search of a telephone pay station to place a call. I found one in the lobby of the Rookery. I called my dear friend, Professor Josiah Everett, and arranged to meet. Then I hurried to the South Side Elevated and took it down to the University.

Nearly an hour later, I found Josiah sitting in the Hutchinson Courtyard. I'd heard this part of the University had been designed in imitation of Oxford University in England. I'd once seen a postcard of Oxford, and it seemed to be true. He sat on a stone bench reading a book while eating a bagged lunch his landlady had packed for him. He'd spread the bag across his thin knees and was part way through a sandwich made with thick bread and what looked like deviled ham.

Josiah was pale with fine yellow hair that flew about in the light afternoon breeze. His eyes were milky blue and his skin translucent. It seems foolish now, but at the time Josiah seemed old, mature, though he was likely only thirty-one or two. His hair had begun to recede and there were crinkles at the corners of his eyes. His face brightened when he saw me coming, and he put aside the book he was reading and his sandwich.

In lieu of a greeting, I blurted, "I have horrible news. My mother has suffered a financial reversal and I've been forced to take employment."

"Dear Lord, that means you won't be able to stay with me to finish our research," he said with an expansive sigh.

I sat down next to him, close enough to press my thigh against his. He moved his away, quickly saying, "This is tragic news, my friend. Can't anything be done?"

"At the moment, no," I said. "I'm not sure whether to believe Mother. She claims to have money difficulties, but I've seen no evidence of it other than insisting I take employment. She continues on as though nothing has happened."

"If your mother says she has difficulties I am sure it must be true," he said. "What kind of position have you taken?"

"I have been taken on as a Pinkerton detective."

"But you mustn't! They're thugs, they're goons!"

It didn't surprise me he felt this way. I knew Josiah's politics were radical. The Pinkerton's reputation as strike-breakers would certainly horrify him.

"Why on earth did you accept that sort of situation?"

"My mother arranged the interview."

"Your mother?" he said with some horror. "But she's a woman of refinement, a freethinker. Why would she want you to engage in something so… so base?"

"Freethinker is, perhaps, an exaggeration."

When he'd come for dinner, Josiah had been very impressed with her—though as I'd come to find, she did not return his regard.

The night of the dinner, once he was gone, she'd very casually asked, "Why hasn't he a wife? He's well over thirty."

"You do realize, Mother, one doesn't simply mail-order a wife from the Sears, Roebuck Catalogue."

"Don't be naive, Lewis. Brides are ordered through the mail all the time."

"Not from Sears, Roebuck," I'd mumbled weakly and slunk out of the room.

Josiah was giving me a stern look, squinting with the sun in his eyes. "You shouldn't disparage your mother. She's a fine woman. With a sharp intellect."

"My father was a Pinkerton."

He looked at me in surprise. "Have you told me that before? Have I forgotten it?"

"I don't think I've kept it a secret." Perhaps I had.

I knew I had mentioned it to other professors, but only if I thought it might improve a sagging grade.

"But wouldn't your mother want you to improve yourself? You are well on your way to becoming a professor. I can't fathom why she wouldn't want to see that happen."

"My mother is a woman of unusual opinions."

Josiah returned his half-eaten sandwich to the waxed paper it had been wrapped in. Then set it down next to his book, a well-worn copy of *Crime: Its Causes and Remedies* by Lombroso. Apparently, my news had caused a loss of appetite.

"I don't expect I'll be very good at the job," I said, hoping to reassure him.

"No, I don't imagine you will be. Not if beating hungry miners to death is what is expected of you."

And he was right; I couldn't imagine myself beating anyone to death, even if they were frail and starving.

"You're far too gentle for that," he said, looking at me fondly. I forgot myself and placed a hand on his thigh. Under his breath he hissed, "Lewis!"

I withdrew my hand. My friendship with Josiah had been intense. We were alike in our criminality, I knew that. I knew Josiah's secrets, not because he'd told me, but because I knew my own. Together we had fought off our baser natures and chastely hid ourselves in theories and hypothesis and the ephemera of study.

Recovering myself, I said, "As you can see, the situation may resolve itself rather quickly. I'm bound to fail dismally."

I attempted to sound cheerful when I said it, but Josiah did not seem cheered.

"I'm afraid for you."

Smiling at him, I said, "Thank you, friend."

"You will take notes though, won't you? Should you meet any actual criminals, you'll take note of their appearance."

"Of course."

We sat awkwardly for a moment, then he said, "I shall begin to work up something for you in the fall. Something with a stipend or perhaps a small salary."

Neither of us mentioned that his relative unpopularity with other professors might make that a difficult task. Physiognomy was, if not exactly frowned upon, not widely endorsed. Nor was he the sort of man who smoothed over things with personal charisma.

"I would like that," I said, rising to leave.

Standing there, I was reluctant to go. I blurted, "And we'll continue... our friendship."

"Yes, of course, you are dear to me. Perhaps I'll find a lecture series we can attend together."

Sitting next to him, silently, in a stuffy room listening to some old man drone on and on was not what I'd had in mind. "Or... a night at the theater, a late dinner and a night at the Blackstone. I wouldn't want to wake Mother returning so late."

"Lewis. You know how much I care for you. I would never sully that... the way men like us redeem ourselves is by remaining chaste. You know that."

"I hadn't meant... it was an innocent suggestion."

I'll admit it was not.

When I returned home, Mr. Cuthbert had already telephoned Mother. Ignoring her obvious pleasure, I hid myself in my bedroom, pining for things I barely understood, and refused to come out for dinner. I waited for the lights to go out, telling me Mother had gone to bed. During the night, I snuck into the kitchen and made a sandwich, so I was able to nonchalantly pass up breakfast, as well.

"You needn't act like a condemned man," my mother said when I refused the oatmeal the Polish girl had made.

"I *am* a condemned man," I replied, fantasizing that it might be the last thing I ever said to her. And then I stalked out of the apartment to begin a job I already hated.

* * *

ON MY FIRST day as a Pinkerton agent, I was given almost nothing to do. Bored, I managed to put my hands on, or perhaps someone gave me, a sales tract entitled "An Endorsement of Pinkerton's Bank and Bankers' Protection." It was about seventy-five pages in length, most of which were testimonials by Bankers and Chiefs of Police from dozens of states, Canada and England. The far-flung nature of the company was impressive; there were more than thirty Pinkerton offices.

The floor below William Pinkerton's office, the eighth floor, was composed largely of small offices lined up in two rows. Some of the other agents called it the rabbit warren. We weren't assigned offices. As I later learned, most of us were rarely in the office to begin with, and there were often visiting detectives from other locations. Therefore, offices were claimed willy-nilly.

I chose an office toward the back of the building. An uncomfortable, airless little room that I thought none of the more senior agents would fight me for. That first afternoon, aside from the sales tract, I spent my time reading case reports and other materials Mr. Cuthbert sent down, and wondering how to get myself out of this dreadful predicament.

The office boasted two boys of about twelve who ran errands. My second morning there, one of the boys, the one who wore a very adult sneer on his face, showed up in my doorway and informed me: "Mr. Cuthbert wants ya." He then ran off, presumably to other errands.

Avoiding the creaky elevator, I took the stairs up to the ninth floor. I assumed I was to be given more cases to read. But when I presented myself to Mr. Cuthbert, noting that the famous Mr. Pinkerton was still not in residence, he said, "I have a case for you."

A large ledger was spread in front of him. He didn't

bother to look up. I had no idea what he was doing, but I imagined he made notes on the progress of every case run from the Chicago office, possibly all Pinkerton offices. He glanced up for the shortest moment and pushed a brown folder to the edge of his desk. "It's an insurance claim filed by one Mrs. Jurgis Rudkin. This past February, her husband died in a fire at their home."

I picked up the folder, asking, "Do you think her husband was the victim of foul play?"

"I don't know, and I don't care. And neither do you. The insurance company doesn't want to pay the claim. It's your job to find them a reason not to."

"All right," I said, thinking that had Mr. Rudkin met with foul play at the hands of a family member it would be reason enough not to pay the claim. It would also feel good to deny a claim like that. If I found a reason to deny the claim that was not foul play, that was not Mr. or Mrs. Rudkin's fault, well, that wouldn't be fair and was unlikely to feel good.

"What sort of name is Rudkin?"

Mr. Cuthbert shrugged. "Slavs, I think."

I nodded as though that somehow helped my investigation and began to leave the room. Mr. Cuthbert stopped me. "Before you go, I want you to read through the file and tell me the order in which you're going to conduct your interviews. Sit down and study the file for a moment."

I sat in the same occasional chair I'd occupied a few days earlier. Opening the file, I discovered there was little there. It held a smudged carbon copy of the application for life insurance, which was for one thousand dollars; a handwritten duplicate of the death certificate; a handwritten note from a Dr. Thacker saying he'd identified Mr. Rudkin's body; a brief transcript from the inquest in which it was decided that the death was accidental; and a scant police report.

When I was finished reading, I said, "A thousand dollars seems a small amount of money for a life insurance policy."

"Did you look at the address?"

I went back to the application. Mr. and Mrs. Rudkin had lived at 4728 1/2 South Justine Street. That didn't mean anything to me. I looked at Mr. Cuthbert blankly.

"Packingtown," he said simply. "Mr. Rudkin was a butcher at Libby McNeil."

I knew of Packingtown, of course, but little more than the fact of people living in squalor there. I couldn't imagine why someone from a slum, even a butcher, would purchase life insurance. To many, the cost was small, that was true, but still it made little sense.

Mr. Cuthbert offered an explanation without my asking. "Continental Surety & Safety. They specialize in selling policies to immigrants and the impoverished. Their salesmen go back every week to collect a nickel or a dime."

"That can't be profitable."

"It's very profitable. They collect tens of thousands in the course of a year. Most of their clients stop paying long before they have the chance to put in a claim. And those who do put in a claim..."

He didn't say it. He didn't have to. For those who did put in a claim, we found a reason for Continental Surety & Safety not to pay. Whatever my investigation cost, it would not cost anywhere near a thousand dollars.

"Have you decided the order yet?"

"One moment."

Quickly, I went back to the file. I made a mental list. Mrs. Rudkin would have the most information; I should talk to her first. Then the coroner. I'd want the landlord to show me the apartment where the fire occurred. Then I'd want to talk to the neighbors. Last, and certainly least, I would talk to the agent.

I was about to tell Mr. Cuthbert that this was my list, but then I remembered how much I wanted to lose the job. Mentally, I flipped the list over and told him, "First I would talk to the insurance agent, then a few of the neighbors, the landlord, the coroner, and last Mrs. Rudkin."

He smiled at me. Oddly, he seemed pleased. "Working from the outside to the inside. Perfect."

Perfect? Why was that perfect? I was certain I had been wrong.

"Don't just stand there," he said. "Get to it."

In the rabbit warren, there was an office at the front of the floor overlooking Fifth. That office had large windows and its own party line. The next morning I snuck down to that office, and, finding no one in residence, I called the office of Continental Surety & Safety requesting to speak with Roland Harcourt. This was the agent who'd sold the Rudkins their policy. I was told by a rather brusque woman that he wasn't there at the moment but was expected that afternoon.

I dawdled for the rest of the morning. I could have gone to Packingtown and attempted to speak with the Rudkin neighbors, but to be honest, I was a bit concerned about going there. What I knew of Packingtown came from the newspapers and exposés. The workers lived in terrible, unsanitary conditions. And worse, it was a hotbed of social-ism. Clearly, a dangerous place.

The offices of Continental Surety & Safety could be found in a rather anonymous brick skyscraper on LaSalle near Monroe, kitty-corner to the much less anonymous Women's Temple where Mother spent a great deal of time.

Entering the building, I took the stairs rather than the elevator, as the company was only on the third floor.

I found Harcourt in a large room filled with desks, ledgers, wire baskets, and ten to twelve women of assorted ages. The room was stuffy even though two of the large windows had been raised a few inches to let in the spring air.

With a flirtatious wink, Harcourt shooed a young woman away from her desk. When we sat, he leaned back in the wooden swivel chair and put his feet on the desk. An older woman nearby clucked at him, but the look on her face said she approved as much as she disapproved.

Roland Harcourt had a strong jaw, clear skin, hair neatly combed with a tonic that smelled of apples. His tan suit was well-tailored—perhaps too well-tailored. *He could be an Arrow collar man*, I thought, remembering the magazine ads which often brought my heart to a stop.

"You got questions?"

"Yes, I do," I said, quickly adding, "Only a few. I won't take up much of your time."

I gave him an involuntary smile. I wanted him to like me. I stumbled about for a moment. In all honesty, I didn't have any questions at all. I hadn't given the interview much thought other than that it needed to happen. If I was lucky, he'd call to complain about me. Finally, I asked the very general, "What can you tell me about the Rudkin family?"

"Not much. These people are all the same. Don't speak English. Got these sad, surprised looks on their mugs. Like they don't understand why coming to America didn't turn them into J.D. Rockefeller. They sure didn't come here expecting to work as hard as they did where they come from."

He was crude. My mother would find his manners an affront, but I could easily see how he managed to charm nickels and dimes out of illiterate, homesick women.

"You don't remember anything specific about the Rudkin family? Don't you see them every week?"

"They got a daughter. Fifteen. Sixteen. A looker. She sure does make the visit worthwhile."

I tried to frown at him, but it was hard to be disapproving. Then he said something that might be useful: "The girl's the one who speaks English. That's how it works with a lot of them, you see. The parents don't learn English, but the kids do."

"You completed the transaction through their daughter?"

"Yeah, you could say that."

"Tell me about Mr. Rudkin."

"Never met the man."

"You never… But you sold him a life insurance policy."

"I sold it to his wife. She had him sign the form and go to the doctor."

"No one actually saw him?"

"The doctor saw him."

"But no one from Continental?"

"You're kind of hoity-toity," he said, looking me up and down.

"I beg your pardon?"

"For a Pink, you're hoity-toity."

"I have an education, if that's what you're referring to."

"Most Pinks don't got an education. Except what life gives them."

The way he said that suggested he didn't value education. I raised myself up, just as my mother would have, and said, "I didn't come here for a personal critique, Mr. Harcourt. I came to discuss the Rudkin family."

"Don't give yourself vapors. It was just something I noticed, that's all. I gotta notice things in my business, too."

He gave me the same flirtatious wink he'd used to get his chair.

"I find the Rudkins suspicious," I said, wishing to cover the fact I was blushing.

"What do you think? You think these people are grifters? I don't think so. You have to be at least a little smart to be on the grift. None of the people I deal with are smart. Besides, you make one mistake and the claim don't get paid, right? That's why you're here, ain't it?"

I nodded uncomfortably. I'd never heard the term grifter before. From the context I assumed he was talking about confidence men. At the same time, I had to wonder *How could we be shocked when the poor tried to steal if we, as their betters, did nothing but steal from them? Were we only shocked at the shabby nature of their efforts?*

"If I need to reach you after hours, how would I find you?" There was a lump in my throat as I asked it. I wasn't entirely sure why I was asking.

"Whiskey Row. Most evenings."

"That sounds familiar, but…"

"It's in Packingtown. I grew up there."

Embarrassed, I said as formally as I could, "If you think of anything helpful, you can reach me at the Pinkerton office."

There it was again: Packingtown. As I left the building, I asked myself what I knew of it aside from the squalor and the socialism. From time to time my mother sang the praises of the Armour family and their support—well, founding of the Armour Institute of Technology, a college where anyone could attend, that offered evening classes for workers.

When I was much younger, Mother went with her temperance group and attempted to shut down the saloons in Packingtown, the same ones Harcourt spent his nights in. She talked of the terrible filth and poverty she saw, which she attributed to the presence of saloons. It was impossible for her to connect the poverty to poor wages, since so many residents of Packingtown had a dime for a nightly bucket of warm beer.

That afternoon, after working up my courage, I took the South Side Elevated as I normally would to get home, but at the Indiana stop I got off and waited to change to the Stock Yards Branch. The weather had turned cool. My wool suit didn't require an overcoat, but I was thankful when the Elevated came quickly its windows were closed.

Still, as we got closer to the yards, the car I was in filled with the pungent smell of live pigs and cattle. And no wonder. I looked out the window and saw we were traveling directly over the pens. Each pen was full to bursting, and the animals struggled to get away from the sound of the Elevated crossing above them.

Suddenly, their panicked mass disappeared and I was staring at the side of a brick building. The smell began to change, making the shift from the stink of living beasts to the stench of death. These were the slaughterhouses.

A few stops later, the Elevated would turn around and make its way back to the world I knew. Even though I wanted very much to stay on and return to my clean, sweet-smelling home, I forced myself to get off the train at Packers, which seemed to be the most southerly station.

I'd consulted a city map before I'd left the Pinkerton office, so I knew that to get to Justine Street I had to walk even further south. I wasn't sure exactly how far. When I reached street level, I took my bearings. Behind me were the yards and in front of me the beginnings of Packingtown. The smell of dead animal was even stronger and hung in the air like damnation.

I stepped to one side of the station, sure that I would vomit, but then, luckily, did not. Remembering my scented handkerchief, I retrieved it from a pocket and held it under my nose hoping to shut out the riot of smells that assaulted me.

The street was unpaved. There were no trees or lawns or streetlights. Nor were there street signs. Soot from the nearby city dumps hung in the air. Children seemed to be everywhere, all under the age of seven or eight, adorned with worn clothing and dirty faces, with no mothers or older siblings to scold them. They stared at me as I picked a direction and began to walk. I must have looked wrong to them in many ways.

My gray suit was brushed just that morning by the Polish girl. I was clean. I bathed frequently, while these urchins seemed not to bathe at all. Most surprisingly, I was an adult male wandering about mid-shift in a four-dollar derby. They likely never saw a man during those hours, nor a hat that cost more than a butcher's daily wage.

The houses hunched close together, constructed of unpainted clapboard graying from the elements to match the coal smoke that rose from each chimney. Most of them had ten to twelve wooden steps leading up to the front door. Another set of steps descended into the ground, leading to an apartment half sunk into the dirt.

Over my shoulder, I caught a glimpse down several blocks of brick buildings shoved up against one another. Music drifted out of them; a polka, I think. Whiskey Row. The establishments Roland Harcourt visited each evening and that my mother was determined to close. From where I stood, I could see that the building on the end had a sign-painted onto its second and third floors. DRINK COCA-COLA, it commanded. Underneath it said, "RELIEVES FATIGUE."

The handkerchief was beginning to lose its effectiveness, so I put it back into my pocket. I had to find 4728 1/2 South Justine Street quickly so that I could get back on the

Elevated. I returned the urchins stare, saying, "Pardon me, what street is this?"

"Forty-fifth," he said in a mumble.

Given the way Chicago streets were numbered, that told me I was approximately two blocks from where I wanted to be. Or rather two blocks north of where I wanted to be. I could still be many blocks east or west of my destination.

"And do you know where Justine Street is?"

He waved toward the west.

"How many blocks?"

"Two."

I had a few pennies in my pocket, so I gave them to the boy. A mistake, apparently, because shortly thereafter a herd of children walked with me the two blocks to Justine. Once on Justine, I knew I had to walk about two blocks south. Except, Justine ended after one short block.

"I'm looking for the Rudkin family. They live at four-seven-two-eight and a half South Justine." This earned me a crowd of blank looks. I added, "There was a fire there a couple of months ago."

The last registered and they dragged me east a block, then down a diagonal street, which seemed to cut across where Justine should have been. Part way down that street they pulled me into a tiny walkway between two houses—I might have been afraid if they weren't such young children—then we crossed an alley, which doubled as a foul-smelling drainage ditch. Finally, we were on another unpaved east/west street, hurrying toward what I would learn was Justine. We came to a stop in front of a frame house, among a row of sagging houses. It looked weathered and unhappy, but I couldn't see any evidence of fire.

"This is it?" I asked the urchins.

"In back," one of them said and the whole crew began to run down the narrow walkway between the two houses. I squeezed down the walkway, having to turn my shoulders so they didn't scrape. I thought they'd meant that the fire had been in the back of the house, but when we got there I saw that there was another, smaller house built behind. That house, little more than a two-story shack, had blackened windows and a front door hanging slack on its hinges.

The crowd of youngsters stared at me expectantly. I reached into my pocket to find that all the change I had left was four nickels. There were at least ten urchins. I handed out three nickels to the three oldest looking children, keeping one for my return ride on the Elevated, explaining as I did, "This is what I have. You're going to need to share."

Of course, the boys with the coins simply bolted off. It took the other children only a moment to chase after them screeching. I had the disquieting feeling I had just begun a slum riot.

Pushing through what was left of the front door, I stepped into the small house. It smelled of smoke and char, though it was something of a relief after blocks of rotting carcass. It was quiet. I could hear the floorboards creak as I walked across them. Then, unexpectedly, a train went by a block or two away. One of those bringing livestock, the squealing of pigs mingling with the squeal of metal on metal.

The parlor was small and scorched. On one side of the room sat a potbelly stove. The furniture was scant and had likely been ruined long before the flames touched it. A couple of straight back chairs, a sprung couch, a stained carpet, each item scarred by fire. The parlor opened onto a small kitchen. It struck me as odd that there wasn't a dining room or even a wall between the kitchen and the main room. In the center of the floor, traversing both rooms, there was a long deep char. It looked to be about the length of a body and about as wide. I decided not to step in that direction, since the blackened spot had nearly burned through the floor.

I glanced over the rest of the kitchen. There was no cook stove. I imagined what cooking they did was over the potbellied stove, even though it was in the parlor. There was an icebox—not what we call an icebox now, but a cupboard with a spot beneath it to put the ice and a rusted tray to catch the water when the ice melted. There was a linoleum countertop, a couple of cupboards and a cast iron sink. Other than soot, the room seemed as untouched as the parlor. I wondered how the fire had started. The police report had been uninformative and didn't give any indication that I recalled. I stood in the sooty room trying to imagine what had happened.

It almost seemed Mr. Rudkin had been the source of the fire himself. Most of the damage seemed to be in the spot where he would have fallen. Could he have been taking something from the potbellied stove and his clothes caught fire? It seemed possible. I wasn't familiar with Eastern Europeans. Would a man be doing the cooking? That seemed unlikely in most cultures. Perhaps he was stoking the flames. The fire had happened in February. It might have been a father's responsibility to stoke the fire and keep his family warm.

But where was his family when he caught fire? Were they at home? Did they try to put him out? A horrible scene ensued in my mind. A wife, several children, attempting to extinguish a burning man. Surely, they would have succeeded. The man might still have died from his injuries, but there wouldn't be a deep scar in the center of the floor which indicated he'd burned for some time. No, either he was alone or his family had stood and watched him burn.

On one side of the parlor, a rickety staircase led to the second floor. I would have climbed it, but the ceiling sagged and I was afraid if I went up I'd come right down in an undignified way. I decided I should leave and try speaking with some of the neighbors.

Moments later, I was climbing up the wooden stairs that lined the back of the front building. On the second floor, laundry had been hung out to dry, suggesting there might be someone at home.

I knocked on the door. A minute or so later a woman opened it. She was not much older than me, though she looked worn and beaten down. She rested an infant on her distended belly. I blushed immediately. Of course, I knew that she was pregnant, but I'd rarely seen a woman in this advanced state. Among the women my mother socialized with none would dare show themselves in such a condition. Behind the woman's skirts two toddlers peaked up at me.

"Do you speak English?"

"Yes, much good." She smiled, proud of herself.

"I'm here about the Rudkin family. About their fire."

"Yes, much bad. Much… sad."

"Do you know where they've gone?"

"Ah… yes. They go Swift."

My first thought was that they went somewhere quickly, but then I remembered that Swift was one of the meatpackers. Presumably, after Mr. Rudkin's death the family had to go to work in the slaughterhouses.

"And where do they live now?"

She shrugged, looking a bit confused.

I tried another question. "How big is the family?"

Uncertain, she shook her head.

"How much family?" I asked, mimicking her limited English.

"Ah, two boy, girl and mother."

"Tell me about Mr. Rudkin. What was he like?" That was too much, too fast. I tried again. "Mr. Rudkin. What look like?"

"Ah. Is tall. Much man."

I tried not to sigh too heavily. 'Is tall. Much man.' That

was not useful. Not useful at all. Despite her much good English, this woman wasn't helping my investigation. I smiled, about to take my leave, and said, "Well, at least the fire department did a good job. Half the neighborhood could have gone up."

That earned me another confused look. I explained, "Firemen. Big truck. Bell."

"Ah." Her brow wrinkled. "They no come. We put out."

"You and your neighbors, you put out the fire?" I was sure she was misunderstanding my English.

"Yes. We. Snow."

She smiled at their cleverness. I glanced around the alley. There must have been some plumbing, but not a great deal of it. It would have been a great challenge to collect enough water to put out a fire. But in February there would have been snow. Much snow.

"The family was here when Mr. Rudkin..."

She nodded.

"Do you know how the fire began?"

She looked confused again, though whether it was my question or the difficulty of answering in another language I wasn't sure. Finally, she said, "Is light stove. Make fire much."

A chill shook me. As I'd thought, he'd been stoking the flames and caught fire. His family had been there. Watching. They were unable, or just as likely unwilling to put him out.

"Was Mr. Rudkin a good man?"

She shrugged, saying, "Is man." Apparently, she didn't have a high opinion of men. Though given the evidence in her arms and in her belly, she was well liked by one man.

I smiled again and said good-bye. It took me less than ten minutes to walk back to the Elevated. As I did, I was flooded by not only relief but also pride. I'd come to the notorious Packingtown on my own, examined the scene, interviewed the neighbors—well, one neighbor. And gathered information for an actual case.

I went through the things I'd learned, which I had to admit were not many. A tall man, no better or worse than other men, accidentally caught fire and died in his kitchen. His family may or may not have tried to put him out.

This paucity of information should have heartened me since my aim was to lose the job, but I'd been a good student and disliked not doing good work. And, if I was honest, I was doing a bad job of it. I should have stayed longer. Knocked on more doors. Found more adults to speak to. I could come back at night. *Did I dare?* There would be more adults around, adults who spoke better English and knew more than the woman I'd spoken to.

As I entered the Packers Elevated station, I knew I wouldn't come back in the evening. My courage did not extend beyond daytime visits. No, it was time for me to return to the world of Ellis Street, with its cobblestone lanes, sidewalks with careful curbs, glowing streetlamps, and the delivery men who regularly came to the door; the milkman, the iceman and, in winter, the coal delivered into the basement through a chute. It was a civilized life and I was grateful for it.

I would be home in fifteen or twenty minutes. Ellis Street was, after all, less than a mile away—which was not a reassuring thought. Places like Packingtown should exist on the far horizon, they should be an arduous journey away, impossible to stumble across by accident. It should be an easy thing for decent people to deny places like Packingtown existed.

Except, of course, it wasn't.

CHAPTER 4

When I stepped into our parlor, Mother was not alone. On the grim horsehair settee sat a young woman near my own age. She was petite, her feet hovering an inch above Mother's prized Mosul carpet. Her hair was brown, as were the lively eyes with which she investigated me. I felt as though I were the prize in some sort of scavenger hunt. She was fashionably dressed in a maroon velvet dress, with a long, tapered skirt that buttoned on one side, and had white lace at the collar and sleeves. On her feet, she wore delicate shoes that perfectly matched her dress. Next to her, given a seat all its own, was a ridiculously large hat with feathers.

My mother smiled widely. "Lewis, this is Miss Edna Riggins. We met at a lecture last week. I've invited her for dinner."

I told the young woman it was a pleasure to meet her, though it was no such thing. She insisted I call her Edna. Turning to my mother, I said, "I'm sorry Mother, but I'm done in. If you don't mind, I'll just have a sandwich in my room. My apologies, Miss—"

"I most certainly do mind," Mother said, standing and coming toward me. As she got closer, she smelled the stink of Packingtown on me. Her nose wrinkled. "Come now, you'll feel better when you've freshened up. Edna and I will have another glass of lemonade while we wait."

I smiled weakly and walked out of the room. I'd been trapped; Mother knew I wouldn't make a fuss in front of her guest. I went through the kitchen to my bedroom. Logically, one might have put a maid's room next to the kitchen, but it was the largest of the bedrooms and I doubted my father had ever intended it for anyone but himself and his bride. Mother had kept it for years, but when I turned eighteen, she had given it to me. She was a suffragist but not a radical.

Some kind of concoction bubbled in a cast iron pot on the stove. There was no sign of the Polish girl, which made me wonder if the dinner wasn't somewhat impromptu. On the rare occasions we had guests, Mother had the girl stay to serve.

In my bedroom, I stripped off my suit. It would have to be aired and brushed again. Mother would give the Polish girl detailed instructions on just how to do that. I should probably say, should probably have said earlier, I don't remember the Polish girl's name. For that matter, I don't remember which girl she was at the time. There were several through the years.

Mother's habit of giving overly detailed instructions in a language they barely understood often led to their finding other employment. The smart ones would simply ignore Mother and do things as they saw fit. That usually worked out better than if they'd followed Mother's instructions to the letter—though it never worked out for long.

After taking off my suit, I put on a robe and snuck into the bathroom. I could hear Mother and her friend chatting quietly in the living room. The whole thing was humiliating. And it was not the first time.

Mother had an unfortunate habit of attaching herself to marriageable young women. Sometimes they came with stern unhappy mothers, or hovering maiden aunts, or even brothers who paced in the street while they visited. That Edna Riggins had come alone was different, and I wondered for a moment if that meant anything other than my mother was becoming increasingly desperate.

The Victrola began to play in the parlor and Enrico Caruso filled the apartment with Italian virtuosity. Conversation stopped when Mother played the Victrola. She insisted everyone sit in the parlor as they would during a concert performance. I dressed in the dark blue blazer I favored for evening. With it, I wore a pair of flannel slacks and a white shirt with a fresh collar, and a light blue tie.

The pitcher of lemonade sat on the dining room table. I poured myself a glass before I entered the parlor. Thankfully, Caruso had finished.

"Edna and I met at the most fascinating lecture. It was given at Cobb Lecture Hall." She referred to one of the halls at school where I'd had two or three of my larger classes. She continued, "Several women were there who'd attended the Woman Suffrage Procession in the Capitol last month. The stories they told were exhilarating and brutal."

"The newspapers said two hundred women were injured," Edna added. "Though from the stories we heard it was likely many, many more."

"You remember, Lewis, there were several long articles in the *Examiner* about the Procession."

"Yes Mother, you read them to me."

My mother frowned at my less than enthusiastic response.

"Are you interested in suffrage, Lewis?" Edna asked.

"I don't know that I have a choice in the matter."

"You're a man," she pointed out. "Men always have choices."

"Well, if it's my choice then women can have the vote. If for no other reason than to change the subject."

Edna laughed, but I caught a glimpse of my mother's deepening frown. She took my comment for the slight it was meant to be. She stood up and said, "Let me just see to dinner. I hope you don't mind eating *en famille*, Edna. The servant girl took ill."

"Not at all," replied Edna. "Please don't make a fuss."

Mother left the parlor, leaving Miss Riggins and me uncomfortably alone.

"Would you like to hear another recording? I believe Mother has the arias from *La Traviata*."

"Dear God, no." She smiled at me, something I wanted her to stop doing. "Your mother tells me you're a Pinkerton detective."

"She tells me that, too."

"It must be terribly exciting."

"I suppose. If your idea of excitement is spending the day in Packingtown."

"That's a horrible place, isn't it?"

"It's not too bad if you're fond of dirty street urchins and the smell of rotting meat."

The girl cringed and was quiet. I wasn't flirting with her, as I'm sure she expected. The hat alone screamed for compliments. I was barely making polite conversation. I'd probably offended her, which was fine with me. I wanted to offend her right out of the apartment.

"You're in low spirits, aren't you?" she said abruptly. "I can see why. I've visited the Stock Yards. Of course, the yards themselves are an engineering marvel, but at the same time… You've read Upton Sinclair, haven't you?"

"Mother would never allow that," I said, tersely. Of course, Josiah spoke highly of his work. He may have read some of it aloud on occasion, but…

"What exactly sent you to Packingtown?"

"An insurance claim. A woman's husband burned to death in their kitchen. She'd like to collect a thousand dollars."

"But that's a fortune for a person like that. Do you think she killed her husband?"

"I have no idea. It doesn't matter, anyway."

"It doesn't matter if she killed her husband? Isn't that what you're there to find out?"

"No, it doesn't matter to the insurance company whether she killed her husband or not. What matters is that I find a reason not to pay the claim."

"But, what if she's innocent?"

"It's not about guilt or innocence. It's about a thousand dollars."

The look on Miss Riggins' face was satisfying. I was sure she thought me a monster, which was excellent. I had just used the job Mother forced upon me to rid myself of the girl she was attempting to force on me. I was pleased with myself. I smiled at Miss Riggins. She didn't smile back.

Mother came out of the kitchen wearing an apron and carrying the cast iron pot I'd seen on the stove. For the first time, I wondered if the absence of the Polish girl was Mother's way of economizing. Perhaps her money problems were real after all.

Miss Riggins and I joined her in the dining room. The table was already set with Mother's prized Blue Willow. After she set the pot down, she went back into the kitchen, and brought out a bowl filled with egg noodles and another with fresh green peas.

At that time in my life, I knew little of housekeeping, but I imagined the peas had been expensive since they weren't in season—very little is in season at the beginning of April in Chicago. Most people ate canned goods and home preserves during the winter. Though vegetables were becoming available year-round, they were not for those on a budget any more than they are now.

Mother sat and began to serve us what she called Beef Stew a la Française. There was a delicate baguette, which she'd clearly bought at a bakery. The Polish girl made bread for us, but it was thick and hearty, not at all like French bread.

After complimenting the food, Edna said, "Lewis was telling me about a case he's working on."

"They gave you a case? You hadn't mentioned." There was a bit of hurt in my mother's voice. Normally, she was like steel, but my keeping this from her stung even more than my gentle reproaches in the parlor.

"It's nothing really," I said, brushing it off. "Just a simple insurance claim."

"And a possible murder," Edna added. "You know, upon reflection, I think the wife did it and deserves whatever happens to her. She has to have done it. If a man is burned to death in his own kitchen who else is there to blame but his wife?"

"Nonsense," Mother said. "Women by nature are nonviolent."

I wasn't surprised by this comment, my mother's primary argument for granting women the right to vote was that women's empathetic natures would make them superior at governance to men. In fact, I suspected if she could grant women the right to vote while removing that same right from men, she would.

"What about the Dietz woman, Angelica?" Edna mentioned a case that had captured the public's imagination and was being tried at that very moment.

"I should think that proves my point. She didn't kill her husband; she had her lover do it."

"I think women are fully capable of doing anything a man can do," Edna said flatly. "That includes the best *and* the worst."

"That would be taking things to an unnecessary extreme," Mother replied.

"What do you think, Lewis?" Edna asked. But I was barely paying attention. I was thinking how fascinating it would be to go to Joliet and catalogue the crimes of the women there and compare those crimes with the men's... When Edna asked again what I thought.

"Well, it's a difficult question. In theory, I suppose a woman could do anything a man could do. But then, society and biology restrain them."

This answer, while as honest as I could make it, pleased neither woman. To change the subject, Edna generously complimented the stew again. Her generosity was all too apparent as the stew was greasy and had too many onions. Mother seemed quite pleased with it, though, and her apparent ingenuity.

"The recipe is French. It called for wine, but I ignored that. The French ruin everything with alcohol."

I told her I particularly liked the peas, which did nothing to prevent her from going into a long-winded lecture on the evils of liquor. I watched Edna's reaction. She seemed not to share my mother's interest in temperance the way she shared Mother's interest in suffrage. When we finished eating, Mother took the dishes into the kitchen and promised to make coffee.

"Do you like art, Lewis?" Edna asked.

"I suppose."

"The International Exhibition of Modern Art is at The

Art Institute. It's quite controversial. I read that students from the Institute have burned the paintings in effigy."

"In effigy? Do you mean they copied the paintings and then burned the copies?"

It seemed a lot of effort when you could simply say you didn't like something.

"Yes, I think that's exactly what they did."

"They must have strong opinions."

There was a long silence. Finally, Edna said, "Lewis, I'm hoping you'll invite me to go."

"Oh." Trapped by her boldness, I had little choice but to ask, "Would you like to go with me to the exhibit?"

"That would be lovely." She continued, "The exhibit closes soon. Do you think we could go Monday next?"

"Yes, of course," I said, increasingly annoyed by the enterprise before it had begun.

"I have to return a few purchases to Carson Pirie Scott. Perhaps we could meet at say five-thirty. In front of the lions?"

"Yes, all right."

I stood abruptly. "If you'll excuse me, Miss Riggins, I think I'll forego coffee and go to bed."

"I've asked you to call me Edna. I hope when we meet again you will."

After a curt smile, I walked into the kitchen. The percolator was on the stove already boiling, while mother cut slices out of an apple cake the Polish girl had made.

"None for me, thank you," I said, as I passed on my way to my bedroom.

She followed. "Lewis, you're not being impolite, are you?"

"Not at all. I said, 'good night'."

"Oh, you're terrible."

"I promised I'd take her to an exhibit at the Art Institute. Happy?"

"Yes, very. When are you going?"

I was in my room by then, looking for something on my bureau. I found it. It was a small, brownish envelop with my first week's pay in it. One of the boys had given it to me first thing that morning. Inside were two ten-dollar bills, a two-dollar bill and a fifty-cent piece. A full week even though I'd only worked two days. I wondered if I should thank Mr. Cuthbert.

Back in the kitchen, I told Mother, "I have my first pay envelope."

Then I reached in and pulled out the ten-dollar bills offering them to her. Instead, she took the envelope out of my hand and looked inside. She extracted the two-dollar bill and the fifty-cent piece and stuffed them into a pocket hidden in the folds of her skirt. "Thank you."

"Mother, you either need money or you don't."

"If you're going to keep company with a girl like Edna Riggins, you're going to need money to do it. I'll consider it an investment in your future. Get yourself a new collar and buy her a corsage for the exhibit. And remember not to slouch so."

CHAPTER 5

$\mathcal{A}$ Pinkerton agent was expected to work until Saturday noon, unless they were on an assignment requiring they keep special hours, in which case they often worked longer. I began my Saturday morning attempting to track down the doctor who'd seen Mr. Rudkin and declared him healthy. The note the doctor had written for Rudkin was on a piece of stationery with his address. I'd copied out the address on another sheet of paper. In fact, I'd copied a number of things onto the piece of paper, since I couldn't see myself wandering around Chicago with the file under one arm.

The doctor, one Wallace D. Thacker, M.D., had an office at 2415 S. Leavitt Avenue. That morning, I took the Elevated into the Loop and switched to the Metropolitan line, which I then took to Marshfield. Walking the few blocks to Taylor, I basked in the bright, brisk morning. That part of Leavitt was a street of shops on the edge of Little Italy. With the temperature well above fifty degrees, the shops had opened their doors to the spring air. I could hear snippets of what I assumed was Italian coming from the tailor and the cleaner. I walked by an Italian restaurant and then a bakery. I was tempted to go inside the bakery, Ferrara's, since I didn't know what Italian pastries were like.

I was working so I didn't, but still, I was distracted enough that I walked right by Thacker's office. I stopped in front of a saloon at 2425 S. Leavitt and turned back the way I'd come. 2423, 2421, 2417, 2413. There was no 2415 S. Leavitt. I hadn't missed the doctor's office; it wasn't there. Unless I'd copied the address wrong. I took out the folded piece of paper and checked it again. 2415 was what I'd written down. Leavitt.

Taking a lesson from my time in Packingtown, I attempted to look behind 2417 and 2413 in case the building was in the rear. It took a bit to find the alley and prove to myself that there was no such address as 2415. Returning to Leavitt, I walked back to the Ferrara bakery.

Stepping inside, I walked up to a glass case and studied its contents. There were butter cookies dipped in dark chocolate, delicate pastries shaped like bowties, white cookies twisted around rich red jellies, sugary logs dipped in sesame seeds. A large gentleman of about forty-five wearing a very white apron looked me up and down, and asked, "What you want?"

"Do you know of a Dr. Thacker in the neighborhood?"

"No."

"And there's definitely no 2415 South Leavitt Avenue?"

"No."

I almost turned and left, but the surly look the baker gave me made me point at a stack of cookies cut into long arcs and ask for half a dozen. He filled a paper sack with six of the cookies and charged me twelve cents. That seemed outrageous. I knew Mother bought butter cookies at the A&P for ten cents a pound.

"What are they called?"

"Biscotti."

I made a guess at translation, "Biscuit?"

The man shrugged. The cookies didn't look like any biscuits I'd ever seen. They barely looked like cookies. I left the store, thinking more about the cookies than the nonexistent doctor's office.

As I walked down Leavitt, I desperately wanted to take out a cookie and eat it. Of course, respectable people did not eat while walking down a street. I resisted for a block before I remembered that I was hardly a respectable person. For one thing, I was a Pinkerton agent, which was not what I nor many others thought of as respectable. I had hoped to one day be a professor, a profession that is quite respectable. Indeed, I might still become a professor. In the meantime, there was no reason not to eat an Italian cookie on the street.

I took one out of the bag and bit an end off. It was annoyingly hard, crisp, and dropping crumbs down the front of my wool suit—which I suppose was reason enough not to eat a cookie on the street. Briefly, I wondered if the baker had sold me a sack of stale cookies, but then the biscotti began to do its work and my mouth filled with the flavors: vanilla, almond, sugar, butter, and another flavor that was more exotic. A flavor that was similar to Black Jack chewing gum, but not exactly that. Deciding I liked the cookie no matter what was in it, I took another bite.

While I was chewing, I wondered about Dr. Thacker's address being wrong. His note was written on stationery. Printed stationery. Someone had invested in stationery for an office that didn't exist. Unless Dr. Thacker had the stationery made with an incorrect address. By mistake? Or was there something more nefarious at hand? And if it were a mistake, why use it? Was there even a Dr. Thacker? I decided I should check the city directory when I arrived at the Pinkerton office.

I finished the Italian cookie while walking down Blue Island Avenue, past Robey, and was considering whether to have another when I stopped. I was about to cross Ashland. That sparked a thought. I took out the sheet of paper on which I'd written information from the file. The morgue was at Ashland and Polk.

As a room full of dead people couldn't be more frightening than Packingtown, I hopped a streetcar on Ashland and went north. Reaching Polk, I found myself in front of what looked like a large campus, not unlike a university. Two city blocks covered in brick buildings and green lawn. The old hospital was at the south end of one block, while the new hospital, which they'd scarcely begun, was being excavated.

The transcript of Mr. Rudkin's inquest noted that it had taken place at the morgue. It was scarcely two pages, though, and said little more than that Mr. Rudkin had accidentally burned to death. There wasn't anything in the transcript that actually supported that conclusion. As I walked toward the Cook County Morgue, I wondered if there was anyone there who could tell me how that verdict had been reached.

The morgue was a three-story, brown brick building shaped like the letter T; a lazy T lying down on the lawn, or perhaps a T that had died in the night. The front entrance was up a few steps, and I almost went in that way, but then decided to follow the paved driveway around to the back. If I went in the front, I was almost certainly to be treated like a relative or loved one. I wanted to be treated like a professional, so I went around to the back.

There, I found a kind of loading dock with a four-step stairway on one side. I climbed those stairs and entered the building. The smell. It was unforgettable. A strong soap, not dissimilar to the one the Polish girl used in our bathroom, had been used to excess. It covered a hint of something sweet that has turned. Repulsive in a way few things are. Right before I found the attendant in his small, airless office, I had the thought that it was as though someone had taken the smell of Packingtown and mixed it with rotting apples to a stomach-turning effect.

The attendant was a man named Hoffman. I found him squeezed behind a small wooden desk in a cramped office. A diffident fellow, dressed for an afternoon in a bar; he gave me an exasperated look when I told him I was a Pinkerton. Morgue attendant was a patronage job, meant to be simple and require little effort beyond showing up, and sometimes not even that. Hoffman seemed especially perturbed that I required him to betray that ethic.

After squeezing out from behind the desk, he led me down the hallway to a narrow room with a wall of small, square white enamel-painted doors resembling neatly stacked ovens. The windowless room was noticeably cooler than the rest of the building. He began to open one of the doors and I stopped him.

"Wait, what are you doing?"

"You said you was here about Rudkin."

"The fire was two months ago. How can he still be here?"

"The wife said she'd bury him when she got the insurance money."

"What if she doesn't get the money?"

"He goes to Potter's Field in a few more weeks."

And with that, he opened a square door and slid out a thin metal drawer, nearly knocking me over in the process. Catching myself, I stared at what looked like a man who'd been spit-roasted. And with a certain amount of horror, I realized that was very nearly what he was.

His arms were drawn up as though he were warding off a punch, his blackened face distended into a permanent scream. His features had been burned off. The smell of smoke joined the other disgusting smells of the morgue. I was struck by how small he looked in death. Small and powerless.

"What do you got in the sack?"

"Cookies," I said, simply staring at the corpse. I handed the sack to Hoffman. At that moment, I doubted I'd ever eat again. He had the bag open in a flash, and shoved a whole biscotti into his mouth.

"I've had these. *Italian*," he said, crumbs tumbling out of his mouth.

"There was no autopsy," I noted.

"Nope. Died in the fire, don't you think?"

I blushed. It was obvious he'd died in a fire, and I couldn't think of a good reason they should have done an autopsy when the cause of death was so clear.

"And his wife identified him?"

"Yep."

"How? How did she identify him? If he was a friend of mine, I wouldn't know him."

Hoffman thought for a minute, then said, "His feet. Woman knows her husband's feet, don't she?"

It was true; his feet were relatively unscathed. If you knew him, intimately, you'd recognize his feet.

"Wait, you said his wife would bury him, is that right?"

"Yup."

"*She* told you that? I have it on good authority she doesn't speak English."

He squinted at me and kept eating my cookies.

"It was the daughter that said it for her. Same difference."

"Did they seem upset?"

He shrugged. "What do you expect from foreigners? They ain't like us."

I sincerely hoped Mr. Hoffman and I were not similar in any way. People could be so presumptuous in their use of pronouns. Us? I think not.

"Surely they regret the loss of income, if nothing else."

Naïvely, I assumed that Mr. Rudkin supported his family like a good husband. Now the whole family had gone to work for Swift, as the neighbor said, to make up the loss.

"Well, the insurance is going to take care of things for them, ain't it?"

"Did they mention the insurance? Other than in connection with the burial, that is."

"Yep, couple times. They wanted to make sure they had the right papers to turn in. Didn't want nothing to go wrong, they said."

* * *

"Do you see it? It is the wine-cup of *pleasure.* This is the first cup at the banqueting house of Satan. The young man takes it and sips the liquor. At first it is a cautious sip; it is but a little he will take, and then he will restrain himself. He does not intend to indulge much in lust, he means not to plunge headlong into perdition."

Mother and I were members of City Tabernacle, a protestant church only a few blocks from the Ellis house. I wish I could say we went out of convenience, but that would not be true. We went because Mother enjoyed the preacher, Reverend Cade Thompson; a robust man of about forty-five with excellent oratory skills and a taste for fire and brimstone. That Sunday his subject was, as it often was, sinners. He'd divided sinners into groups, making sure no one in the congregation felt left out.

Of course, I was barely paying attention. I was thinking of Josiah. It hadn't been long since I'd last seen him, but I missed him. Or rather, I missed him because it was unlikely I'd see him again for a very long time. He was right about everything. The highest form of love was a friendship between two men, a chaste friendship. It was terrible of me to attempt to lure him to a hotel. My criminal nature. And yet when I pressed my thigh against his...

"There is the table set for *secret sinners,* and here the old rule is observed," the minister went on. And on. "At that table, in a room well darkened, I see a young man sitting today, and Satan is the servitor, stepping in so noiselessly, that no one would hear him. He brings in the first cup—and oh how sweet it is! It is the cup of secret sin. Stolen waters are sweet, and bread eaten in secret is pleasant."

And then I made connections. *I* was a secret sinner. I found myself blushing. Humiliating. Worse, because my cheeks had reddened, everyone would know. I tried not to think about what Reverend Thompson was saying. I decided to think about the Rudkins. It was certainly a more appropriate topic than Josiah and his ideas about romantic friendship, murder was a topic that might keep me from blushing.

Logically, I knew I should return to Packingtown. I knew I should track down more of the neighbors and get a better idea of exactly who Mr. Rudkin was. But I was loath to do that. The place had disgusted me thoroughly and I would be happy to never go there again. In fact, I would be happy to stop being a Pinkerton agent, so there really was no point in returning to Packingtown.

What I needed to do was go into Cuthbert's office and admit defeat. If I threw up my hands and showed him how badly I'd botched the case, then he'd have no choice but to fire me. I must admit; I did not enjoy the idea. I was not a person who enjoyed failure. The success I'd found in my schooling had been my saving grace. It had made up for my other deep flaws. It felt wrong to fail deliberately. And yet the idea of remaining a Pink was untenable. Wasn't it? Without my noticing, the sermon had mercifully come to an end. We sang one more hymn and it was time to leave.

"I'm proud of you, Lewis," Mother said, as we stepped into the aisle.

"Why is that?"

"You managed to stay awake during the Reverend's entire sermon. You must have enjoyed it."

There was no appropriate answer to that.

CHAPTER 6

In the morning, I read the newspaper as I ate my corn flakes. An anarchist had attempted to kill the King of Spain; the pope was ill, and since he was very old likely to die; ministers were testifying before the Senate to explain why girls went wrong. Most importantly, in my mind at least, John Barrymore was playing in *A Thief for a Night* at the McVicker's. There was a matinee on Wednesday.

If Mr. Cuthbert didn't fire me right off the bat, he'd surely do it by Wednesday morning and I'd be free to see Barrymore. It would be my reward for outsmarting Mother. Maybe I should also see the *Ziegfeld Follies* before they left town.

When I arrived at the Pinkerton offices, I went directly to Mr. Cuthbert's office and saw that he was in, and that Mr. Pinkerton still was not. I walked across the floor and tentatively leaned my head into the large office. "Mr. Cuthbert, do you have a moment?"

He slipped a pencil into the crease of the ledger he'd been studying. "Come in. Come in." He stayed behind his desk.

I positioned myself uncomfortably in front of it. "I'm

afraid I've failed on the Rudkin case. I cannot find a reason not to pay the insurance claim."

This earned me a suspicious look. "You haven't had the case a week."

"Yes, I know that, but I feel I've exhausted every avenue." This, of course, was not true but my only other option was to promise to work harder and go back to my uncomfortable, temporary office.

"Tell me what you've done?"

I went through the steps I'd taken very slowly, hoping that if I did so slowly it would sound like more than it was. After I completed the story of my somewhat pathetic investigation. Mr. Cuthbert began asking questions.

"You haven't spoken to Mrs. Rudkin, yet?"

"I'm afraid she doesn't speak English. And at this point, I'm not sure what I'd ask her."

"Nonsense. You had enough sense to leave her for last. You know perfectly well you ask her questions based on what you've learned. Preferably questions you already know the answers to. Get her to tell you a lie. Get her to slip up and show her true colors. What are the two most important things you learned from the insurance agent?"

"I learned that Mrs. Rudkin uses her daughter as an interpreter. And that the agent, Roland Harcourt, never actually met Mr. Rudkin."

"And from the neighbor, what two things did you learn there?"

"That Mrs. Rudkin and her older children have begun working for Swift." That was only one thing. He'd said he wanted two, so I threw in the only other thing I could remember that the woman had said, "And... I learned that Mr. Rudkin was tall."

"And does that match the doctor's recollection?" Mr. Cuthbert's face was reddening. This was almost over. I was certain I was about to be fired. I could tell my mother I'd tried, and I was simply not fit to be a Pinkerton. The whole episode would be over. I struggled to feel relief.

"I wasn't able to locate the doctor. I went to the address listed on his stationery; there was no office at that location."

"But you did go to the morgue. What did you learn there?"

"Mrs. Rudkin identified her husband by his feet, which were relatively intact. The rest of his body—"

"What else?"

I struggled to remember some other useless bit of information I'd learned at the morgue. In my mind's eye, I saw the corpse laid out on the metal shelf. There was room at the top and room at the bottom.

"Oh, my Lord," I said, realizing something.

"What? You've remembered something?"

I stared at Mr. Cuthbert's desk for a moment. It wasn't that wide, not as wide as the shelf had been. I spun around and looked at Mr. Pinkerton's desk across the room. It was much wider. The gurney was about as long as Mr. Pinkerton's desk was wide.

"We need a yardstick," I said.

At that point, Mr. Cuthbert should have told me I was unstable and thrown me out. Instead, he went out into the main office area and yelled for a girl to bring a yardstick. A few moments later, he handed me a wooden yardstick with most of the individual numbers rubbed off. I took this over to Mr. Pinkerton's desk and measured it. The desk was just over two yardsticks long. Six foot and possibly two inches. The gurney had been roughly the size of the desk, but the corpse I'd looked at had been much shorter than the shelf. Shorter by seven to ten inches. The corpse was no more than five foot four or five foot five.

"How tall are you Mr. Cuthbert?"

"I'm five foot four and a half."

"Has anyone ever called you tall?"

"Not since I was in short pants, no."

"It's not Mr. Rudkin," I said, unable to keep the excitement of being right out of my voice. "Mr. Rudkin was tall. The corpse I saw was not tall. Not tall, at all."

Mr. Cuthbert relaxed. "Congratulations. You've solved your first case. Now go write your report."

I hurried back to the office I favored in the rabbit warren. Taking out several sheets of paper from the top drawer, I began to write my report. Essentially, I wrote down much of what I'd just said to Mr. Cuthbert. Except I did try to make myself look smarter in the process, making my conclusion seem more inevitable than serendipitous.

Part way through, I wondered what I was doing. I was excited when I ought to be upset. I didn't want the job, but there I was trying to make myself look good. I *had* wanted to be fired, but when I'd figured out the body wasn't Mr. Rudkin, that I'd done some good since the Rudkin claim did not deserve to be paid—well, I was glad. I was happy. I liked what I was doing. But then I wondered how I could be happy. A man had burned to death. A man I couldn't identify. Who was he? And where was the real Mr. Rudkin? I wondered if there would ever be answers for these questions.

As Mr. Cuthbert had instructed me, I took my handwritten report up to the ninth floor and gave it to one of the typewritists. She dropped it into a wire tray, letting me know in no uncertain terms that my report was no more important than anything else she had to type.

I went back to my office, deciding on the way that I would still reward myself. I'd simply have to go to see John Barrymore in the evening. And I was going to have to find another way to lose this job.

I did not buy Edna Riggins a corsage as my mother instructed. That would have indicated an interest in her I did not have. As I walked the five blocks between the Pinkerton office and the Art Institute, I plotted excuses I could use to cut the evening short. The best, of course, was health. Or rather lack of it. I could claim a headache or a peptic stomach. Then I could tell Mother we weren't suited and that would be the end of it. Well, until she found another young woman eager for matrimony.

The Art Institute sat alone in Grant Park on the east side of Michigan Boulevard. Across the street, half a dozen skyscrapers ten, twelve stories tall seemed ready to march across the wide street and kick the dwarfed museum into the lake. It was a classical building about a block wide with grand columns and arched windows. Once it had been white, but its limestone was stained in soot, so on that day it was a brownish gray. Twilight had begun and the sun hunched in the west behind the skyscrapers leaving much of the city in shadow.

Arriving earlier than I'd expected, I stood by the bronzed

lion to the south. While I waited, I pondered Edna Riggins. Why did she want to see me? At dinner, I was certain I'd been rude enough to repel most young women. And yet she'd insisted on this meeting. I hoped—futilely I'm afraid—that she was simply an appreciator of art. And, as a woman, couldn't attend the exhibit without an escort. Maybe that was it. It wasn't me she wanted to see, it was the art.

Quite a number of people flowed in and out of the building. Apparently, she'd been right, the exhibit was drawing attention. Checking my pocket watch, I saw that Edna was ten minutes late. For a few minutes, I savored the hope she might not come at all, but then I saw her scurrying up the steps on her delicate feet. She wore a soft gray suit and a black felt hat with a pointless buckle in the front.

"I'm late, I know. I always am. I'm afraid you'll find that I'm simply riddled with character flaws."

I had no idea what to say to that. It would be too rude to agree with her, but in our short acquaintance I'd have to say she was right. I smiled weakly, and said, "Should we go in, Miss Riggins?"

"Edna, please. Don't make me ask you again. That would be rude."

I capitulated. Stiffly, I said, "Edna, then."

She smiled, victorious. I steered us forward. Upon entering the Institute, we were confronted with a row of ticket-takers standing in the crowd. It cost fifty cents to enter: twenty-five cents each. It was a reduced fee. If we'd come first thing in the morning it would have cost a full dollar. That price seemed absurd. I couldn't imagine what they had inside that would take all day to see, no less be worth an entire dollar. After I paid, we were given programs and directed to climb the stairs in front of us to the galleries on the third floor.

"Tell me about your case. Have you solved the murder

yet?" Edna tucked her arm in mine as though we were old friends.

"Yes. I mean, no, not solved exactly. The insurance company will not be paying the claim because the body identified as Mr. Rudkin was much too short. His wife identified the wrong corpse," I explained.

"But she must have known."

"Yes, I imagine she did."

Reaching the third floor, we stepped into the entrance of the exhibit. Edna's mind was working over the information I'd just shared. I looked around. The ceiling of the Institute was unfinished, with exposed metal braces holding up the wood-lined roof. The walls were white-washed brick. Around us on false walls, the exhibit began with several large paintings. No, they were screens. Painted screens.

"Who is the man who burned to death? Do you think he's a friend or a relative? Could he be the wife's lover?"

"I have no idea who he is. Though I suspect the answer is less sensational than you'd like."

"Tell me how you're going to discover the man's identity."

"That isn't my job. I imagine the insurance company will inform the police. Clearly this woman is guilty of fraud. And likely murder."

I could see that Edna was about to complain about the injustice of it all. And certainly, I was aware of that, but had no urge to discuss it with her. I changed the subject.

"So far, I would hardly say the exhibit is scandalous."

"Hold onto your hat," she said, leading me into the next gallery as I quite literally held onto my hat.

"You've been before?"

"Oh yes, this is my second visit. And I was here in January to see the German Art, which was also quite exhilarating."

We found ourselves in a large room with an elaborate checkerboard skylight and electric lights hanging on chains that ended in glowing electric orbs. They seemed to me an orderly galaxy of suns shining down on us. The artwork was hung in such a way that the paintings sat on a picture rail that circled the room. In the center, double-sided benches faced a collection of statuary, most of it nude. Edna brazenly stared at the statue of a large nude woman, and I took the opportunity to detach myself from her.

I took a few steps away and found myself studying an over-sized red painting that seemed to be of the artist's studio. The gallery was full of people drifting slowly past the artwork, many of whom seemed entranced while others merely sniffed. As they passed, I attempted to study the red painting. Its images were primitive. Perspective ignored. It could have been done by a child. I wanted to dismiss it entirely. Certainly, I could do something similar myself. But then, it did have a certain charm—

Abruptly, Edna grabbed my arm again and pulled me over to a small marble sculpture. It seemed to be of a woman resting her head on her hands except it looked like no woman I'd ever seen. The sculptor had made the woman's eyes far too big for her head and her nose a tiny sliver between them. *Where was I?* Paintings that could be done by children; statues of women that didn't look like women; I began to see what the uproar was about.

"What do you think?" Edna asked.

"Well, it's certainly unique."

"It is, isn't it? I love everything Brancusi does."

"You didn't say, but I assume you live with your family?" I asked to avoid expressing an opinion on the Brancusi, which I found curiously disturbing.

"I live with my older brother. We have an apartment on East Lake Shore Drive."

"So, your parents are deceased?"

"Practically. They live in Detroit."

"Oh. Then you grew up in Detroit?"

"I did, yes."

"Why did you and your brother come to Chicago?"

"It pleased our parents," she said, curiously. For most parents, certainly for my mother, children living hundreds of miles away would not be pleasing. She continued, "We need to go to Room 52. That's the most remarkable room. We'll want to spend time there."

She pulled me along and a moment later we were in an unadorned, medium-sized room. It was more crowded than the first two rooms we'd been in. The room was dedicated to only three artists. All French. Or so I thought.

Edna pulled me between a couple knots of people until we stood in front of a series of paintings that were all done in a flurry of brushstrokes. "Van Gogh," she said, as though it was supposed to mean something. Several of the paintings were landscapes; a few others were portraits; one was of a pair of shoes. *Why would someone paint a pair of shoes?*

"What do you think?" Edna whispered.

"Well…" I really wasn't sure what I thought. "They're so, so obviously paintings."

"Yes! Exactly. That's brilliant."

I struggled with the idea, wondering why it would be desirable to be so obvious. Fortunately, Edna elaborated. "It's ridiculous to expect that painting should do what photography does. No, it needs to distinguish itself. It needs to do what photography cannot."

"I suppose that's true."

"Don't you think it's an exciting time to be alive? So much change. The world is reinventing itself. And we… Well, we can reinvent ourselves however we'd like to be. How would you like to be, Lewis?"

I hesitated to answer. I think what I really wanted to be at that particular moment was alone in my room with a good book. Possibly something by Dickens. Or Forester. Something solid and true. I wasn't sure I wanted to reinvent the world; inventions so easily go wrong. But that was hardly the passionate response Edna was looking for.

"It is a very exciting time, yes," I said, limply.

She studied me a moment, then said, "I'll crack your shell. You'll see. Come this way."

And she dragged me out into a hallway and then to yet another gallery. When I gathered my bearings, I discovered I was in the most surprising gallery of them all. In this room, it wasn't exactly the way the paintings were made that was so surprising; instead, it was what the paintings depicted. Or perhaps what they didn't depict. The paintings were composed more of shapes than figures. Shapes that depicted motion more than anything else. The entire room seemed to be swimming in motion; it was terribly unsettling.

Edna must have read the discomfort on my face since she said, "You're not liking it. And I so thought you would." She licked her lower lip as though she were about to say something profound. "Your mother tells me you're fond of Mr. Whitman."

"Do you mean the poet?"

"Yes, I mean the poet. Did you think I meant the chocolatier?"

"No, I didn't think you were… I have read his poetry, yes. Mother insists he was temperance."

"Yes, I know. Don't you think it interesting that in poetry, and art too, people most often see themselves reflected?"

That was, perhaps, true but I didn't want to admit it. It wasn't so much Whitman's poetry I liked as his subjects. I knew what that said about me.

"Do you always lecture on art appreciation when you come here?"

She was silent, and I thought perhaps I'd won. Though

won exactly what I couldn't be sure. I turned my attention to my program, learning that the strange, blocky paintings surrounding us were by Francis Picabia, Marcel Duchamp and Pablo Picasso. There were enough similarities between the paintings that it was as though a whole new school of art was bursting onto the scene right in front of us.

"Which is your favorite?" Edna asked.

"I'm afraid I'm not fond of any of them."

"I meant Whitman. Which of his poems is your favorite?"

"I like them all. Equally." I blushed. Yes, there were certain poems, certain images, I found more intriguing than others, but I certainly wasn't going to tell that to Edna Riggins.

"Do you? I'm rather fond of this one, 'We two boys together clinging/One the other never leaving/Up and down the roads going, North and South excursions making/Power Enjoying, elbows stretching—'"

"Edna, really… Could you please stop?"

There were far too many people around for her to be reciting what was probably Whitman's most scandalous poem. And, yes, one of those that I found intriguing. She soldiered on for another moment or two with the poem. But then stopped. My mind was spinning. I could not see the point in this. It was as though she knew things about me that I did not want her to know. That she couldn't possibly know.

"Would you mind very much if I saw you home? I'm afraid I've developed a headache." What I'd developed was the wish to be rid of her as quickly as possible.

Her face turned stiff, nearly unfriendly, and she said, "Yes, of course. If you're not feeling well."

I walked out of the gallery and made my way through the winding hallways until I was back at the stairs. Edna trailed a few feet behind me. I was careful not to get too far ahead of her, since I was technically escorting her, but I was also careful to stay out of her reach.

When we got to Michigan Boulevard, I slowed down. Seeing her home was the decent thing to do. But it meant finding a taxicab or a streetcar and riding further north. And then finding a way to retrace my steps. It seemed a ridiculous expense, but what I really wanted to do was hire a taxi to take me all the way home. Of course, since I wouldn't be seeing Edna Riggins again, perhaps I could spend some of the money Mother had wanted me to spend courting the girl.

As I debated, Edna reached into her bag and pulled out a crumpled package of Turkish cigarettes. Murad, they were. And right there in plain sight on Michigan Boulevard she struck a match and lit a cigarette. Still holding the package of cigarettes and the box of matches, she extended her hand and asked, "Would you like one?"

"No, of course not." I said stiffly. "I'm temperance. And so are you. Aren't you?"

"Not at all, I'm afraid. Please don't tell your mother. She'll be so disappointed in me."

"I'm sorry. I assumed since the two of you seem to be great friends that you had similar views."

"Actually, it's always been you I was more interested in. Your mother talked about you quite a lot and I had the feeling... I thought we might be kindred spirits."

"Yes, well, I think you've made a mistake. We best start looking for a taxi. Or would you rather take a streetcar?"

"I am sorry if I've upset you. I just, well, I thought it best to declare my intentions."

"Intentions? Women don't declare intentions."

"No, we have them declared upon us. But I'm not like other women, Lewis. Any more than you're like other men. Do you know what a *mariage blanc* is?"

"Is that French? I don't speak French."

"White marriage. You've never heard of it?"

"I think you're quite possibly the most unpleasant woman I've ever met."

"I'm afraid I have to agree with you, but that doesn't mean we can't be of use to each other. Your mother would like very much for you to marry. She's said as much to me… And my parents have offered me a significant payment if I marry."

I knew I should storm away, leave her standing on Michigan Avenue alone in the dark. But I didn't. She continued, "A white marriage is when two people marry for convenience or profit or safety… a boy like you and a girl like me. We'd still have our lives and our love affairs, our privacy, but we'd have each other for protection."

"Protection?"

"I think you know what I mean."

I did, of course.

"And we wouldn't… consummate?"

"No. Not unless we decide to have a child, which of course my parents would pay dearly for. But even then, I've heard of ways… to avoid unpleasantries. Dairy farmers for example…"

"Oh, my Lord! This is an absurd conversation." I decided I needed to be rid of her that minute. I gave up looking for a taxi and said, "There's an Elevated station at Wabash. Just a block away. I'll see you to it."

"Oh no, no thank you. For one thing, the El doesn't come anywhere near my apartment. For another I'm quite capable of getting home alone."

"A decent woman does not traipse around alone after dark." It was something my mother would have said, but I had no reason to disbelieve it.

"After our conversation this evening, Lewis, you can't possibly think me a decent woman." She stared at me for just a moment, then said to herself. "I suppose I should have known this was hopeless."

Then, she reached into her bag and brought out a card. Handing it to me, she said, "If you change your mind, please telephone."

Like a faerie dancing away on the mist, she ran down the steps to a Ford taxi that had suddenly appeared at the curb. The front of the car was open, but the passenger seat in back was in a sealed cab. Quickly, it sputtered off and she was gone. I wanted it to feel like she'd never been there at all.

Instead, it felt like she hadn't left.

CHAPTER 8

I lived in humble terror for the next few days, my thoughts torturing me, *How had she known? How had she so easily determined my nature? My criminal nature?* I felt naked, as though every single person I came into contact with knew my deepest secret. Was she right? Did I need to marry to protect myself from discovery? I had thought, hoped really, that if I lived the quiet, introspective life of a scholar I could drift into a confirmed bachelorhood; that I could live peacefully, alone with my desires and my secrets. But now that seemed impossible, owing to my mother's intervention. It now seemed foolish to have even hoped.

Thursday morning, I was summoned to Mr. Cuthbert's office by the more insolent of the errand boys. I was certain I was about to be fired. I'd done virtually nothing most of the week. In fact, I'd snuck out to see George M. Cohan in a matinee of *Broadway Jones* the day before. The story of a city boy inheriting a gum factory was well worth the dollar I paid to see it. Mr. Cuthbert must have found out I'd gone to the theater. Well, that was fine.

At that point, I wasn't sure I cared why I was being fired. Of course, since I'd had a success with the Continental Surety & Safety claim, perhaps I'd be able to negotiate with him as to the reason he told my mother for firing me. I hoped I could convince him to tell her that they simply had too many agents and didn't need me. He could even leave the door open to some future employment—provided he never followed up.

A few minutes later, I walked into Mr. Cuthbert's office only to find him sitting there with a bosomy, blonde woman somewhere in her thirties. Her dress was the brightest blue I'd ever seen, and she wore a hat with a veil and a fluffy white feather that was bigger than her head. Even standing in the doorway, I could smell her perfume which was thickly sweet. On her lap was a photo album, Mother had one like it. This was filled with tintypes, wanted posters and newspaper drawings.

I realized instantly that the errand boy had tricked me. Mr. Cuthbert was in the midst of a meeting, and I was completely humiliated.

"Excuse me, sir. My mistake."

"No, no, Lewis please come in. This is Mrs. Hempstead."

Without taking her eyes off the book, she raised a gloved hand and let it hover in the air. I suspected she wanted me to kiss it, but I held my ground and said, "It's a pleasure to meet you, ma'am."

"This one," she said, pointing at a tintype. "This is definitely the man."

It couldn't be, of course, the tintype was probably forty years old and the man in the photograph in his thirties and very likely dead.

Mr. Cuthbert explained, "Mrs. Hempstead was burgled a little more than a week ago. A watch was taken, a small amount of cash and a necklace. Mrs. Hempstead is convinced the culprit is the elevator operator who works the day shift. A man named Evans."

"He has shifty eyes," she added.

"How interesting," I said, thinking to put my schooling to work. "Are you referring to how his eyes are shaped or how he uses them?"

Mrs. Hempstead looked at me blankly. Then pointed at the tintype again, and said, "He looks like this."

"At nine o'clock tomorrow morning you're to go to 585 Surf, apartment 1020," Mr. Cuthbert said, producing a set of keys and holding them out to me. "Don't take the elevator we don't want Evans to see you. Wait in the apartment to see if he attempts to burgle it again."

"But why would he do that? He's already gotten whatever there was to get, hasn't he?"

"On my suggestion, when she returns home this morning Mrs. Hempstead will ride the elevator with a good friend and say to her friend that she's relieved the thief hadn't found her 'good' jewelry. If it is indeed Evans, he'll be back to look for the 'good' jewelry."

"I see. How many days am I to go there?"

"Mrs. Hempstead has agreed to three days. If he hasn't incriminated himself before then we'll meet again and decide whether to continue. Do you have a gun?"

Somewhat to my own surprise, I immediately said, "Yes, of course."

And I did have a gun. My father's. Well, perhaps it was truly my mother's gun, but she always referred to it as mine. It was a Colt Lightening Revolver with a shortened barrel. My father also left a leather holster which allowed the gun to be carried beneath a suit coat. It was the preferred way of carrying a gun for contemporary lawmen. I knew that because as a teenager I'd been mad for *The Argosy* magazine and had briefly imagined myself the sort of man who might conceal a weapon. A short and embarrassing episode, I'll admit. And one that was now coming true.

"Can you use the gun?"

"Yes," I said, refusing to take offense at his doubtful tone.

At the end of my infatuation with *The Argosy's* seaman, soldiers, jailbirds and Chinamen, Mother had hired a rig and taken me out to a bit of prairie a mile or two west of the Ellis house. She insisted I shoot through an entire box of ammunition. I hadn't enjoyed it as much as I'd thought I might, but I'd been more than able.

"It's your gun, Lewis. It's real and true. Not at all a thing of fantasy. Respect it," she said, and then told me to "Stand straight."

My reading habits changed, and I didn't have occasion to touch the gun again. That did not amount to a lot of practice, but it would have to be enough.

"Make sure to bring your gun with you tomorrow morning," Mr. Cuthbert said.

"Do you think an elevator operator could be truly dangerous?"

"Oh, I'm certain of it," said Mrs. Hempstead. "He has the look of a real devil."

Mr. Cuthbert smiled at her indulgently. Then to me he said, "Even if he doesn't look like a devil, I find that the less suspect a person is, the more dangerous they turn out to be."

Mrs. Hempstead looked dutifully impressed.

He continued, "But you're right, Lewis; I doubt you'll need the gun. I'm only suggesting you bring it as a precaution." He looked at me oddly, and added, "I wouldn't like anything to happen to you. I don't know how I'd explain it to your mother."

He stood, to indicate the meeting was over. I hadn't even sat down. Mrs. Hempstead rose, too. Cuthbert continued,

"Please don't worry about a thing, Mrs. Hempstead. This will all be resolved in within the week."

"Oh Mr. Cuthbert you've been so kind to a widow in distress. I can't thank you enough." She held out her hand again; in the same limp way she'd held it out to me. Mr. Cuthbert bent over and kissed her knuckles. She giggled and left the office.

I took a step to leave, but Mr. Cuthbert said, "Lewis, please stay for a moment." At that point, I did sit down.

"Mr. Pinkerton was pleased with the work you did for Continental Surety & Safety." I glanced over at Pinkerton's still empty desk as Mr. Cuthbert continued, "Tell me what you've been doing for the last few days?"

"Very little. I've helped a few agents with their reports. That's all." It was most of the truth. Obviously, he knew I'd been to the theater. I didn't have to tell him.

"Yes, I have noticed that grammar in our reports has shown unexpected improvement. Feel free to continue lending a hand when you're between assignments."

"Between assignments?" I should have realized this earlier, but I was not being fired as I'd hoped.

"You have your father's curiosity. I've a mind to keep you in a back pocket, as it were. Saving you for our more challenging assignments."

Strange. He couldn't be suggesting I was better than the other agents. Well, grammatically perhaps. But in truth, any fool would have seen that the Rudkin corpse could not actually be the Rudkin corpse. I was trying *not* to see it and couldn't avoid it.

"May I ask, why hasn't Mrs. Hempstead called the police? They're not so bad they couldn't handle a simple burglary."

"Mrs. Hempstead requires discretion." I waited for him to explain why but he didn't. "Discretion is part of our service, Lewis. Don't forget that."

That evening, I sat in the kitchen with the Colt spread out in pieces in front of me. Before leaving the Pinkerton offices, I'd had the good sense to corner another agent, Len Dorchester, and get instructions on how to clean a gun. I chose Len because his adventurous spelling and hazardous grammar made it less likely he'd tease me about my own, trivial deficiency.

Once home, I collected a makeshift set of tools: a thin rag, a handful of cotton balls my mother used to remove the cosmetics she swore she didn't wear, a wire from one of the kitchen whisks, and a small can of oil we kept for resolving squeaks.

Luckily, when I found the gun in the bottom drawer of my bureau there were two boxes of ammunition, one unopened. Though I don't know why I thought it was lucky to have seventy-some cartridges when I didn't expect to use one. Still, at least I didn't have to find a shop to sell me bullets first thing in the morning.

I had taken the wire, wrapped the rag around it and was running it through the barrel when I heard my mother enter the apartment. As she walked through, she called out my name. I didn't have time to answer before she was in the kitchen pulling the pin out of her hat.

"The Polish girl left you a sandwich in the ice box," I said.

"She shouldn't have gone to the trouble. I had high tea at the South Grill Room with Edna Riggins." She set her hat down on the counter.

The skin on the back of my neck tightened. Stiffly, I said, "I'm sure that was charming."

"It was. Very charming. I don't know why you won't give her a chance, Lewis. I can't imagine a young woman coming along who's more suited to you."

I had to admit in a way she was right, though I couldn't

conceive of Mother understanding why. Nor did it make the proposition any more attractive.

"I don't wish to discuss it."

"But we *are* going to discuss it. Left to your own devices you'd be alone in a room with a book. You can't truly want to live such an arid, bloodless life."

Bloodless. She'd used that word to describe Josiah. And I had hoped to lead a life with Josiah. I wouldn't call it bloodless. Circumspect perhaps. Quiet. The opposite of where my life seemed to be going.

Her accuracy annoyed me though, and I asked, "Is that why you've maneuvered me into dropping my studies and taking a humiliating position I don't want or need? Because you think me bloodless?"

"I can't image what you mean."

She could imagine exactly what I meant, and I stared at her for a long moment to make sure she understood we both knew that. Then I asked the less inflammatory question, "Shouldn't I be the one to decide what kind of life I live, Mother?"

"No, you shouldn't. Young people should never be trusted with deciding their own lives. They make such a mess of it."

"That sounds like regret. Are you trying to tell me you have regrets about the way you've lived your life?"

That took her aback. Through grit teeth she said, "I regret nothing. Nothing at all."

"And neither will I."

I wanted to get up and storm off, but I was only part way through cleaning the gun. The smell of metal and oil was thick in the air. I tried to concentrate on what to clean next, but it was challenging. The silence between us swelled, and for a moment it seemed that the room would capsize and we'd be bounced into an ocean of anger.

Mother watched me struggling to clean the gun, saying, "You're not wearing your ring."

"I don't want to damage it," I lied. I hadn't worn the ring because it reminded me of her machinations; that she'd cried poor and then given me a gold ring.

"Edna Riggins has invited us to dine with her on Saturday evening. You can wear it then."

She picked up her hat and left the room.

CHAPTER 9

The next day was deadly dull. I took the Elevated into the Loop and transferred to the North-western line. I got off at the Diversey stop and walked east toward the lake. The building I was looking for was north of Diversey just off Broadway. It was a twelve-story, yellow brick building that had two wings on either side of a court-yard with landscaping that was still a bit sparse having only been put in a year before.

The lobby was small and faced entirely in marble. In the center, sat a podium-like desk and two benches with red velvet cushions. A doorman stood at the podium giving me a sour look the moment I entered. Rightly, he determined that I was not a tenant and was therefore more likely to cause him some kind of trouble. I noted that the elevator was not on the ground floor as I walked over to the podium.

"I'm from the Pinkerton agency. Mrs. Hempstead has engaged us to protect her apartment from theft. Can you point me to the stairway?"

As soon as all of that came out of my mouth, I thought how I'd been stupid not to make up some other kind of story.

The doorman could be in league with the thief or might in fact be the thief himself.

"Stairway is right there around the corner. But Mrs. Hempstead lives on the tenth floor. Elevator will be back shortly."

"That's all right. I prefer the exercise," I said and zipped around the corner to the stairs. I ran up the first five flights but then having winded myself slowed down. By the time I reached the tenth floor I was sweating and bored with climbing stairs. I found apartment 1020 and, using the key I'd been given, let myself in.

The largest apartments were in the front of the building. Apartment 1020 had four wide rooms, a parlor, a dining room, a large bedroom and a roomy kitchen. Behind the kitchen was a small bedroom for a live-in maid. There were windows on three sides—I immediately opened one to help myself cool off—with a partial view of the lake, a view north to Evanston and a sweeping view west. I noted the apartment was attractively furnished—except for the maid's room, which was empty but for a couple of wooden crates.

For the first half hour I sat stiffly in the parlor. It was a large room with a comfortable sofa and two less comfortable chairs. There were a couple of standing lamps, a Victrola and a small writing desk. Next to the front door, a small alcove was set into the wall about four feet from the floor. It was the kind of thing you saw in churches, filled with the statues of saints. Mrs. Hempstead had filled hers with a telephone, which I imagined was the architect's intended use.

I wanted to snoop around, but that seemed impolite. But then I convinced myself it was important I be familiar with all aspects of the apartment. It would, for instance be a terrible thing if the thief were hiding in the bedroom closet while I sat in the parlor.

Armed with a vaguely reasonable excuse, I wandered into

the bedroom. It was a feminine room with a large canopy bed featuring peach-colored bedding. The walnut bureau had six drawers, three on each side and a wide mirror attached at the back. Its top was quite full, boasting a large jewelry box, a mirrored tray holding a surplus of perfumes and atomizers, and two round boxes of powder. I lifted the lid on the jewelry box. Though no expert, I didn't see anything that looked particularly valuable. There was a good deal of garnet, a dozen gold-plated bracelets, a couple of broaches set with colored glass, and a complete, black mourning set: carved necklace, bracelet, earrings and an ugly pin. I remembered Mrs. Hempstead saying she was a widow. It certainly explained the possession she'd taken over the bedroom.

But then I noticed a pair of men's slippers on the floor on the far side of the bed. There was also an awkward valet chair, with a low seat and a wooden back that ended in a hanger at the top. A man was meant to put his suit jacket on the hanger and fold his pants onto the seat. Everything neatly organized and ready to wear again in the morning. *How recently had Mrs. Hempstead been widowed?* She seemed not to be in mourning, so it couldn't have been recent. Would her husband's slippers still be beneath the bed?

I opened the closet door and found nothing but women's clothing. I glanced around the room and saw that there was no other closet. I went back out into the hallway, which did not have a closet, only a built-in linen pantry. A peak inside showed me only extra blankets and bed sheets.

The bathroom was very modern, with clean, white tile that was level with my nose, which meant there had to be more than five feet of it. The claw foot bathtub glistened under a small window, while the toilet and a heavy sink sat side by side. I opened the medicine cabinet and found tooth powder, a tonic that looked to be for women's complaints, a

William's shave stick and a safety razor. On the back of the bathroom door, I found a man's flannel nightshirt hanging on a hook. I checked the two remaining closets, the one in the maid's room: empty, and the one by the front door holding only women's overcoats.

I was sure that Mrs. Hempstead might not get rid of all her husband's things, but would she keep his slippers, a nightshirt and shaving equipment? No, it seemed that Mrs. Hempstead had a male visitor who slept in her bed, shaved in her bathroom, neatly folded his clothes on a valet but didn't leave anything there other than a single nightshirt. The mourning jewelry suggested Mrs. Hempstead had not been lying when she said she was a widow, but now it appeared she was a gentleman's mistress. And that explained her desire for discretion.

Settling back into the sofa in the parlor, I let my mind wander. The situation with my mother and the audacious Edna Riggins weighed on me. I certainly had no intention of having dinner with her on Saturday evening or any other evening. I supposed I could tell my mother that Edna smoked tobacco and, though I had no proof of it, likely drank liquor as well. That would end her in Mother's eyes. Of course, it would also set mother off looking for other suitable young women, a possibility every bit as if not more distressing than Edna Riggins.

I spent a good portion of the morning imagining that the apartment was mine, and mine alone. Now that I was a working man, I could afford to live on my own, though obviously not in an apartment as nice as this one. No, I would only be able to afford a single room. What they sometimes called a bachelor. But even that sounded wonderfully peaceful, wonderfully private. Of course, I couldn't leave Mother to live on her own. That would not be appropriate. I imagine Mother assumed that Edna, or whomever, would eventually move in with us. Which reminded me again, just how severely Mother had misjudged Edna's character.

The sandwich I'd had the Polish girl make me that morning was finished by ten thirty, and then I drifted in and out of sleep for an hour or two. Once or twice I thought I heard someone in the hallway, but, if indeed I had, they must have been one of the neighbors. Out of boredom, I began to read a book I found on an end table next to what was probably Mrs. Hempstead's favorite chair. The book was titled *The Romance of a Plain Man* and not the sort of thing I would have picked up on my own since it was clearly meant for women. The novel was set in Virginia and had to do with a young man's resolve to make his way in business and win the heart of a young woman from a fine old Southern family. After the first few chapters, it began to make me drowsy again and I nearly dropped it onto the floor, but then I heard something in the hallway. Footsteps. Getting closer. A key in the door. Doorknob turning.

I nervously aimed my gun at the front door as it opened. He was tall, very tall, and seemed to be held together by his tightly tailored suit. He looked at my gun and calmly asked, "Well, are you going to shoot me, or not?"

His name was Joseph Bankhead, he was about thirty, brown-haired, and somewhat freckled. He had been a Pinkerton agent for three and a half years and his spelling was almost passable. I knew him from the rabbit warren, of course. He was there to relieve me for the day.

"I'm not going to shoot you. I know you," I said, stating the obvious.

"Yeah? Isn't it usually a good idea to know who you're shooting?"

"You know what I mean."

He eyed my gun carefully, so I put it back into the holster.

"You don't want to carry a semi or an automatic?" he asked.

"It's my only gun right now. It belonged to my father."

"I guess it's okay as long as you don't have to reload in a hurry."

"I'm not planning to be in a gunfight. In fact, I'm not planning to use it at all."

"I don't plan to be in a gunfight neither. But I got a semi-automatic pistol just in case."

He reached into his suit pocket and pulled out a black gun with a white pearl handle. It was all barrel on top and did not have the revolving chamber that my gun had. "Thirty-two caliber Savage, semi-automatic, holds ten rounds."

I blushed. "I'm fine for now, thank you."

"Suit yourself. It's been quiet here, huh?"

"Yes, it has been. It's not a noisy building."

"Guess that explains the book you're reading."

With hot cheeks, I grabbed Mrs. Hempstead's book from the sofa and put it back on the end table exactly as I had found it.

"I should have brought my own," I said flatly.

From a pocket, he pulled out this month's *Adventure* magazine with a sheriff holding a rifle on the cover. "I like to think ahead."

"I should probably go," I said, brushing by him to get out of the apartment.

"See you tomorrow," he called after me.

It took nearly an hour to climb down the ten flights of stairs, walk to the Elevated, and catch a train to the South Side. But I was in no hurry to get home and spend the evening with my mother. When I walked into the apartment, she was in the spare bedroom off the parlor working on her Singer. It appeared she was making yet another black skirt.

My guess would be that she had eight or ten of them, all nearly identical. But I might have been wrong.

Dinner was curtly announced as chicken pot pie and was eaten silently at the dining table. The telephone bell rang twice during dinner, but mother didn't get up to answer it. I was sure the calls were for her. There was some hope that the legislature might take up suffrage in the coming session. A great deal of strategizing, canvassing, and leaflet distributing was underway. We both ignored the noise. I thought there were too many potatoes in the pie but kept silent.

"Did you have an interesting day?" she asked stiffly.

"I spent the day sitting alone in an apartment waiting for it to be burgled. It wasn't. I suppose some people would call that interesting. Rewarding even."

Mother picked up her plate and took it into the kitchen. A few moments later, she came out and went into the parlor to sit. On the small mahogany table next to the Lincoln rocker she cherished, there was a milk glass candy dish in which she kept lemon drops, her one vice. I listened as she lifted the lid and snuck out a candy, something I knew she'd be doing every twenty minutes for the next few hours. When I finished my dinner, I took my dish into the kitchen, then went into my bedroom and read *Howards End*. The Schlegel sisters, while no less contentious than Mother, were infinitely more entertaining.

I had no idea what Mother was upset about, and I had no intention of asking.

CHAPTER 10

The next morning, I was relieved to find Mother had beaten me out of the apartment. Part of me wondered if she was in a hurry to avoid me. *No,* I told myself, *that wasn't it.* She and her suffragist friends were likely handing out pamphlets somewhere in the Loop. Somewhere with a lot of foot traffic, Marshall Field's or Carson Pirie Scott or, more likely, the Chicago Stock Exchange. None of it was likely to be productive. The women they'd encounter at department stores could not easily hand themselves the vote; nor were the financial wizards of LaSalle Street, who *could* change laws, all that disposed to.

I'd read more than one editorial hypothesizing that the minute women got the vote they'd want to run for office or, worse, take seats next to their husbands at the stock exchange itself. After I washed and dressed, I asked the Polish girl for a sandwich. I slipped into my father's holster with the loaded Colt, grabbed *Howards End,* took the wax paper-wrapped sandwich, and headed off to the north side.

That second day at the Hempstead apartment was similar to the first. Except, instead of worrying about how Edna

Riggins had determined I was an invert, I now had to wonder at my mother's sudden mood change. Did it have something to do with Edna? Would that explain why she was so cold the night before?

To distract myself, I looked around the apartment for changes and determined that Mrs. Hempstead had decided to stay somewhere else while we Pinkertons were in residence. I made myself comfortable and spent the morning struggling to read Forster. The thing about British novels was, no matter how dramatic the situation, things always seemed to be handled in a much more civilized manner than in American novels. British characters knew that attempting to rise above your station was in bad taste, even as they attempted it. American characters, though, believed *not* attempting to rise above your station was the only real social faux pas.

I tried to wait to eat my sandwich, since eating early the day before had made for a very hungry afternoon. I made it all the way to eleven o'clock. The Polish girl had packed me a deviled ham sandwich with a wilted lettuce leaf and a slice of tomato, along with a sugar cookie placed on top.

Of course, I worried about what to do about Mother. I couldn't tell her the truth, but I had also never been especially good at lying to her. It was only then I realized she must still be angry about the things we'd said the night before. How long was she likely to be angry about that, I wondered. I didn't relish the idea of her being angry with me for the rest of my life. Or even a few more days. Was I going to have to apologize? At this point, I wasn't even sure what to apologize for. What exactly had I said?

Of course, the best thing to do with Mother was always to go along with what she wanted. It seemed I was going to have to go to Edna's for dinner with her. Mother could forgive me anything if I managed to seem more interested in

Edna. I didn't have to go to the extreme of marrying her, but if I spent a little time with her Mother could assume her matchmaking scheme was working.

Edna's calling card was in my wallet. I decided it might be wise to call her and tell her I would be joining them for dinner in case Mother had already called to say I wouldn't. Or, if they did speak in the meantime, Edna might mention my calling. I went over to the telephone alcove, took Edna's card out of my wallet. Picking up the earpiece, I waited for the operator to ask for the number.

As I waited, I heard a key in the door. It was far too early for Bankhead to relieve me. The door opened and a man walked into the apartment without seeing me. From behind, he was short with a spreading bald spot on the back of his head. He wore a lumpy, ill-pressed gray uniform. As I studied him, the operator came on the line and said, "Number please."

Hearing the voice, the man spun around. He did actually resemble the tintype Mrs. Hempstead had picked out. I dropped the telephone's earpiece and reached into my jacket. As I attempted to pull the Colt out of the holster it caught, and I had to try again.

"Don't move," I said, yanking on my gun.

Evans, I was sure it was Evans, bolted through the door as though I'd just shot a starter gun. I finally got the gun out of the holster.

Snatching up the earpiece to the phone, I said, "This is Lewis Wait, Pinkerton, call the police and tell them I've apprehended a burglary suspect at 585 Surf. I'll meet them in the lobby."

Then I hung up and dashed out the door. I ran down the hallway toward the elevator. When I was less than ten feet away, I saw Evans about to step into the elevator. He saw me, quickly calculated that he would not be able to shut the elevator door before I reached him, and changed direction. He ran down the hallway and around a corner toward the stairs. I was hot on his trail.

I caught him just as he was attempting to open the door to the stairs. Grabbing him by the collar with my free hand, I pulled, and he was quickly on the floor. I aimed the gun at him. I was very happy with myself. I'd just apprehended a criminal. I really was a Pink.

The poor man held his hands in front of his face.

"You're Evans, aren't you?"

"How do you know that?"

"Mrs. Hempstead suspected it was you who burgled her apartment. Where did you get the key?"

"Doorman."

"That's a lie. The doorman knows I'm here. If the two of you were in this together, he'd have told you not to come here."

"Not this doorman. The one they fired. Couple months back."

That made sense.

"All right. Get up."

"No."

"What?"

"I said, no."

"I've got a gun."

"You're not going to shoot me."

He happened to be right. I grabbed him by the collar again and started to drag him. I considered the stairs but quickly rejected them. I didn't like elevators, but dragging him down ten flights seemed as though it would have a lot of risk involved. Not to mention the effort.

Slowly, I dragged him toward the elevator. It wasn't easy. He was like a large sack of potatoes. His jacket and shirt had come loose, and it looked like his pants might be slipping from all the squirming he was doing. Then he began whimpering. It took me a moment to realize he must be getting a rug burn on the small of his back.

I pulled harder.

"All right, all right!"

I stopped, and he got up.

"Are you going to cooperate?"

"Yeah, yeah, sure."

Still holding the gun on him, I followed him to the elevator. It was still standing open, as there was no one to operate it. We stepped inside. First he closed the outer metal door and then he pulled the accordion metal gate shut. On the wall next to him was a lever in a round casing. It looked like a large yo-yo. He pushed the lever forward and we began to go down.

Then, unexpectedly, he changed his mind and pulled the lever back. The elevator began to rise.

"What are you doing?"

"I'm not letting you hand me over to the cops."

I sighed heavily. I had hoped this would be easier. The elevator rose steadily the two floors to the top of the building, then lurched to a stop. It swung in place for a moment. My stomach flopped. I tried not to think of the twelve floors of emptiness below us.

"Take it down."

"No."

I reached over him and pushed the lever. The car lurched downwards much faster than I'd have liked. Evans grabbed at my gun. I pulled it away from him, attempting to keep hold of the lever, but he grabbed the barrel. With one hand he was reaching around to get hold of the handle when the gun went off. I don't know how, maybe he pushed my finger, or maybe I squeezed trying not to let go of the gun, but suddenly, after the loud clap of the shot, there was blood everywhere and he was screaming, "You shot my fingers off! You shot my fingers off!"

And it was true, I looked down at the floor of the elevator and in a growing puddle of blood were pieces of Evan's fingers. His middle finger and his ring finger, each from his right hand. The hand he used to hold the…

The elevator smelled of gunpowder and blood, making my stomach churn. I slipped the gun back into its holster, feeling it's heat against chest. I doubted he'd try anything else. We needed to bandage his hand somehow until he could be gotten to a doctor. I suggested he take off his jacket and wrap it around his hand.

"It ain't mine," he said. "It belongs to the building. They'll make me pay for it."

Though I hardly thought that the worst of his problems, I decided it best to simply lie.

"The jacket will need a good washing afterward, that's all."

Besides, it was already bloody. They were going to make him pay for it regardless. The only possible use for it now was to keep him from bleeding to death. He looked at me like he didn't believe me but then he slipped the jacket off. We had just gotten it wrapped around his hand when we reached the lobby with an ominous thud.

I pulled open the gate and then the outer door. As soon he saw us, the doorman came over and, seeing the blood, began saying "Oh no, that won't do. That won't do at all."

Evans began to yell, "He's killed me! He's killed me!"

"Is there a doctor in the building?" I asked.

The doorman shook his head.

"I'm going to die!"

"Is there a hospital nearby?"

"Augustana at President's Corners."

"Where is that?" I asked. Truth be told, I was not well acquainted with the northern neighborhoods.

"About seven, maybe eight blocks south."

I was about to take Evans out to the street to look for a taxicab to take him to the hospital, when two beat cops walked into the lobby. Both were young, barely older than I was. One was named Flynn and the other Quinn. It must have been somebody's idea of a joke to put them together.

Flynn took one look at the situation and asked, "Who's the Pink?"

"I am."

"You shoot this guy?"

"He's killed me!"

"He reached for my gun in the elevator. It went off."

Flynn nodded.

"I did not do that. He just shot me. For no good reason."

"Oh yeah? Where'd he shoot you?" Quinn challenged.

"In the hand. Shot my fingers clear off."

"Because you was reaching for his gun," Officer Quinn corrected him. "You see how his story and your missing fingers fit together and make sense? Him grabbing your hand and shooting your fingers off for no good reason, that don't make no sense."

A blank look crossed Evan's pale face as he tried to come up with a way to counter the argument. Flynn and Quinn stepped away and conferred over who was taking the burglar to the hospital. It was decided that Quinn would drive, and we walked out to the curb where there was a little black Ford Runabout with two seats. We installed Evans in the passenger's seat and then Quinn drove him off to the hospital—and not a moment too soon, as the man had turned remarkably white and looked as though he might soon faint.

Flynn asked me to explain the whole event step by step. Which I did. We walked back into the lobby. The doorman had wandered off and come back with a galvanized pail and a mop. Flynn stopped him.

"Can you leave that for now? I need to make sure I know what happened."

The doorman stared for a moment at the bloodied floor, as though he couldn't fathom how leaving it unclean might help the police officer, but then he shrugged and wandered back to his podium.

We followed the blood across the lobby and into the elevator. Evans' finger bits lay there, lifeless. Flynn and I crammed into the corner of the elevator that was not soaked in blood. We closed the doors and then Flynn pulled the lever back to take us to the tenth floor. He was very close to me and smelled of cigarette smoke, Bay Rum and pomade. He was a bit taller than I am and I found myself looking at the poor work he'd made of shaving his chin and jawline. His whiskers were dull brown, a few shades darker than his hair.

I could feel myself blushing, though there was so much blood everywhere I doubt he noticed. I was having thoughts, criminal thoughts about him, at a time like that. It was humiliating. I really was a degenerate.

"Thank you for believing me," I said.

"What you said was logical and right. It don't take anything to believe you."

Finally, we got to the tenth floor. I led him to apartment 1020 and immediately saw that I'd been too occupied to shut the front door. Once inside, I began my tale. "I was attempting to place a telephone call when Evans opened the door with a key."

"How'd he come by a key?"

"When I questioned him, he said he got it from the previous doorman."

He nodded.

"Who were you calling?"

"A friend. I'm invited for dinner on Saturday. I wanted to confirm."

"Did the call connect?"

"No, the operator was on the line when Evans entered the apartment."

Our conversation went on like that. Flynn asked questions here and there, but it was obvious he continued to believe me. The whole thing was straightforward. Evans entered the apartment, I held him at gunpoint, called the police, and then we went to the elevator. It was simple, I had a bit of trouble staying focused though. The fact that Flynn and I were alone in the apartment kept crossing my mind.

Before we left the apartment, he asked, "The key. Did you take it away from him?"

"No. I imagine it's still in his pocket."

Unless he'd had the presence of mind to throw it away somewhere on the way to the hospital, but that seemed unlikely. Blood loss and presence of mind did not go hand in hand.

We went back to the elevator, and I explained what had happened there. Flynn asked, "Why didn't you operate the elevator yourself?"

"I suppose… because I was holding the gun." Not to mention, the levers can be tricky at times.

"And why not take the stairs?"

I couldn't help but blush. In retrospect, it probably would have been wiser to take him down the stairs. I said, "We're ten flights up. It seemed there'd be more opportunities for him to escape if we did that."

Flynn nodded.

We squeezed ourselves back into the tiny corner of the elevator not covered in blood. Flynn studied the elevator as we descended back to the lobby. I tried not to study Flynn but couldn't help myself. He was such a handsome fellow and I was standing so close to him. I thought for a moment he noticed my appraisal. I quickly looked away. I cursed myself;

a man had been badly injured and my thoughts… well, they were criminal.

Back at the lobby, we stepped out carefully to avoid walking in Evans' blood.

"Show me how he reached for the gun," Flynn instructed.

I took the gun out of the holster, emptied it of bullets, then demonstrated how Evans' hands were positioned. Flynn's hands were on the barrel and reaching for the handle which entangled our hands. His were warm and softer than you'd expect.

When he was satisfied, which seemed to take a very long time, he said, "I'm going to need to write this up and I'd like you to read over it and attest to it. Then it will go to a detective. He may have some questions."

"Do you want me to come with you now?"

He looked me up and down. I was covered in blood. "It might be better if I put you in a taxicab. You can come to Town Hall Station tomorrow. It's just off the Addison Elevated stop."

Then he said he'd go down to Diversey and see if he could find me a taxicab. I offered to do it myself, but he worried I might frighten any ladies I came across.

When he left, I found it terrible to be alone in the lobby. I'd shot a man. It seemed an impossible thing to believe. I'd shot a man. It was something I couldn't undo. Something that would always be there. I'd always have shot someone.

When I described the high points in my life—that I'd seen the Columbian Exposition at four, that I'd watched Sarah Bernhardt perform in a tent when I was seventeen, that I'd been to university—I would now have to add, 'and of course, I shot a man when I was twenty-two.'

The doorman came over, and asked, "Can I mop up now?"

"I suppose you can. Officer Flynn—"

The front door opened, and I turned expecting to see

Officer Flynn, but instead watched as Bankhead walked in, ready to relieve me of my post. It took a few minutes to explain everything that had happened. When I was done, he nodded twice and said, "The boys in the rabbit warren won't believe this, they had you pegged for a brownie."

"A what?"

"A fairy."

CHAPTER 11

I wanted to go home, desperately. But when I told Bankhead I was leaving and that I'd be in the office to submit my report in the morning, he asked, "How in blazes do you think you're getting there?"

"Officer Flynn has gone to get me a taxicab. He said I'd frighten people if I went to get it myself."

"He's right, you can't go round like that. For Pete's sake, you're soaked in blood. Did you telephone Mr. Cuthbert?"

"Oh, no… This has all happened very quickly."

"I'll do it then. I'll use the telephone in the Hempstead apartment." Then he looked me up and down, saying, "Don't go outside until the taxi comes." Then he walked away.

Looking down at myself, I took inventory. The left side of my suit coat was soaked in blood. My vest and the right side of my coat were splattered. My pants had a spray down my left leg, and my shoes looked as though I'd marched through a bloody marsh. There was blood on my hands that had become sticky and uncomfortable. I couldn't be sure, but I'd have laid money there was blood on my face and in my hair.

Seeing so much blood, I began to wonder if Evans had made it to the hospital in time.

I preferred to think of him surviving his injuries. I was uncomfortable enough with the idea that I'd injured the man in a way he'd never be able to forget, I wouldn't want to be responsible for killing him.

I began to worry about whether I had enough money in my pocket to pay for a taxi. It was at least ten miles to 54th and Ellis Avenue. It would cost five dollars, at least. I knew I'd left a ten-dollar bill at home, and I might have left a five-dollar bill with it, leaving me with a couple of dollars and some change. I could have reached into my pocket to check, but with blood everywhere on me I wanted to stay as still as possible.

Stop thinking about it, I told myself. Once I was home, I could go inside and take whatever I needed out of my top dresser drawer to give to the taxi driver. But that would require explanations both to the driver and, more than likely, my mother. Then I wondered if the latter was what really worried me.

I was still reeling from Bankhead's comment. The agents I worked with had suspected I was a brownie, a fairy, an invert. Edna Riggins. Bankhead. Did people think of nothing else? Or was it something about me?

Well, now that I'd shot someone they wouldn't think that anymore. Although honestly, that didn't make any sense. It's true that I felt different. But not in *that* way. I didn't feel… changed. In many ways I was only just learning the sort of person I was. But even then, I didn't see any reason in the world an invert couldn't fire a gun. A pansy could shoot a man's fingers off. One thing had nothing to do with the other.

"You're going to be the man of the hour, you know,"

Bankhead said, coming up behind me. I couldn't help myself; I jumped.

"Why? Why would I be the man of the hour? I don't want to be."

"I don't think anyone at the Chicago office has shot a suspect in at least two years. Mr. Pinkerton will be very happy with you."

"Because I shot someone?"

"No, because you apprehended a burglar."

"But it wasn't a very important case. There can't be a very large fee attached."

"You've got something more important than a fee. You've got a story. I'll bet Mr. Cuthbert is already on the line with *The Daily News*."

"But..." I stopped. Mrs. Hempstead had hired us for discretion. Was telling the newspapers a good idea?

Just then Flynn returned on foot.

"I couldn't find one," he said. "Maybe we'd better call a taxi company and have them send one just for you."

"No need, it's taken care of," Bankhead told him.

"What do you mean it's taken care of?" I asked.

"And who are you?" Flynn asked.

"Joe Bankhead, Pinkerton agent."

"Where were you when the shooting occurred?"

"Riding a turtleback in from Logan Square."

"You weren't here then?"

"No, I'm the next shift. If Evans had just waited a few minutes, I'd be the man of the hour." He said the last as if it had just occurred to him and with notable disappointment.

Flynn glanced at me as though to verify. I nodded.

"So, you don't have anything to add to the investigation?"

"Only that we're all very proud of Mr. Lewis Wait."

"I think we really should call a taxicab. I'd like to go home."

Bankhead nodded at the street out in front of the building. I looked through the lobby windows and saw a large, deep maroon Peerless pull up in front. A chauffer dressed in a black suit with silver buttons up to his neck and a cap climbed out. "Mr. Pinkerton's driver. Cuthbert sent him to take you home."

The idea horrified me. "I can't get into that automobile. Look at me. The seats." Though I would have willingly soiled a taxicab.

Bankhead went over and asked the driver if there was a blanket we could use. The driver went round to the boot, opened it, and took out a plaid carriage blanket. Then he spread it across the tufted leather of the backseat. He nodded at me, and I climbed in. Bankhead climbed in behind me.

"What are you doing?" I asked. "You don't need to see me home."

In a whisper he hissed, "I know I don't need to. But this is my chance to ride in a Peerless model 48. With a chauffeur no less."

The driver climbed into the front seat and turned to look at us. "Where am I going?"

"Ellis and 54th," I told him.

Bankhead made himself comfortable, happy to take a long ride to the South Side.

"Isn't this the life?"

Covered in blood, I couldn't say I agreed, but still I smiled. For some reason a half-remembered image popped into my mind: Someone had taken mother and I to the Chicago Automobile show. I couldn't remember who. I must have been about twelve, so it's odd that I didn't remember the event more clearly. I did remember I was allowed to pay a dime for a ride in some kind of automobile up and down Wacker, one that looked more like a buggy and had a stick to steer with rather than a steering wheel. Sitting in the Peerless, I couldn't but marvel at how far we'd come in such a short time.

"I *almost* shot a man once," Bankhead said, as though that were the topic of conversation. He told me a story about being sent to discourage strikers at a shirt factory. I didn't pay much attention. I had too much on my mind. "I was glad things didn't get out of hand, on account of it was mostly girls, young girls. I didn't much want to shoot a girl."

"I can't imagine that would be something to be proud of," I said, glancing out at the lake, which was bluer than it had a right to be, given the smoke gray sky. The driver had taken us out to Sheridan Road and then down to Lake Shore Drive going south. Once we reached the Loop, we'd have to cut over to Highland Avenue, which we'd take the rest of the way to Hyde Park.

"No...I didn't want to shoot no girls," Bankhead said. "I got four sisters."

I asked him to tell me about his family, mainly because I didn't want him asking me any more questions. His family came from back East. He couldn't place them any further back than that, but they'd obviously come from some part of Europe. His parents were disciples of Mary Baker Eddy but had died young, leaving Bankhead to raise his sisters alone. He'd wanted to go into the army to be a soldier, but with his need to take care of his sisters he'd found work with the Pinkertons instead.

"Of course, I didn't start where you started. I did mostly guarding things and keeping watch. You started right up with detecting."

I felt like I should defend Mr. Cuthbert's decisions, though they really didn't make much sense to me. "I went to university."

"Book learning. That ain't good for much."

"I studied crime. Or rather criminals. Among other things."

"Criminals. That's not a subject."

"Physiognomy. It's the scientific study of facial features and their differences in criminals."

"You mean you could tell that elevator man was a thief just by looking at him?"

While Evan's brow had seemed a bit heavy and his eyes close, the primary indication he was criminal had been his walking through the apartment door with a stolen key.

"There's quite a lot more to it than simply looking at people." Like calipers and statistical analysis.

He seemed to think about that, deciding whether physiognomy was science or magic. I expected him to ask more questions about it, but instead he said, "My one sister is married but the other three are out for husbands."

It took me a moment to understand that I was being offered a hero's reward: one of his sisters.

"Ah well, as it happens, I'm courting a young woman. Miss Edna Riggins."

"I see. You're full of surprises today, ain't you?"

We arrived at the Ellis house shortly thereafter. The driver pulled up in front of my mother's two-flat and I quickly got out. I thanked them both and hurried into the house before Bankhead could get any idea of being invited in.

The parlor was empty when I got to the second floor. The door to Mother's bedroom was closed. She might have been laying down for a nap, or perhaps she'd just come home from the Women's Temple and decided to change her clothes. Either way, I hurried past and was in the kitchen, thinking only of stripping off my foul clothing and taking a long, hot bath. Before I could get across the room to my bedroom, the Polish girl screamed.

Using signs and simple English I managed to convey that I wasn't injured, but it was too late. The scream had caught Mother's attention and before I was even sure she was in the room with us, I heard her asking, "What happened? Have you been hurt?"

"I shot a man."

Now that the shock had worn off, the Polish girl began to mumble in her native tongue. Presumably, she was not pleased that she would now have to attempt to save my suit.

Mother stared at me a moment, and then said, "I'm proud of you, Lewis."

"Proud of me? You don't know what happened."

"I don't need to know. I'm sure you did the right thing."

"I blew off a man's fingers."

"A guilty man, I assume."

"Yes, but that doesn't mean he deserved to lose his fingers. It seems a harsh punishment for a little inept burglary."

"I believe the loss of a hand is a punishment for theft in some countries."

"Primitive countries."

"Well... Did you entice him to become a burglar?"

That was a difficult question. The answer was no, of course. But we did entice him to attempt to burglarize that particular apartment a second time. He was, however, *already* a burglar.

"No," I said, finally.

"His bad actions resulted in your shooting him. He is, in fact, responsible. Even if it's not a fair punishment, it's not a punishment you doled out purposely, is it?"

I couldn't help but wonder if she was being guided by motherhood or logic. Any mother would view her child as innocent regardless of whom they'd shot or what the circumstances were. But since I hadn't woken up that morning wondering whom I could shoot that day, her response might be logical. Circumstances I had not created caused me to shoot a man. In fact, I wasn't even sure I'd pulled the trigger deliberately.

Mother instructed the Polish girl to run a very hot bath. "Lewis, you need to get out of that disgusting suit."

"I'm afraid it may be very difficult to clean."

"Clean? I think it best we burn it. It's time you bought a new suit anyway."

"I don't know that we can afford to do that. A suit will cost me half a week's wages."

"A good suit will cost a whole week's wages, and you'll spend it, too," she said, as though we'd never had a conversation about money problems. I suspected she'd lied to me for some reason, but then again, she might simply be a spendthrift.

I took my jacket off, folded it, but then wasn't sure what to do with it.

"Set it by the door," Mother said. "I hope this won't prevent you from having dinner with Edna tomorrow night," she said, as though in passing.

"I haven't decided," I said, even though I *had* decided earlier in the day. I didn't have any intention of pleasing Mother until the last possible moment.

"It's not like you're accepting a marriage proposal. It's only dinner." Her voice sounded measured, careful.

As I peeled off my vest, I said, "You can use that excuse for weeks and weeks, and then one morning you realize you've unfairly led someone on."

"Perhaps this time things will be different."

I already knew things were different but was hardly going to explain how to Mother. I took my pocket watch out of my vest and set it on the table. Even inside my vest pocket the watch had become smudged with blood. I kicked off my shoes. "Can we at least try to save the shoes?" I asked mother.

"All right. I'll have the girl work on them. Give me the pants."

Blushing I undid my pants and let them drop to the floor. That left me in my linen union suit. I was covered, certainly. Though it was humiliating to stand there in little more than a thin sheath of cotton, and my socks and garters. I turned and walked across the kitchen to the bathroom.

The Polish girl was coming out as I entered. She took one look at me and made a little squeak. Quickly, I shut the door. The tub was nearly full of hot water, so I turned off the tap. Stripping off my remaining garments, I stepped into the hot tub. Seconds after I was completely under the water it began to turn pink. I picked up a bar of soap and washed my hands, turning the water even pinker.

I couldn't help thinking about the blood belonging to Evans, the pink belonging to him, and it was now so very far away from wherever he was. That eased me into a reverie about what it meant to be alive. Which made much of what lately I'd been thinking small and ridiculous. I lay back and followed my train of thought until I was near drifting off. In the distance, I heard the telephone bell ring.

About a minute later, there was a knock on the bathroom door. Then my mother said through the door, "Lewis, there's a man from *The Examiner* on the phone. He wants to talk to you about what happened."

"Tell him thank you but I don't want to talk about it."

Mother hesitated outside the door. I sensed that she wanted to say something—possibly encouraging me to talk to the press—but then I heard her walk away.

CHAPTER 12

The sun was just rising when I woke the next morning. The Polish girl didn't begin until six, so I walked through the apartment, opened the door to get our milk delivery—a quart of milk, a half-pound of butter and a pint of cream—and the *Daily News*. Both the milkman and the paperboy would climb the stairs to leave our things just there, for which we tipped generously at Christmas.

I carried everything back to the kitchen, set the dairy items on the counter, and sat down with the newspaper. I could have made myself a cup of tea but decided to wait until the Polish girl arrived and put on coffee.

I unfolded the newspaper and began to read. Five people were injured in a streetcar crash, the children of dancer Isadora Duncan drowned when the chauffeur drove them into the Seine, and a Pinkerton agent named Louis Wait foiled a burglary. They'd spelled my first name wrong. I wasn't happy about that, but I also wasn't happy about making the front page of the *Daily News*.

That changed my plans for the day. I had intended to go into the Pinkerton office and write up my report. But now I was not inclined to see the other Pinks and accept their gentle, and not so gentle, ribbing. I decided I'd write the report from home and drop it off at the Pinkerton office on my way to Edna Riggins dinner that evening.

I pushed the newspaper aside and attempted to put my life into some kind of perspective. The last two weeks had been eventful to say the least: A job I didn't want; my first successful assignment; a marriage proposal of sorts, and shooting a man, which I suppose was my second successful assignment. It was a great deal to absorb.

There was a decision to be made about Edna. Simply showing up for dinner was a commitment of sorts and I didn't want to give her the wrong idea. Could I marry her? It would make Mother happy, of course. It would please Edna's parents and increase Edna's bank account. And it would give me something to say to people like Bankhead who attempted to push miscellaneous female relatives on me. But there really ought to be more to it than that.

A marriage is not simply entered into and then forgotten. Shouldn't Edna and I be, at very least, friends? And if we couldn't be friends, was the marriage worth considering?

The Polish girl arrived, percolated some coffee, and then set to work making Mother and I breakfast: potato pancakes, sausages and eggs. She glanced shyly at me a few times and I wondered if I'd made the Polish-language newspaper she sometimes brought with her.

Then Mother bustled into the kitchen dressed for her day. I noticed she wore her second-best suit: light brown with a dark pinstripe and pearl buttons at the cuff. She smiled pleasantly at me.

"You'll have to wear your summer suit to Edna's this evening," she said as she sat down at the table.

My summer suit was a beige sack made from lightweight

wool. It was not at all appropriate for an evening affair. "No, Mother, I'll wear my blazer with my flannel slacks."

"But—" she stopped when the Polish girl set her coffee in front of her.

"What are your plans for the day?" I asked.

"I thought I'd call on a few of the neighbors."

"Please don't," I said before I'd even thought it. She was going to brag about her son, the hero, to people she barely spoke to the rest of the year. I was mortified.

"I have every right to be proud of you, Lewis." She sugared her coffee, and continued, "I should go with you to the tailor. I think we should get you more than one suit. We'll replace your winter suit, of course, and then I thought you might need something—"

"I think I'll buy my own clothes, Mother."

"Lewis, I think Edna travels in different circles than we do. And you might need—"

"I wouldn't say you and I travel in any circle."

Pursing her lips, she gave me a stern look. "Stop being contrary. You know exactly what I'm talking about."

"I've noticed that Miss Riggins dresses very fashionably and I think she mentioned something about her parents settling some money on her, but I haven't really given her social status much thought."

"Well, you're going to need to."

"If I'm not good enough for the woman, then that certainly settles things."

"You're good enough for any woman, Lewis. That's not what I'm talking about."

CHAPTER 13

orth Lake Shore Drive was being turned from large lake front homes to ten, fifteen, even twenty story brick apartment buildings. The northward trajectory of the drive was broken by a short jog called East Lake Shore Drive, just above Upper Michigan Avenue. Along East Lake Shore Drive, half a dozen brand new apartment buildings faced north to the park and the rare southerly winds that blew in off the lake. One of the buildings might have been under construction, I can't be sure.

The Riggins' apartment was on the sixth floor and took up fully half the floor. When I got off the elevator—unexpectedly, the elevator had seemed less frightening than it would have just days before, though the operator was now a bit of a concern—I found myself in a short hallway with two doors. Edna's door was 6A. I knocked. A squat little maid in a formal uniform answered, glared at me, took my hat, and asked that I wait in the foyer.

The foyer had a marble floor, crisp white walls and a small chandelier. Around the room were arranged three velvet benches in the event a guest got tired and needed to sit.

In the center, sat a large table, in case I'd like to set something down. On it, there was a delicate silver tray. Should I not be seen, I could leave my card on the tray. Minutes passed. I began to wonder if I should avail myself of a bench, when Edna entered. She wore a formal gown that was largely white but had a black pattern stretching up to her knees and short sleeves in the same pattern. Her waist was tightly cinched, and the neckline quite exposed. I had an amusing thought of my mother, who I was sure had already arrived, being confronted with the horror of Edna's décolletage.

"I'm sorry. I didn't realize it was a formal evening," I said. I did have a tuxedo suit; Mother had made me purchase it when I was a freshman at the University of Chicago. She assumed, wrongly, that I'd take an interest in fraternities and the formal parties they gave.

"I don't stand on ceremony. I'm just glad you came," she gave me a genuine smile then led me into the parlor. The room was larger than my mother's and my entire apartment. There were two seating areas, both with large, matched sofas. At the front of the room a window seat with velvet cushions curled into the elaborate bay window. Beyond the window was a view of the lake, which given the hour was very dark. We could see the sporadic lights of the city traveling northward up the coast. On one side, the parlor opened onto a paneled study with another sofa and a sturdy desk. Bookshelves lined one wall, filled to bursting. The south end of the parlor opened onto a large, window-less dining room with a table that had seating for ten, and beyond that what looked like a solarium.

Sitting in the window seat, a young man with very long legs, dark hair that refused to find any kind of order despite being slick with Pomade, and eyes blacker than the night behind him. Edna introduced him, "Lewis, this is my brother, Hal."

I said it was a pleasure to meet him and then stepped over to offer my hand. He didn't move, just ran his eyes over me and said, "Charmed, I'm sure."

"Has Mother not arrived?" I asked Edna.

"She telephoned. Apparently, she has a crushing headache and won't be able to come. It's just the three of us this evening. You can't be too disappointed. You see your mother all the time."

It had to have been a deliberate plan of hers to have a headache. As nearly as I knew, Mother did not get headaches. Or rather, she never got them inconveniently. But why had she wanted me to come alone? Did she think me more likely to fall for Edna's charms if she wasn't present?

"Would you like something to drink?" Hal asked.

"Lemonade if you have it," I said.

Edna laughed. "He meant a cocktail. Your mother's not here. There's no reason not to have a little fun. What are you having, Hal?"

"I was thinking of a gin rickey."

Edna turned to the maid who I'd forgotten was standing there and said, "Paula, gin rickeys please."

Paula gave Edna an injured look as though the request was offensive but left the room to make the drinks. To be honest, I didn't want a drink. I didn't care one way or another whether other people drank. In fact, there was something about my mother's fascination with what other people did that seemed somehow impolite. But I also didn't have any inclination to drink something that by all accounts caused a great deal of trouble.

"Lewis is a Pinkerton detective," Edna told her brother.

"Yes dear, you've mentioned that a dozen or so times."

"Tell us what exciting things you've done this week," she continued. "Last week, Lewis solved a murder."

"That's not exactly true. Last week I exposed an insurance fraud, it's different."

"Pish-posh. It was terribly exciting, all the same."

They stared at me a moment. I'd only done two things that week. I'd corrected the grammar and spelling of my fellow agents, and I shot a burglar while apprehending him. I didn't think they were much interested in grammar, so I said, "I did, well, shoot a man yesterday."

Edna gasped then turned to her brother. "See, I told you he was fascinating."

"No one's calling you a liar, Sissy."

Edna attempted to get the full story from me, but I refused to give more than the broadest details. Since the story had been in the papers that morning, I wasn't interested in adding to what was already public.

Around that time, the maid came back with the drinks. Deciding not to make a scene, I took my drink off the tray. It was served in a tall glass with a lot of ice. I took a tentative sip. It was tart, bubbly and left an aftertaste reminiscent of pine needles. Edna seemed inordinately pleased that I'd taken the drink. I remembered myself, and asked politely, "And how have you been, Edna?"

"Bored to tears. It's a crime to be born a woman *and* rich."

I smiled weakly. It was so obviously not a crime to be born a rich woman. Hal smiled and whispered, "She wants you to ask why."

"Hal, he doesn't have to."

"I'm sorry. Why is it a crime to be born a woman and rich?"

"Well, if I was born a man and born rich, I could spend my time doing exactly what I pleased, and no one would stop me. And, if I was born a woman and poor, I'd have so many children by this age that there wouldn't be room for a single thought in my head."

"But can't a rich woman have a large number of children?"

"Well, of course she can. But she wouldn't take care of them herself. Hal and I were raised by nannies, weren't we?"

Hal nodded in agreement. "Some of them were quite nice. Not that I remember their names."

"We make it a rule not to learn the names of servants," Edna explained. That was an obvious lie. I'd heard Edna call the squat little maid who was standing at the end of the parlor by her name. Or was I to assume that her name was not Paula? That Edna had just called her by a random name? As I was thinking that Paula gave out a little squeak. I turned to see her leaving the room.

I said to Edna, "I think you'd find poverty much less interesting than you imagine."

"I'm sure you're right," she said, almost distracted by the maid's departure. "The thing you need to learn is that while having cocktails it's more important to be clever than it is to be right."

"Well, I don't think I'll be having cocktails often."

"Don't say that," Edna said breathlessly. "Hal and I are hoping to spend a great deal of time having cocktails with you. Aren't we Hal?"

"Yes, of course," Hal agreed. "A great deal of time."

I very nearly asked why. It's not that I didn't think I was an interesting fellow; it's that I didn't know why *they* thought I was an interesting fellow. With their money and their charm and their cocktails, they could be spending time with someone whose appeal was more apparent.

I was halfway through my drink. My cheeks were a little warm but really that was it. I'd expected more from the demon rum, as my mother's crowd called it. Fortunately, the conversation drifted away from me and onto some friends of the Riggins' who, I was assured, despite the somewhat unpleasant things being said about them, I would adore.

Our drinks were finished. Edna looked around the room and noticed that the maid had not returned. "Where is Paula?" She got up and floated out of the room.

Hal and I smiled at each other uncomfortably, then he said, "So, you're Sissy's latest plot."

"That's a way to look at it. Though from my end, your sister is my mother's latest plot."

"Do you think it's a particularly female sort of thing? Plotting?"

"I don't know," I said honestly. "I've never paid much attention to women."

It was an exhilarating thing to say. There were so few situations where I'd have felt comfortable saying it. Hal smiled at me, his black eyes shining. And then Edna was back, chattering about the difficulties of dealing with servants. She promised there would be more cocktails in just a few moments. She glanced at her brother, and he rose. "If you'll excuse me, I have some reading to do before dinner." He got up and with a nod to me walked out of the room.

I felt like Edna had dismissed him, as though through some pre-arranged signal she told him she wanted to be alone with me. This was confirmed moments later when Paula walked into the room with just two gin rickeys on a tray. As soon as we'd accepted the drinks and thanked Paula, whose mood did not seem to have been improved by having been dealt with, I said to Edna, "I'd like to ask you a question. How did you know? When you announced your intentions, how did you know that I… that I'm one of them? I mean, one of you, I suppose."

"Oh, my dear, the look on your face. I'm so sorry. Did I make you feel obvious? No, darling you're not obvious. At least not to anyone who isn't already familiar. It was things your mother said about your being shy with girls, that you preferred reading, and then, of course, the things you read give you away."

I must not have looked reassured, because she continued, "I believe we inverts have a secret code that we use to identify each other. A normal woman wouldn't have thought twice. You're just as virile and manly as anyone else." She smiled charmingly and said, "There. Can we put the subject to rest? Have you thought anymore about my proposal?"

"I'm not sure I understand the situation completely. You said that your parents would settle money on you if you married, though they seem to have settled quite a lot on you already."

"My family has an absurd amount of money. The quite a lot they've already settled on me is quite a little to them."

"And you'd like more?"

"I'd like as much of their money as I can get my hands on. It's the only thing my parents understand. They've sent Hal and I away for fear of scandal. Though they don't really care what other people think, they only care that a scandal might cost them money."

"But isn't sending you away costing them money?"

"I'm not talking about money they have; I'm talking about money they intend to have. A scandal could close certain doors to them. They might not be invited to the right parties, the right dinners. Fortunes can be made or lost over cigars and cognac."

"The fact that I don't know that… well, doesn't it demonstrate how unsuitable I am? Clearly, I don't travel in the same social circles. In point of fact, I was probably more passable last month when I was simply a college student on his way to becoming a professor. Now I'm a Pinkerton man. They can't think that appropriate for their own daughter."

"That's why you're perfect," Edna explained. "If I chose some effete little pansy from our own social set, my parents would know exactly what I was doing and quite possibly welch on the deal they offered. But if I insist on marrying a Pinkerton detective everything is different. They can believe that it's real. Certainly, their friends will believe it's real. It's scandalous enough that my parents will be met with sympathy rather than outrage. Exactly the kind of scandal they'd appreciate."

"You've thought it all through."

"I don't make proposals lightly."

Dinner was many courses, most of which I don't recall. There was a fish course featuring some kind of fish I'd never had before served in browned butter, and the main course was a rack of lamb with tiny paper chef's hats crowning each rib. There must have been a cook in the kitchen because things ran too smoothly for Paula alone. She continued to scowl at us, mainly me, as she took plates up and put them down.

Hal and Edna ate lightly. They took several bites of each course and then waited for their plates to be taken away and replaced by new ones. Edna must have noticed I was cleaning my plate each time because she leaned over and said, "It doesn't go to waste. The servants take it home. I mean, I assume they do. I would never be so crass as to ask what happens to the remains."

I had no idea what to say to that. Of course we fed the Polish girl lunch, but a meal like this would be saved, and mother and I would spend days eating it.

During the dinner, several bottles of wine were opened. They were all tart, one with a little more sweetness than the others, and one that barely had a taste at all. Conversation seemed to surge with each bottle that was opened, though I can't for the life of me report what we talked about. By the end of dinner, I had a warm, happy feeling and had become quite fond of both Hal and Edna. I wanted to hug them. Well, Hal more than Edna.

After dessert was served, poached pears in cream, Edna abruptly stood and said, "If you gentlemen will excuse me. I think I need to freshen up."

Leaving barely enough time for us to nod, she went through the door that led to the kitchen. Hal gave me a lazy smile and said, "Follow me."

Though I would have liked a bit more time with my dessert, I followed him to the window seat in the parlor. The view of the lake had become even darker, with only the thinnest trail of lights running up the beachfront. From a nondescript box, he took out a pouch of tobacco. It said DRUM on the label, beneath that the word GRANULATED. The small cardboard-wrapped stack of cigarette papers was French with LE NIL written on the outside of the package. From it, he took a single piece of paper. Carefully, he folded it and then, pinch by pinch, filled it with tobacco from the pouch.

"Why do you roll your own when you can buy them premade?"

"Because I'm not lazy like my sister."

When the cigarette was full of tobacco, he rolled it back and forth between his fingers. Then he licked it from end to end. As his tongue traveled up and down the short cigarette, he turned his eyes up to me. They were very large and far too knowing. Happy with his handiwork, he offered me the cigarette. I took it. He struck a match and lit it for me.

That first inhalation of smoke was like a horse kicking me in the chest. I almost coughed the smoke out but was determined to be every bit as sophisticated as Hal Riggins. The smoke was dry and tasted of old shoes and dirt—but I liked it. Hal set to work rolling another for himself.

"They know about the two of you? Your parents?"

"They do."

"How? How do they know?"

"Edna has always had a weakness for serving girls." Which explained Paula's behavior through most of the evening. "It was one thing when the girls worked for us, but then she fell in love with the maid of a dear friend. They were found out. The girl was fired. Edna tried to find a placement for her, but the girl grew despondent and drank carbolic acid in Palmer Park."

"Oh, my goodness!"

"Yes. Well, too many people knew the story and rumors began. She was sent to live with me."

"You already lived here?"

"Yes. I was always much more discreet than my sister. Which didn't stop my younger brother from discovering my proclivities. He told on me and is now being groomed to run the family business."

"Is that what you want to do? Run a business?"

"Oh, I don't know. It isn't going to happen, so why ask a question like that? I don't think about it."

He smiled but it wasn't an easy smile.

We smoked for a bit. I wanted to ask what he did think about. Wanted to know everything that went through his mind. But those were foolish thoughts. I barely knew him. I inhaled the last possible bit of smoke from my cigarette, then clumsily laid it in the ashtray that Hal had set between us. He reached over and put it out properly.

"Why don't we go downstairs and find you a taxicab?"

"What about Edna? Shouldn't I stay until she comes back?"

"Oh, she's not coming back. She always ends an evening like that. I think she hates to say good-bye. Not that she'd admit it."

It seemed an odd thing. To suggest you were coming back and then not. But then, there was little about Edna that was normal or expected. We retrieved my hat from a closet near the foyer and went out to the elevator. While we waited, I said what every good guest says, "I had a lovely time."

"The first of many," Hal said, though it had the feeling of being rehearsed—or at least too often repeated. I wondered if he liked me or had I mistaken curiosity for interest.

The elevator arrived and an operator opened the door for us saying, "Good Evening."

Hal asked for the lobby and then whispered in my ear, "Don't get any ideas about shooting our elevator man. We rather like him."

The man must have heard but didn't react. I was too distracted by the smell of Hal close to me to respond. He smelled of alcohol and cigarette smoke, lavender soap and pomade. I wanted to touch him but knew how foolish the thought was.

When we reached the lobby, we got off the elevator and walked out to the street. It was empty. Reluctantly, I suggested "Maybe I should walk down to Michigan Avenue. There might be taxis there or maybe a late streetcar." Though I was planning to walk to an Elevated station and take that home, saving the expense of a taxi.

"No, don't," he said. Then he pulled me into a service door near the edge of the building. "Let's wait here, out of the wind."

There was no wind to speak of that night. As soon as we were out of sight, he pulled me into his arms and kissed me. I felt a wave of relief wash over me. I hadn't realized how much of the evening I'd spent waiting for that moment. He was just an inch or two taller than I was, I had only to tilt my head and fit myself into him. It felt glorious. What didn't feel glorious, though, was our location. Yes, we were somewhat hidden in a deep doorway, but we were still risking discovery. I pulled away from him, and said, "We could have done this upstairs. It would have been much safer."

"Don't you think a little bit of risk makes everything better?"

Before I could answer, he was kissing me again. Pressing his body into mine. I liked the way he felt against me. He was lanky, even standing still his limbs arranged themselves around me in a relaxed, uncalculated way. I cupped the back of his head, pulling him further into the kiss. I didn't want it to end; I wanted to stay in that moment forever. But it was not to be. We heard the sputter of an automobile on the street and peeked out to see that it was indeed a taxicab. Hal took a few steps out to the curb and hailed it.

I took a moment in the dark doorway to arrange myself before I re-entered the world. I ran to the curb and climbed into the taxi. I didn't say good-bye to Hal but also didn't take my eyes off him, even as we pulled away. Had we really just kissed? Had my life just changed?

The weekend was full of fantasy. I spent much of the weekend in my bedroom pretending to read *Howards End* while fantasizing about what a life with Hal would be like. Of course I would marry his sister. That now seemed like the perfect idea. No one would think it odd that her brother lived with us. No one would think it odd that I liked to spend time with him. It all fit together in a way that was more intoxicating than a gin rickey.

Not being a complete ogre, I did stop to give some thought to where Mother would live. Obviously, she couldn't live with Hal and Edna and me. She'd have to go on living at the Ellis house by herself even though that wasn't entirely proper. Perhaps I could convince her to advertise for a companion. For some reason it wasn't acceptable for a woman to live alone, but two women living alone was acceptable.

No matter. I was sure I could figure something out. And, as long as I got to be with Hal it didn't matter what that something was. I wondered when I'd see him again. I wanted to call the apartment on East Lake Shore and at least say hello. Obviously, it wouldn't be all right to invite myself to dinner again, but I could call Edna and suggest that we meet and talk about her proposal again. She could help me decide what to do about Mother.

I resolved to call the Riggins' on Monday evening. Hopefully, they'd call me first to arrange another meeting. The thought crossed my mind that I should try to keep mother away from Edna and Hal. It would be a terrible thing if she found out they weren't temperance. But then I thought, no. What could she do about it? She was the one who'd pushed Edna on me. She couldn't very well change her mind. And if she did change her mind, it hardly mattered. Once I married Edna it would all be decided.

On Sunday morning, we went to church. Though we were members of City Tabernacle, it suited Mother to visit other churches from time to time. That Sunday we attended a South Congregational Church that stressed good works and was at 40th and Drexel in the mostly Irish neighborhood of Oakland.

The heavy stone church dominated its corner. Businesses had nudged right up beside it and the whole area was bustling, even on a Sunday morning. I was drowsy and caught up in my fantasies. I barely paid attention to the service, until the sermon. That caught my attention. The minister told the story of the fall of Adam and Eve. He became quite theatrical while describing how the snake enticed Eve to eat from the apple, the fruit of the tree of knowledge. That annoyed me. Ultimately, it is a bad thing that Eve eats the apple and then convinces Adam to eat it too. Knowledge. I didn't see how knowledge could be evil. And therefore, how it could be divided into good and evil. I didn't see how this was mankind's original sin: To know.

Did God truly want us to remain as ignorant, illiterate children frolicking in a garden? Was that a vision of happiness? For me, happiness was knowing, knowing everything about, well, everything. It all seemed illogical. If the tree had been the tree of un-knowledge or the tree of stupidity, then it would have made perfect sense that Adam and Eve had thrown away everything that mattered. But really, by the time the minister finished the only thing that Adam and Eve seemed to have lost was a free place to live and the desire to run around naked. Next to the ability to know, to learn, to grow, those losses seem insignificant.

After the service, we took a turtleback down Cottage Grove to 54th and then walked the four blocks to Ellis. I'd wanted to discuss my thoughts on the minister's sermon the whole time we were on the streetcar, but it was too public for such a conversation. Of course, I knew that Mother would likely side with the minister, but I liked the opportunity to bring out my ideas and listen to them myself. And Mother had been known to make a good point or two.

She had tucked her arm in mine, and I was just about to bring up my objections to the sermon, when she said, "You left the clothes you wore last night in the kitchen."

"Yes. I assumed the Polish girl would launder them tomorrow."

"Your jacket smelled of smoke and alcohol. Did you go to a bar after dinner? Did it have to do with your investigation?"

I suppose it was kind of her to offer me an easy escape. I

could tell a very small, very simple lie and the conversation would end. I could tell her that, yes, I stopped in a bar. I didn't even have to say it was for an investigation. I could simply tell her that I was curious, that I went in and had a drink, which only horrified me. I could tell her that I left, shamed by my curiosity. And then promise I'd never, never do it again. But I didn't. I told the truth knowing it would come out eventually.

"The Riggins aren't temperance, Mother."

"What? No, that isn't true. Edna and I have had several conversations. She would have said."

"No, she wouldn't have said. Why would she?"

She was quiet. I could see her mentally erasing Edna, removing her from all consideration. Finally, she said, "Well, it's just as well you're not interested in the girl then."

"But I am interested. In fact, I'm planning to marry her."

CHAPTER 15

If I'm remembering correctly, I spent the first few days of that week looking over fellow agents' reports and, as a special favor to Mr. Cuthbert, checking the hours that agents charged on their timecards against hours billed to clients. Just to make sure we weren't selling ourselves short. I was something of a celebrity after several newspaper stories came out about the shooting. Agents would come over and loiter for a few minutes in the tiny, unpleasant office I'd claimed for myself.

You'd have thought, given my newfound fame, that Mr. Cuthbert would have found some prime assignment for me, but there wasn't anything until mid-week. I was untangling the grammar in a report on the investigation of a bank robbery, when I looked up and there was one of the office boys telling me Mr. Cuthbert wanted to see me.

A few minutes later, I sat in front of Mr. Cuthbert's desk. "We've received a rather curious request from Continental Surety & Safety."

My hackles went up. Had I done something wrong with the Rudkin claim? Had that really been Mr. Rudkin after all?

That didn't seem likely. Was I finally about to be fired? That was a horrible thought. I no longer wanted—

"What is it?" I managed to ask.

"It's the Rudkin claim."

I nearly said *Oh God*, but instead nodded as stoically as possible.

"It seems Mrs. Rudkin has filed a second death claim for her husband."

"What? No. We've already proven her claim a fraud."

"It seems there is a new corpse."

"Was this one also found burned beyond recognition in the lady's kitchen?"

"No, this one was found next to Bubbly Creek. Four days ago. Stabbed to death."

"Is there reason to believe that this is the real Mr. Rudkin?"

"Continental sent their agent, Harcourt, and the doctor who examined him for the policy. They both agreed with Mrs. Rudkin that this corpse is indeed her husband."

Something bothered me about what he'd just said, but I was too agitated to examine the thought. Mr. Cuthbert held out the brown folder to me. I took it, worrying he was about to ask me what order I planned to use for my interviews. I really had no idea what the right or wrong way would be to pursue this. And now, it mattered to me. Now I was more interested in finding the right way to investigate than the wrong way.

"In order to deny the claim, we need to find that Mrs. Rudkin had something to do with her husband's murder," I said, to clarify my assignment.

"Or that her husband did."

It took me a moment to catch his meaning. "Stabbing is rarely a method of suicide," I speculated.

"Not for the Japanese. Seppuku."

I frowned. I knew that Japanese Samurai did sometimes stab themselves to death, since I was—or at least thought I was—well-versed in world history. But Mr. Rudkin was not a Japanese Samurai and therefore it was unlikely he'd eviscerated himself. I decided not to point that out. Instead, I promised Mr. Cuthbert I'd get right to it. I stood, about the leave, when I remembered two important facts from the earlier investigation.

"I remember Harcourt telling me he'd never met Mr. Rudkin. And also, the doctor who examined Mr. Rudkin for his policy seems not to exist."

"Excellent," Mr. Cuthbert said. "You have a place to begin."

Back in my rabbit hole—which is how I'd begun to think of the dank little office at the very end of the rabbit warren—I opened the brown folder. Like the first claim, the file was very thin. It included the same smudged carbon copy of the application for life insurance I'd seen before—presumably it had been moved from one file to another; a handwritten duplicate of the new death certificate; two handwritten notes from Dr. Thacker—one saying he'd examined Mr. Rudkin and found him healthy and another attesting to his identification of Mr. Rudkin's body; a hand written statement from Roland Harcourt agreeing with the identification of the body; and another scant police report.

I had a sinking feeling in my stomach. Sooner or later, I would have to go back to Packingtown. I assumed Bubbly Creek was nearby. I should probably see the spot where the body was found. Well, there was nothing to be done about it.

I took a piece of paper out of the desk drawer and began to make notes about exactly whom I needed to speak to. I would need to make another trip to the morgue. I wrote that down and then took a quick look into the file. *How long had this Mr. Rudkin been dead?*

The police report said the body was found four days ago, confirming what Mr. Cuthbert told me. The death certificate put his death one day before that. If I remembered correctly, that was two days after Continental Surety & Safety denied the claim. That left the question open: Where was Mr. Rudkin between the time the first man was burned to death and the time his own body was found? I wrote the question down, even though it was much more complicated than "go to morgue."

Another important question came to mind: Who was the first corpse? It would be foolish to think that the two corpses were not in some way connected. Off the cuff, I imagined that Mr. and Mrs. Rudkin had worked together. They'd wanted the insurance money, so they killed a man in their kitchen and attempted to pass him off as Mr. Rudkin. When that failed, they killed someone else. Or, possibly, Mrs. Rudkin decided she wanted the insurance money more than she wanted Mr. Rudkin and she killed him. I considered this for a moment. It was an interesting theory. In fact, as long as the theory was even a remote possibility, Continental Surety & Safety would not have to pay the claim.

That led to an epiphany. During the first investigation, my original thought had been to talk to Mrs. Rudkin first. But when I attempted to be wrong and put her last, Mr. Cuthbert thought *that* a good idea. Now I understood why. As the person most likely to have killed her husband—since she was the beneficiary—it followed that I needed to know as much as possible before interviewing her. I put her name at the bottom of the sheet in front of me.

I scribbled down a few names without giving them much thought. The insurance agent, Roland Harcourt. The doctor. There were two statements from Dr. Wallace Thacker. A man I'd thought did not exist. Both were on his stationery. Glancing at the addresses, I saw that they were both on Leavitt, but one was not the part of Leavitt I'd gone to. That was curious. I'd have to look more closely at that before I attempted to find Dr. Thacker a second time.

Then I read through the police report, which turned out to be more than simply a report of the incident. It was their entire investigation. In three pages. The first page was the handwritten incident report filled out by the first officer on the scene. Then there were carbon copies of two typewritten pages attached to it with a paperclip.

As Mr. Cuthbert had said, the body was found next to Bubbly Creek. The man had been stabbed and his pockets emptied. That was the basic information from the first page. The second two pages, the typed pages, outlined the steps the police had taken and their conclusion. They'd spoken to the coroner, half a dozen customers of the nearby bars, and several barkeeps. The final sentence of the report read:

It is concluded that the demised ran afoul of a thief in the night who stabbed him and stole his wallet. This is not an uncommon occurrence on Whiskey Row as individuals are often times flush with cash from gambling. Bar patron said demised had recently won a large pot at poker. Attempts to find thief are judged to be futile.

At the bottom of that page, it had been stamped CASE CLOSED.

Their investigation seemed rather perfunctory. I also wondered if Continental Surety & Safety would pay out the claim even if it was, exactly as the police said, without an actual killer. To me it seemed that they were asked to pay on the mere suggestion of the killer. But then, I supposed it didn't matter as long as the killer wasn't Mrs. Rudkin. If she were truly uninvolved, then the matter of who killed her husband would be moot. The claim would be paid.

The neighbors. I'd have to speak to more neighbors this time. As many as I could find. And then, *then* I should talk to

Mrs. Rudkin. I was going to have to bite the bullet and spend one or even two days in Packingtown. The idea of it nauseated me. The smell alone.

But first, I should go upstairs and do something I'd forgotten to do the first time I investigated Mr. Rudkin's death: Check the city directory for the doctor's correct address.

As I stood to go upstairs, there was a knocking on my doorjamb, and I looked over to see one of the office boys standing there. Not the one who'd come to get me earlier but the other, the one who always wore an adult smirk. "Oi, lady here to see ya."

"Don't say 'oi'. Say 'excuse me' or even 'excuse me, sir.' It's not polite to simply oink at people."

"Yous coming, ain't ya?"

He was right, of course, I was already walking out of the office. I couldn't imagine who this lady was. I'd only really worked two cases so far, which meant it could be Mrs. Hempstead come to thank me for capturing her burglar or, more disturbingly, it could be Mrs. Rudkin here to hurry her claim along.

When I got to the ninth floor, I found Edna Riggins standing in the reception area. Today's hat was large brimmed and topped with a purple feather. She wore a well-tailored brown overcoat that had at least two-dozen buttons down the front and a skirt that was cut tight to her ankles in the same color. Her boots were delicate and buttoned up the side. Several of the typists eyed her enviously.

Edna's eyes brightened when she caught sight of me. "Lewis Wait, you terrible man. You never sent a thank-you card after our dinner last week." She was right. I hadn't. And my mother had taught me better than that.

"Perhaps I was too busy fondly recalling the evening to think about a card." Which was almost the truth.

That made her smile. "I'm hoping you'll want to make up for your social faux pas by taking me to lunch."

I calculated for a moment. I should get started on the Rudkin case, but it was nearly lunchtime and I could leave for the morgue after lunch. "All right. I can manage a short lunch."

"You've been put on a new case?" She guessed. "Something exciting I hope!"

"I probably shouldn't talk about it," I said, and by that I meant I probably shouldn't talk about it in the office. I didn't want anyone to get the impression I couldn't keep a secret. "Give me one moment."

I took a few steps toward the receptionist, Daisy I think her name was, and asked for the city directory. She walked back to a cabinet behind the typewritists, opened one door, and came back to me with the directory. Taking it from her, I quickly flipped through the pages until I found Dr. Wallace Thacker. He was at the same address used on his *new* stationery. I wondered what that meant? The doctor whom I'd thought did not exist, did. Handing the directory back to the girl, I wondered if that was important or not.

"It's from last year," she said.

"What?"

"The directory is from last year. They might have moved."

"Yes, that's true. Thank you." I turned to Edna, and said, "Let me get my hat and we can go."

We agreed to have lunch at the South Grill Room on the seventh floor of Marshall Field's. It was only a few blocks away. As we walked, Edna talked about the differences between Detroit and Chicago, "They call Detroit the Paris of the West. I think the French would take exception to that." And her family, "My father is very intelligent and completely immoral. We're in building materials: lumber, bricks, iron. They're building hundreds of factories in

Detroit. My father saw that would happen thirty years ago. He's made money hand over fist. After he made his first million, he went to New York to find a bride. My mother comes from a family in Mrs. Astor's 400. Seven girls, and mother far from the prettiest. But a deal was struck and now she lords her family over what there is of Detroit society."

"Are you interested in Chicago society?"

"Not in the slightest. I'm much more the Bohemian."

When we arrived at Marshall Field's, we found the elevator and had the girl take us to the seventh floor. Entering the South Grill Room, we were seated next to a round fountain surrounded by lush, green ferns, as well as a large, stunted palm raised up in the fountain. Our table was white wicker with two matching chairs. The room was meant to have a tropical feel, which felt out of step with the chilly morning we'd just walked through. Edna's unbuttoned her wool coat. The blouse she wore beneath was cream-colored silk.

A waiter arrived with menus and a few minutes later we'd ordered. I chose a combination dish of creamed beef with rice, escalloped tomatoes, and watermelon pickles. Edna chose the cottage chicken with macaroni. We each ordered a lemonade.

"I don't want to keep you in suspense any longer," I said. "I've decided to accept your proposal."

"You have! That's wonderful. You should have said so earlier, we could have ordered champagne!"

"No, I do have work to do this afternoon."

"Of course," she said, then lowered her voice to add, "Hal will be so pleased."

"That would be very nice. If he were pleased." I couldn't prevent myself from blushing. And that seemed to please Edna.

As the waiter set down our lemonades, I said, "There are things I suppose I should ask."

"All right. Ask away."

"Well, should I ask your father's permission? To propose to you?"

"That's so old-fashioned. He won't find it necessary."

"Will we get married here or in Detroit?"

"Here, I imagine. Something discreet."

"Discreet? Your parents don't sound like the discreet sort." Not that I wanted some kind of ostentatious affair, but it did seem more in keeping with Edna's stature.

"I don't want to be rude, but you do remember that my parents will find you thoroughly unsuitable?"

I did remember, though I hadn't thought through everything that might mean. To be honest, most of what of what I'd been thinking about was the possibility of kissing her brother whenever the mood struck and a dark corner was available.

"Are you certain a marriage between us will accomplish your aims? Otherwise, well, there hardly seems a point…"

"My father demanded I marry a man. There were no other requirements."

"And if you marry a man, any man, your father will settle a large sum upon you. Am I understanding this correctly?"

"My father will settle a son's portion on *you*."

"Oh. I see. And I'm to put the money in your control."

"Yes. You'll have an allowance, of course."

"And will we live with your brother?"

"For the foreseeable future."

I was not a fool. I'd kissed Hal but once and the two of us had never had a frank conversation like the one I was having with his sister. While I should like to kiss him again, I also understood what was really on offer was freedom. I wouldn't need to hide myself in an academic life—though, in truth, I hadn't minded that idea. I would be a respected married gentleman able to go where I pleased and do as I please.

"Aren't you afraid I won't give you control of the money your father settles on me?"

She smiled and sipped her lemonade. "I was certain you'd ask that. A man with bad intentions would never ask that question. A thief would want to make sure I was caught unaware. I was certain you were not a thief. In fact, far from it."

I wasn't convinced her assessment was correct. Yes, I was not a thief. I was a man of my word. It wasn't in my character to steal from a woman. But I did think her reasoning unsound. I might simply be a better thief than she supposed. Of course, my mother had taught me it was best not to disabuse women of their notions. It rarely ended well.

Our lunches arrived and the conversation became lighter. The waiter was gracious enough to serve from the right. Edna raised a story that had appeared in that morning's *Chicago Daily Tribune* about a young woman named Ramona Borden who'd been kidnapped from an asylum by two elderly women. I'd glanced at the article that morning but not read it, so Edna provided the details. The seventeen-year-old milk-heiress was now missing after the abduction. My first thought was that she'd brought the story up because of my connection to crime, but then she said, "Of course, it's ridiculous to say she was kidnapped. That's what wealthy fathers do to unruly daughters; put them in an asylum. She escaped captivity. That would be more truthful."

That gave me the sense that our proposed marriage was as much about escape as it was money. Like me, Edna was seeking freedom.

The waiter brought me the bill and I quickly paid it. $1.25. An amount I was quite comfortable with, given the small amount of money my mother had been willing to take from me. Once we were on the sidewalk in front of the department store, Edna opened her purse. I thought she was reaching for a cigarette, making me blush uncomfortably. There were many women on State Street who'd scowl at her in disapproval. But instead, she brought out a twenty-dollar bill and held it out to me.

"What are you doing?"

"I should pay for lunch, don't you think? I ambushed you after all."

"I'm quite able to take a lady to lunch."

"Well, then think of it as your allowance."

"Put that away," I said, glancing around. "We'll discuss an allowance at some point in the future."

She put the money away, looking as though she would have been much happier had I accepted it. Taking my arm we began to walk. Then she said, "Your mother rang me on the telephone. You told her I'm not temperance."

"That's right. I did."

Mother had been so quiet the last few days, I decided it might not matter. But then, apparently, she hadn't been silent at all.

"She told me in no uncertain terms that I am *not* to marry you."

"So, you already knew I'd decided to accept your proposal."

"I knew no such thing. She could easily have turned you against me."

I chose not to admit the truth in that.

"You're not going to let Mother scare you off, are you?"

"Certainly, not. Do I seem like the sort you can scare off?"

"You don't. Should we find you a taxi?"

"Could we walk a bit? It's a lovely day."

It was a lovely day. The sky was clear and blue, the sun warming us gently, and from the east a wind blew across the lake chasing away at least some of the too frequent smells of the city.

"All right."

"Unless you have to get back to the office."

In truth, I didn't have to get back. I needed to get to work on the second Rudkin claim. Briefly, I told Edna about the newest development in the case.

"Interestingly, it's the same case. My first case, come back again. The woman who filed the death claim for her husband who wasn't her husband. She's filed another claim. This time it may very well be her husband."

"How fascinating," Edna said, her eyes shining. "Do you think she killed both men?"

"I have no idea."

"What are you going to do first?"

"I think I'm going to go to the morgue and take a look at this new Mr. Rudkin."

She gasped a little. "I would so like to go with you."

"I don't think that's appropriate."

"I don't think it's appropriate either, why do you think I want to do it?"

"Edna, I can't."

"Think of it as a gift. We've just gotten engaged. There isn't anything you can buy me that I don't already have. Give me this."

And so, my engagement gift to my future wife was a trip to the morgue.

CHAPTER 16

Fortunately, Edna was adventurous enough to ride the elevated, otherwise I would have had to pay for an expensive taxi ride. I suppose she wouldn't have allowed… Well, at any rate. We took the Met to the Hoyne station and then walked south to the hospital. I can't say I recall much about the trip. I have an image in my mind of Edna and I sitting side by side on the leather seats of the noisy train looking blankly at the other passengers, none of whom were of Edna's social standing or even mine. But that image might not have anything to do with what happened. It might be that we chatted happily the whole trip. I do think we were quite pleased with ourselves for having out-smarted the entire world. We would protect ourselves from its cruelties, while at the same time managing to live honestly, at least with each other.

As we walked down the long hallway that brought us to the morgue, the smell crept up on us like a predator in the forest. It stopped Edna in her tracks.

"Oh my. Is that what I think it is?"

"Yes. You don't have to come further. You've been very brave to come this far."

"Lewis, don't even think of becoming that sort."

"What sort?"

"The sort of solicitous husband who blocks his wife at every turn. That's not at all what I'm looking for."

"I was only attempting to be kind."

"Avoid that whenever possible."

When we found Hoffman, he seemed just as uninterested as he had been during my first visit. That probably sounds unfair. Many people, indeed most people, would want to work anywhere other than a morgue. But there were people who would be quite pleased to work in a morgue, excited almost. It seemed unfair they were denied the work by the employment of this bored and sullen man.

The moment he saw Edna, he said, "Excuse me ma'am, are you here to find a relative?"

"She's with me," I said quickly, so that Edna didn't have time to concoct an answer. "Do you remember me? I was here—"

"Yeah, I remember you. I can't allow no woman in the morgue." He waved a dismissive hand at Edna.

"Don't be ridiculous," Edna retorted. "You allow women into the morgue all the time."

"Dead women. Women who got kin here. You got kin here?"

Edna opened the purse that hung from her wrist and pulled out a two-dollar bill. She offered it to the man and he quickly snatched it away. He studied it a moment, though I doubted he'd recognized a counterfeit note even if it were one. Satisfied, he said, "Ain't right, but I'll let you in."

"We're looking for Mr. Rudkin. Jurgis Rudkin," I told him.

"Yeah, I figured. Same as before," he said as he led us over to the wall of small, square doors. He picked out a door about knee height. As he opened it, he said, "Ain't right. Poor man's naked."

"I've seen a naked man before," Edna said. "It's not as frightening as you make out."

"Wasn't your modesty I was worried about."

On the metal gurney lay a nude man of about thirty-five or so. His hair was somewhere between blond and brown. When he was alive it might have been called sandy, but dead it was more like wet straw. He was clean-shaven but for a moustache. It even looked like he'd shaved no more than a few hours before he died. The moustache had been waxed and curled at the ends, though now the curls were limp and bent out of shape. There were a couple of bruises fading away on his face and neck. His body was well developed, with strong muscles. His skin was pale, except for his hands and face, which were darker but not by much. There were several scars on his hands, between two and three inches each. I picked up one of his cold hands and looked more closely.

"Hey there. What do you think you're doing?"

"There are scars on his hands. Where do you think he got them?"

"How should I know?" Hoffman said. It was, at least peripherally, his job to answer questions of that sort, but I decided not to point that out.

"Most of the scars are on his left hand," I pointed out. "Could that mean something?"

"He was a butcher," Hoffman said gruffly. "That's what a policeman told me. Butchers cut themselves."

"Yes, of course," I said. The real Mr. Rudkin *was* a butcher. But I still wasn't convinced this corpse was him. If the Rudkin's had substituted another corpse it would just as likely be someone who worked in the yards. Scars would not be unusual.

I could hear Edna beside me, breathing. I think it was the longest I'd heard her go without speaking. I imagined she was trying hard not to look at the man's prick and balls lolling on his hip. Somehow his genitals seemed more alive than the rest of him. Just below his rib cage was a wound about three inches long. It wasn't a simple cut, there were nicks and gouges at the bottom of the wound.

"It looks like the killer moved the knife around once it was in," I said to Edna.

"Vicious," she whispered.

I looked up at Hoffman again. "You haven't done an autopsy. Is there one scheduled?"

"He died of a knife wound," he said with some exasperation.

Honestly, I didn't know much about autopsies, but there had to be some point to them. And in a case like this, well, it might have been able to tell us many things that we hadn't even thought would be useful.

"How tall is he?"

"Tall."

I frowned at the man. Then turned to Edna, "He's taller than I am. By how much do you think?"

It seemed smart to ask a woman. Women sew and would understand measurements. But as soon as I thought that I remembered that Edna did *not* sew. She instructed others to sew for her—which might still impart an understanding of measurements.

"Oh, well, two inches?" she guessed.

That made him just over six-foot, possibly more.

"Do you have his clothes?" I asked Hoffman.

"I ain't going to dress him up for you."

"I'd like to see them."

Hoffman walked out of the room, and Edna whispered to me, "Is that normal? For his thing to be that… large?"

I glanced at her and realized she was looking at the man's organ. "Honestly, I couldn't say."

"You couldn't say? Don't you know?"

In truth, I hadn't seen many more naked men than Edna. As simply as possible, I said, "I haven't seen a wide range, if that's what you're asking. Nor have I read any scientific studies."

She studied me a moment, and said, "I'll ask Hal."

Which made me wonder if she was really suggesting that Hal might have the kind of broad experience necessary—

Hoffman came back with a brown paper sack. In the center of the room was a large metal counter with a drain at one end. I didn't realize it at first, but that was the counter used for autopsies. That's where Hoffman set the sack.

Inside were Mr. Rudkin' suit, shirt, collar, shoes, socks and union suit. There was a pair of brown shoes, that had been resoled at least once, and a derby hat. I spread the clothes over the counter to study them. The vest, shirt and union suit each had a slit that corresponded with the knife wound. There were blood stains.

In one vest pocket was a gold-plated watch fob. However, there was no watch in the opposite pocket. A quick inventory told me that his collar buttons and cufflinks were also missing.

"Was he robbed before or after he got to the morgue?" I asked.

This earned me a filthy look. I thought it a reasonable question. The way he took Edna's money suggested he was far from honest. "Police took it. Evidence they said."

But then, the fact that he had a watch, collar button and cufflinks worth taking as "evidence" seemed odd… And then, Edna nudged me, saying, "Lewis, the shirt."

"What about it?"

"The label. It's Hart Schaffner & Marx. I buy those shirts for Hal at Rothschild."

I was well acquainted with Hart Schaffner & Marx. I had two of their lovely shirts, which I saved for special occasions. I suspected that when she said she bought them for Hal she meant in a larger number for everyday wear. I checked the label on the suit and showed it to Edna. It was from Montgomery Ward, a catalogue house.

"That is strange," Edna noted. "It's as though one day he's wealthy and the next day he's not."

I went through all the pockets just to see if there was anything the police hadn't taken. In the inside pocket of the jacket there was nothing, but when I pulled out my hand there was tobacco on my fingers. I showed it to Edna. She lifted my fingers to her nose and delicately sniffed.

"Cigars."

Hoffman looked at her with some surprise, though I couldn't figure why. She was a woman who'd bribed her way into the morgue, her knowledge of cigars shouldn't have surprised him. As though to answer his look, she said to me, "My father smokes them. My guess is that Mr. Rudkin wasn't carrying quality cigars."

I didn't find anything else in his pockets.

"Did he have a wallet?"

"If he did, the police took it."

"They don't give you a list of what they take?"

He looked at me like I belonged in an asylum. I ignored him and continued looking at the clothing. On the back of the jacket, there were a few smudges of dirt and some blood, but none of the clothing seemed to have been especially wet. I asked, "He was found next to Bubbly Creek, but not in it?"

"I heard that, yeah."

"Not hidden, just laid on the shore?"

"Wasn't me who found him."

I stared back at the clothes laid out in front of us. Was there anything else I needed to know I wondered? Could they tell me anything else? Suddenly, an idea came to me. I asked Hoffman, "Can we look at the first Mr. Rudkin? Is his body still here?"

"Ain't been claimed," he grumbled, then went back to the wall of doors. He reached for a familiar little door and opened it. Then he pulled out the gurney. On it lay the burned corpse I'd seen before. With a glance, I noticed that Edna's eyes had opened very wide. This was not the nice, clean corpse of the second Mr. Rudkin.

"Look at his feet," I told Edna.

The feet on the burned corpse were rough, toenails thick and yellowed, a flowery burst of veins hovered above the ankle. I can't say I had a great understanding of men's feet at the time. My only real exposure to the feet of other men would have been on the beach at Lake Michigan during the summer. But even without much experience, I said to Edna, "They look old, don't they?"

"Yes, I suppose."

"Now let's look at the new Mr. Rudkin." His feet were unmarred. There were blisters on his heal and under one big toe, both suggesting he'd done a great deal of walking in the days before his death. But his feet did not look old. His toenails were white and clear; they'd have been pink if he were living.

"Mrs. Rudkin came in and identified the burned corpse as her husband. She said she recognized his feet. But if this is the real Mr. Rudkin, then she was clearly lying. She wanted the insurance money and lied to get it. I think it's safe to assume that's still true, regardless of whether this new Mr. Rudkin is the correct one or not."

I thanked Hoffman and we left the morgue. We crossed the street and stood in front of the five-story turreted Rush

Medical College, which was kitty-corner to the hospital. Edna took her pack of Murads out of her elegant bag and shook one out. She offered me the pack. I took one. Then she gave me the box of matches and I lit both cigarettes. I assumed from her behavior that a gentleman was meant to light a lady's cigarette, though that was not among the manners my mother had taught me. There was an etiquette to this that was completely new to me. As soon as she exhaled, Edna asked, "What are your thoughts?"

"I think it entirely possible that this Mr. Rudkin is another fraud."

"You may be right. But doesn't that beg the question, 'Where does Mrs. Rudkin keep finding corpses?' Or, possibly, gentlemen to turn into corpses."

"The first thing I need to do is establish whether this Mr. Rudkin is the real Mr. Rudkin or not."

"We need fingerprints," Edna said, breathlessly. "I read all about the Hiller murder in *The Examiner*. They had absolutely no evidence against the burglar, just fingerprints. But that was enough. They hung him."

I'd attended a lecture or two at school on fingerprinting and read a pamphlet that Josiah had given me. I explained to Edna, "The key to fingerprints is the reliability of your samples. For example, if we had a set of fingerprints that belonged without doubt to Mr. Rudkin, then we could compare them to the second corpse. But we don't. Now, if the second corpse is not Mr. Rudkin and is instead a known criminal, there is a chance his fingerprints might have been collected. But we'd have to have access to the fingerprint cards and that's a needle in a haystack. One that I doubt the Chicago police will pursue given that three people have identified this second corpse as Mr. Rudkin."

"I see," she said and fell to smoking silently. Two older women walked by us on their way into the Rush Medical

College. Both of them gave Edna a vicious look for smoking on the street. Edna didn't notice—or if she did, didn't care. "What you need to do is determine the reliability of the people who identified Mr. Rudkin."

"Yes, exactly. Mrs. Rudkin is already unreliable, having incorrectly or fraudulently identified her husband once. That leaves the doctor and the insurance agent."

"Who are we seeing first?"

"Edna, I think it time for you to go home."

"But why? I was helpful, wasn't I?"

"You want me to keep this job at least until after the wedding, don't you? That might not be easy if they find out I'm bringing my fiancée along with me."

She could not argue with my logic, so she said, "Find me a taxi, will you dear?"

After I put her into a taxi, it occurred to me that I should have a photo of Mr. Rudkin if at all possible. I went back into the morgue and filled out the proper form to obtain a death portrait. Then I gave Hoffman a dollar to cover the quarter for the photo and the fifty cents to pay a boy to run it over to the Pinkerton office. He wrote me out a receipt, and though he owed me two bits refused to give it to me.

*D*r. Wallace Thacker practiced medicine in the front room of his apartment at 5241 S. Leavitt Avenue. The red brick building, which was three-stories and sat in a row of three with cast iron cornices on top, was directly behind a fire station that, given Chicago's history, seemed both a comfort and a curse. The room held a large rolltop desk, the kind you can order from a catalogue, shoved up against the heavily draped front windows. It was jammed with pieces of paper in such a way that it looked impossible to ever find whichever piece of paper you might want. Next to the desk sat an uncomfortable chair for his patients.

Between the desk and the dining room, which was furnished for a family's use, was an examining table. It was the same height as the counter at the morgue, though instead of being metal and containing a drain at one end, this table was covered in cloth over some sort of padding. The room was dark and lit by gaslight. It was strange to hear the hiss of gas. It was a sound of the past, a sound of my childhood.

Dr. Thacker must have seen me glance at the lamps, because he said, "I don't hold with all these newfangled contraptions. Everyday they've got to reinvent the world. World was just fine if you ask me. Now, who are you?"

"I'm Lewis Wait. I'm with the Pinkerton Detective Agency. I'm looking into the death of Jurgis Rudkin."

"Who's that?" His eyes were wet and red, the bags beneath them pulling down his eyelids.

"He's a man you examined for Continental Surety & Safety. And then, recently, you identified his body," I explained.

"All right. Yes."

"Do you remember him now?"

"Of course, I do. Why wouldn't I?" His lower lip hung open, shiny with spittle. I tried not to stare at it.

"Tell me about your examination of Mr. Rudkin."

"I gave him a basic physical. He was young. His heart was strong. His breathing good. He had no complaints. That's what I told the insurance company."

"Did you make note of his height, his weight?"

"To what purpose?" he said, getting quite annoyed.

"Identification."

"Are you suggesting something?"

"I'm suggesting that someone could buy insurance for one person and send someone else for the exam. And there would be no way of verifying that it was the same person."

"That isn't what happened. This man was stabbed. The young man from Continental came and we went to look at him together. He's in the morgue; stabbed to death."

"Yes, I know, I saw the body just an hour ago. You recognized him?"

"I did. And so did the Continental man. We both recognized him."

I thought it very unlikely that he remembered Mr. Rudkin at all. He only identified the corpse because the agent had. I couldn't be certain that the person Dr. Thacker had identified was Mr. Rudkin any more than I could be certain the corpse he identified was.

Of course, there was another issue. "Did you also recognize the first Mr. Rudnick?"

"First— What the devil are you talking about?"

"Was your office ever located 2415 South Leavitt Avenue?"

"No. I've been in this building for fifteen years."

"So, there's no reason for your stationery to use that address on Leavitt?"

"Of course not."

The stationery existed; I had it at the office. That could mean a few things. It was printed in error and not wanting to waste three dollars Dr. Thacker used it anyway. But then he'd admit that now, wouldn't he? It could also be that someone else had the stationery printed in order to commit the fraud, and that person forgot Dr. Thacker's correct address or, just as likely, didn't want the letter traced back to him.

"To be clear, Dr. Thacker, you did not identify the first Mr. Rudkin?"

"What first— Did the man's father just die? Because I have no idea—"

Standing abruptly, I said, "Thank you, Dr. Thacker. You've been helpful."

I hurried out of his apartment. It was just after four o'clock and I had to get to Continental Surety & Safety before five. I knew Roland Harcourt spent most of his time selling policies and collecting premiums in Packingtown. But what did he do with the change he collected each day? My guess was that he went back to the office to turn in the money and update the records.

Excitement coursed through my body. Someone had forged the first letter from Dr. Thacker. Harcourt would be the person who'd supplied the letter to our office. He had to know something about it. Particularly as he also claimed to not know Mr. Rudkin and later identified his body—possibly having influenced Dr. Thacker to do the same.

I was seven or eight blocks from the Elevated station at 47th and Green. I practically ran the whole way. Luckily, a train came quickly and I was getting off at Quincy at twenty before five. I was very near the Pinkerton office, but I didn't think about that. I went directly to Continental Surety & Safety. This time I had the elevator operator take me to the fifth floor. I went quickly to the large room filled with desks and women where I'd found Harcourt before. He was nowhere to be seen.

At the desk nearest me was a woman approaching fifty. She had an air of being in charge, though I don't know if that was true or not. I asked her if Harcourt was in the office or in the field. With a sort of smirk she said, "I think he's in the storeroom down the hall getting pencils. You can go down there if you like."

I thanked her and went out into the hallway. Part way down the hall was the ladies' room, identified as such in gold leaf. Then further down was a door without a description. I opened that door and found Roland Harcourt standing in a small storeroom with a plump young woman next to him. His pants were down around his knees and the young woman's hand was inside his union suit bouncing around with great abandon. I felt myself pale and closed the door.

Standing in the hallway I wasn't sure what to do. I wanted to leave as quickly as possible, but it didn't make any sense to allow Harcourt's bad behavior to get in the way of my investigation. I worried he might not come out at all, but then Harcourt and the plump girl came out of the storeroom. Harcourt had his pants back where they belonged. The girl giggled as she hurried by to go back to work.

"That wasn't very nice of you," he said to me.

"The older woman told me you were in there. It wasn't very nice of *her*. I could have waited."

He nodded. Then he gave me a grin and raised his eyebrows.

"You're not proud of that, are you?" I asked.

"Why not? Nobody got hurt. There won't be any trouble. I know how babies are made. Won't catch me doing that. No, siree."

I decided to get to the point—after all, what he was doing in there wasn't any of my business. "You identified Jurgis Rudkin's body? The second Jurgis Rudkin?"

"Yeah, so what?"

"You told me when I interviewed you before that you'd never seen Jurgis Rudkin."

"No, I didn't. Why would I have said that? It don't make no sense. I'm over on Whiskey Row most nights. Everyone knows Jurgis. When he wins at cards, we all drink for free."

"I'm sure you said you'd never—"

"Yeah, I know you think that. You put it in your report. I almost got fired. If they hadn't believed me, I would have."

Was I wrong? Had he not said what I remembered? He seemed reasonable. And I remembered in our first meeting he'd said he was on Whiskey Row most nights. It was possible I didn't remember correctly. But—

"There's a letter from Dr. Thacker that identifies the first body as Mr. Rudkin. But that's on stationery which lists an address that doesn't exist. You're the one who provided that letter."

"No, weren't me. The Rudkins filed the claim. They're the ones gave us the letter. I just passed it along to your agency."

Suddenly, a new possibility occurred to me. It was Mr. Rudkin who concocted the whole scheme. He had the stationery made. He probably couldn't remember Dr. Thacker's exact address, but he'd been there. That was why it was so similar. When the plot failed, his conspirators decided to attempt it again with the real Jurgis Rudkin.

"Who cancels policies around here?"

"It depends. If they stop paying, I cancel them."

"Why didn't you cancel the Rudkins' policy?"

"They kept paying."

"Mrs. Rudkin identified the wrong man as her husband. That's fraud. Isn't that a good enough reason to cancel a policy?"

"She made a mistake. You don't think—"

"If you think it was a simple mistake, which I don't believe, but if you think that then don't prosecute. But it's not wise to continue the policy."

"Are you accusing me of something?"

"At the very least you were negligent."

"This isn't what you're supposed to be doing. You're supposed to find a reason not to pay the policy. It's no difference if I canceled it or not. The Rudkins ain't gonna get paid, are they?"

"But what if they do?" I asked. "If this does turn out to be Mr. Rudkin and Mrs. Rudkin has nothing to do with his death, then there may not be a way to void the claim."

"I'll believe it when I see it."

Before I could walk away, he said, "That you on the front page the other day?"

"As a matter of fact, it was. What of it?"

He shrugged and said, "You don't seem the type. That's all." And then he walked back into his office, leaving me in the hallway feeling uncomfortable.

When I arrived home, I found that Mother had held dinner for me. She and the Polish girl had made lamb patties, mashed potatoes and canned peas. Unlike the sophisticated fare she'd copied from the newspaper for my birthday dinner, this really was my favorite meal. The meal ended with apple pie and a wedge of sharp cheddar, also my favorite. It was clear that Mother had begun her campaign against Edna in earnest.

After I'd had the last bite of pie, I said to her, "The engagement is official. Edna anticipates there will be an engagement party soon. I hope you'll come."

"I most certainly will not."

"Which would you like? Gout or a weak heart?" I asked, somewhat sincerely.

"I beg your pardon?"

"For your excuse. Which would you like? I suggest gout. It clears up now and then, so if you change your mind you can come to the wedding."

"I will not change my mind. I never change my mind."

"That's hardly true. Three weeks ago, you adored Edna."

"I was tricked. She's an adventuress."

"You think she's after the money you no longer have?" I asked with some bite.

Avoiding the subject of her finances, Mother said, "I don't know what she's after and I doubt you do either. You've allowed yourself to be turned by a pretty face."

That made me smile. Not a happy smile. But a smile all the same. It was working. The ruse of my relationship with Edna was accepted even by my own mother.

"It's done Mother. There's nothing you can do about it."

"Yes, there is. This is my house. Don't think for a moment you'll be moving her in here."

I laughed. Very loudly, in fact.

"I don't know why that's funny?"

"Mother, you didn't notice the quality of her clothing?"

"Lots of young women wear quality clothing. She goes further than most, I suppose. My guess is she's a spendthrift. Another reason not to—"

"Her foyer is larger than our parlor. Her parlor is larger than our apartment."

"She's wealthy?"

"Yes. Very."

Her surprise quite cowed her. She looked down at the table and said softly, "That makes even less sense."

"Thank you, Mother. That's so flattering."

"Don't be a fool, Lewis. Someone of that class wants someone like them."

There was no way to tell Mother she was right. That Edna had found someone like her and that was what interested her in me. We were both inverts, we *were* alike, and we needed each other. Before I could come up with a suitable answer, the telephone bell rang. The machine sat on the buffet next to us. Mother rose to answer it.

"Yes?" she said. Most people said, "Hello" by then but Mother just couldn't get the hang of it. "Oh, yes. One moment." She set the earpiece on the buffet and said to me. "It's your fiancée."

"Thank you," I said as I got up and went over to the buffet. Picking up the earpiece, I spoke into the mouthpiece, "Hello?"

"Lewis, it's Edna."

"Yes. Mother said that."

"I have an idea for tomorrow. Can we meet for lunch?"

"I don't know if I can have lunch with you every day, Edna." I really wanted to spend more time seeing her in the evening when I could see Hal as well. "I do have a job."

"This *is* for your job. For your case."

"I don't think you should get involved—"

"Meet me in front of the stockyard gates at eleven o'clock. Don't be late."

CHAPTER 18

I did not go into the Pinkerton office the next morning. Instead, I remained in bed until nearly eight o'clock. There wasn't anything I could do on the case, so it made sense to go into the office after I met Edna. While still on the telephone, I refused to meet her unless she told me what exactly we'd be doing. She confessed we were to take a guided tour of the stockyards. I didn't expect we'd learn anything earth-shattering, but I had to admit it might prove helpful. After the tour, I planned to go to the office and see if the photograph of Mr. Rudkin's corpse had arrived. If it had, then I could go back to Packingtown and show it to the Rudkin neighbors to see who, if anyone, recognized him.

The ride on the Elevated was quick and I arrived at the entrance to the yards about ten minutes early. The gate itself was an elaborate arch made of stone with imitation turrets. It aspired to be some kind of European castle, but to me it looked more like a theatrical set. Above the arch was a stone carving of a bull—appropriate I suppose, particularly since the corrals began right next to the gate and the smell of manure was thick. In the distance, over the mews of cattle, I could hear a freight train moving lazily as it made its way into the stockyards. The point of the gate, I suppose, was to make us feel something grand was just beyond, but honestly the acre after acre of corrals was more impressive.

Just before Edna arrived, I noted a small group gathering on the opposite side of the arch. There were two ladies in wide-brimmed hats with big bows on top, a short, unhappy looking man, and a very tall, very young one wearing a summer suit. They were all too well dressed to work there, so I assumed they were waiting for the tour. Over my shoulder, I heard a growling automobile approaching and turned to see Hal drive up in a red coupe with his sister sitting next to him.

Most automobiles at the time were black, so red was a startling thing. More startling than that was that the coupe had no windshield; instead it had a round piece of glass sitting in a partial metal frame in front of the driver. It looked like a monocle. Edna waved at me as they zipped by and parked the vehicle a few hundred feet away.

I didn't feel like waiting at the gate, so I strolled over to meet them. I was delighted she'd brought Hal, but at the same time I couldn't let them get into the habit of joining me in my work. Well, the tour was hardly my work. I doubted strongly it would tell me anything of importance.

When I got close, Hal asked, "Do you like it? I bought it at the Auto Show last month. It's a Model T Speedster. It can hit seventy miles an hour if the wind's not too strong."

"Thankfully he didn't go that fast on Lake Shore Drive, I almost lost my hat as it was." Edna smiled broadly, removing a pair of driving goggles. "They haven't started the tour without us, have they?"

"No, I don't think so."

As we hurried back to the gate, Edna said, "I told Hal all

about our visit to the morgue, so he just had to come along today."

"You can't reserve all your charms for my sister," he said with a wink.

"I hope I have more interesting charms than dead bodies and slaughtered livestock."

Hal's smile grew, which made my stomach flutter. I wondered for the briefest moment if we could find a supply closet somewhere and reenact the scene I'd interrupted between Roland Harcourt and the typewritist. What would it be like to let my hand bounce around inside Hal's union suit the way the girl—I forced myself to think of something else. I was afraid my thoughts were all too obvious.

When we got back to the gate, we stood near the others whom I'd assumed were on the tour. Beyond the gate was a long, dusty road that divided the corrals from a row of brick buildings. There were a surprising number of people scurrying about.

A young man in a tweed suit far too heavy for the sunny spring day, walked up the dusty road and waved as he got near. "Welcome! I assume you're all here for the tour." We smiled and nodded agreement. As soon as he was in front of us, he began, "I'm Walter Titus, and I work for the Union Stock Yards. I'll be your guide this morning."

It was such a small group it tempted us to introduce ourselves, but Titus was a sort of servant, and you didn't introduce yourself to servants. He ignored the moment of awkwardness and continued the tour.

"They say if you come to Chicago and miss seeing the stockyards then you've missed seeing Chicago. And truly, the yards are one of the wonders of the Windy City. If you'll step right this way, we'll begin the tour at our viewing stand where you can see over three hundred acres of pens that contain up to thirty thousand animals at one time. Thirteen *million* animals come through the stockyards each year."

We followed him into the yards and over to a narrow viewing platform on the right. It was only a few feet deep with four steps up on either side with a railing to keep you from falling off. The ladies were asked to climb up first. I already had an idea what they were seeing since I'd seen it from the Elevated on my previous visit.

As she ascended the platform, Edna asked our guide, "Will we see any animals killed today?"

"You needn't worry about that, ma'am. I'll give you plenty of warning to avert your eyes."

The other two young women seemed relieved, but Edna plowed ahead, "But how can it be a comprehensive tour if we can't watch an animal being killed?"

"Surely a gentile young woman like yourself doesn't want to see something like that."

She gave him a cool smile, which he ignored.

"Each day cattle, hogs, sheep and horses are brought in from all over the Midwest and the West. They're unloaded and kept in the pens that you see. While in the pens, they're fed and watered. When it's time to slaughter the animal, they're led into the viaducts overhead, which in turn lead to the killing floors at the appropriate company."

It was my turn to climb up onto the platform with Hal. There was only room for three, but the tall man and the squat man both climbed up with us. That left me pressed close to Hal. He leaned in, and said, "It is rather remarkable, isn't it?"

"It's a lot of cows."

Hal chuckled and we walked down the other side of the viewing platform. When we had all gathered again on the street, Titus said, "Follow me. We're going to start with hogs." We followed him. "Very soon we're going to see animals slaughtered. If you're squeamish be prepared to look away."

I don't remember which of the famous meatpackers buildings we went into. It might have been Armour or Libby or Nelson Morris. But I do remember that in very short order we were watching a boy put a shackle onto the back leg of a hog, and then a grown man lifting the hog and hooking it onto a rail. They did it again and again every few seconds. The rail slid the hog down to another man referred to as a sticker, who plunged a knife into both sides of a screaming hog's throat. That, too, happened every few seconds.

The two ladies in hats turned away, covering their faces with handkerchiefs against the stench of the killing floor. Edna, though, didn't look away. In fact, her eyes grew bright as she studied the dying animals with piqued interest.

Before the hogs were finished bleeding to death, they were shuffled down the line and dropped into a pan of boiling water. Several men stood around the pan with poles turning the hogs over and over. At the end of the pan, a metal arm lifted the hog out and workers rolled it onto a table. Titus talked the whole time we watched.

"Most people credit Henry Ford as the inventor of the assembly line, but it's innovations he saw here in the Union Stock Yards during the Columbian Exposition of 1893 which he later adapted into what is now the modern assembly line. And, speaking of the Columbian Exposition, more people came to visit the stockyards than any of the official exhibits. How about that?"

The hogs were stripped of their skin, their heads and hooves cut off, and they were split down the middle. We stood in front of what Titus called "a half mile of hogs" hanging on hooks. He walked us by a room where pork was smoked—which made our eyes water—and another where sausages were made. That room had a table, racks strung with finished strings of sausage, and a dozen children between the ages of eight and ten.

"How much are the workers paid?" I asked.

"Plenty. And if they don't think they're paid well they can go elsewhere, can't they?" The stiffness of his answer suggested he'd gotten this question before. Of course, where he thought children would go for a job that paid more than "plenty" was something I doubted he could answer.

As he led us to the next area, where sheep were slaughtered and dressed, Titus explained, "At the end of each viaduct there is a pen where several leader sheep are kept. These sheep have bells attached around their necks and they have been trained to lead the other sheep from the pens to the killing floor. Cleverly, the leader sheep slips out of the corral at the last moment. These leader sheep become so close to their masters that they take up the habit of chewing tobacco."

That was it. I'd had enough of absurdity and brutality. I pulled Hal and Edna out of line and, while Titus led the rest in to watch the sheep being slaughtered around the corner.

"I've seen enough," I said.

"It's so deliciously brutal," Edna said. "Beautiful in its way."

"Yes, but I really should be working. And I don't know that this is helpful. If you two want to finish the tour..."

"I think we've seen enough delicious brutality," Hal said, gently mocking his sister. She frowned but busied herself pulling a pack of Murads, and offered Hal and I each a cigarette. We both accepted. Fortunately, the tobacco smoke blotted out the smells of blood and death occurring just a few feet away.

"What should we do now?" Edna asked with a mischievous look.

"I should probably go to my office and you two should get on with your day."

"Don't be a wet blanket. We're here. Surely there's something useful we could do?"

"It would be interesting to see you work," Hal added.

Somewhere nearby, Mrs. Rudkin and her children were attempting to scrape together a living. I hadn't planned to talk to her until I was sure that it really was her husband this time, but maybe we could get a look at her. "Well, Mrs. Rudkin works at Swift. So first we need to find where that particular company is."

I remembered that Swift was one of the stops on the Elevated. That morning I'd gotten off at the Exchange station, but I knew the loop around the stockyards from my last visit. It had stops at Morris, Swift, Packers and also Armour. Orienting myself, I decided that Swift was in a south-westerly direction from where we stood.

"This way," I said.

The slaughterhouses were in a loose sense grouped together, so it didn't take long for us to find Swift & Company. The building was brick and had large wooden doors, which opened out into the alley where we stood. There had to be offices somewhere, paperwork had to happen, but I couldn't figure out exactly where they were. The floor in front of us seemed dedicated to the same slaughter we'd just seen.

A man in a leather apron swept entrails into a pile; there was a shovel nearby and a row of three barrels waiting to receive the organs. I tried not to think about where they might be going or what would happen to them. When he got close enough, I leaned over and asked, "Excuse me. Do you know where I might find Mrs. Rudkin?"

He looked at me as though I were unstable.

"She work here?"

"Yes, she does."

"We ain't supposed to get visitors. This ain't no social club."

"I know that. I'm here representing Continental Surety & Safety. Mrs. Rudkin's husband died and she has put in a claim." Instinct told me it might be best not to mention the Pinkerton name to a man denied a union.

"I don't know the woman. But if she works here, she's either on the third floor in the packing room or she's an office girl."

I didn't think she was a typewritist, so I asked, "Where's the packing room?"

"Third floor."

"And where are the stairs?"

He pointed down toward the end of the building. "There's a door down there. If anybody asks, you didn't find out nothing from me." After giving us a dirty look, he went back to shoveling entrails.

As we hurried down the alley Edna lifted her skirt a little, as though she was afraid of what might jump out at her from the slaughterhouse. Hal gave me a sidelong glance, seeming to enjoy the adventure. I was, I suppose, quite proud of myself. Despite the obvious risks, I was showing off for my friends.

The stairway we entered was narrow and dark. There were no windows and no lights. The only light we had to navigate by came from the open door on the second floor. Once we reached the landing, I quickly determined the second floor was devoted to the rendering of fat. The smell and feel of lard was thick in the air. I wanted to wipe my face the moment we went by.

We continued upward to the third floor. Once there, we found ourselves standing in a large room. Three conveyor belts dominated the room. On each side of the belts, women stood at small tables. Meat travelled down the belts—presumably the room on the other side of the wall held a group of butchers—and the women would place it into cardboard boxes. The boxes then went back onto the belt. At the end of the belt, a boy took the box off and set it onto a large flat dolly. Next to the stairs we'd just come up, was a large open elevator. Some kind of matron walked the room, watching everyone, occasionally glancing at a pocket watch she'd take out of her pocket.

A stern looking woman with a thick waist, I stepped over and asked her, "Could you point out Mrs. Rudkin?"

"Who are you?"

"I'm representing Continental Surety & Safety. The insurance company."

"Is this some kind of inspection?"

"I'm not at liberty to say," I said, deciding whatever she imagined was more intimidating than any lie I could tell.

She studied me, then looked over my shoulder and asked, "And who are they?"

"I'm sure you understand the value of discretion in situations like these."

I can't imagine what she thought I was talking about—particularly as I had no idea—but she became quite uncomfortable. "Rudkin, you say? On the right, fourth table down. Don't take no more than five minutes."

"Thank you for your cooperation. It will be noted."

I went back over to Hal and Edna whispering, "Hurry. We have to be fast."

I had no idea how long it would take the matron to figure out I hadn't actually given her any sort of explanation. We walked down the right side of the room to the fourth table.

As we got close, I nearly stopped in my tracks. The woman packing meat was beautiful, truly beautiful. She had the kind of face that painters would stare at for hours and struggle to capture. Her features were perfectly balanced, mouth small, eyes large, skin a healthy pink. She wore a white cap to keep her hair out of her face, but it escaped here and there in thin little curls. Though the room was relatively cool, she was dewy with sweat. It only made her more beautiful.

I remembered Harcourt saying the daughter was a looker. She seemed old to be the daughter. In fact, she was the oldest at the table, but Mrs. Rudkin might be somewhere about.

"Excuse me, I'm looking for Mrs. Rudkin?" I asked the beautiful creature. She looked up but didn't answer.

Behind me, a voice piped up and asked, "Who are you?" I turned and found myself staring at a girl of twelve or thirteen.

"My name is Lewis Wait. I'm with the Pinkerton Detective Agency. We're investigating Mrs. Rudkin's claim with Continental Surety & Safety. Who are you?"

She said something to the beautiful woman in a language I did not recognize, then looked back to me and said, "I am Revka. The daughter."

"And this is your mother?"

"Yes, she is my mother."

I wondered if I had confused what Harcourt said to me a second time. Certainly, the daughter was not beautiful, not even pretty. She was bony with thin hair and eyes that seemed pushed together in a criminal way. She was still young so maybe the next few years would be kind to her, but I couldn't see much hope of that. From the look on her face, I guessed she couldn't either.

Mrs. Rudkin said something to her daughter. Revka responded, clearly talking back. Her mother grew angry.

"She wants to know if you have brought the money."

"I'm afraid not."

"That's what I told her."

"Do you know what fraud is?" She didn't reply so I said, "Fraud is telling lies in order to obtain something you don't deserve. Like money."

The girl translated and they both looked concerned.

"The man found by Bubbly Creek. Is that your father?"

"Yes, it is." The girl stuck out her chin.

"Do you know who might have stabbed him?"

She shrugged. Her mother said a few words, the girl responded crisply.

"What did your father do for a living?"

"He was a butcher."

"He seemed awfully well dressed for a butcher."

The girl shrugged again.

"This is the second claim your family has put in for your father. Tell me, who was the man who burned to death in your kitchen?"

Revka repeated the question to her mother. That led to a brief though somewhat heated exchange. Then Revka said simply, "We don't know who he was. We weren't at home."

"A man entered your home and then somehow burned to death in your kitchen?"

"Maybe he was trying to steal things. I don't know."

"That would be more believable if your mother hadn't identified him as your father."

Revka began to cough. She took a handkerchief from her pocket and held it over her mouth. When she caught her breath, she said, "It's true. She isn't smart."

Mrs. Rudkin seemed to sense that she wouldn't like what was being said, or perhaps she had something to say about the impolite coughing. She began to speak rapidly. They argued for a moment. While they did, I looked over at Hal and Edna. I winked at them. I knew what I was about to do and I thought it would work. I really did.

"Tell your mother that if she doesn't stop lying we won't pay her claim."

After a moment of staring at me, Revka translated this. Mrs. Rudkin erupted in a long string of loud, senseless babble. Unfortunately, many of the women around us understood the babble, and within seconds there were two additional women screaming at me, then four, five, seven, nine. Then the matron was there, pushing us out of the packing room, which seemed to have become one nonsensical howl.

CHAPTER 19

*H*al offered me a ride back to the Loop, and I would have taken it, but the car was a two-seater and that meant Edna would have had to sit on my lap the whole way. Aside from decorum—which was no small issue—it seemed dangerous to drive that way. While I might not be in love with my fiancée, I didn't want to bounce her off my lap and into the street the first time we encountered a pothole. Though I was mortified by the way our trip to the yards had ended, Hal and Edna were thrilled with the experience. They teased me about the look on my face when all those women began shouting at me. Apparently, I turned quite pale.

"Obviously, that woman is guilty as sin. I mean, if that's her reaction when you accuse her of lying, then she must be guilty," Hal said.

I wasn't as convinced. Though I had little experience, it did seem to me that people who were telling the truth did sometimes get offended when you called them a liar. Clearly, my plan had failed. It had been my hope that calling the woman a liar would cause some kind of misstep. I didn't expect her to break down and confess, but I did expect she'd provide more lies to support the lies she'd already told. The more lies I had to work with the easier it would be to prove them false. Unfortunately, I hadn't gotten any new information. At least, not in a language I understood.

It wasn't until I was on the Elevated and heading back to the Pinkerton Office that I began to think about Revka Rudkin. Had I confused what Harcourt said? If I hadn't, why would he tell me Revka was a looker when it was clearly the mother who was appealing? Had *he* confused the two? Was he thinking of some other family in Packingtown?

No, that seems wrong. Harcourt was very aware of women. It would be odd for him not to remember which one was attractive and which one was not. But why would he lie to me? Was he attempting to conceal something? Did he not believe I'd ever meet Revka Rudkin?

When I arrived back at the Pinkerton Office, I inquired to see if the photo of the second Mr. Rudkin had arrived. It had not. Since I'd come all that way, I decided there was still something important I should look at: the two letters from Dr. Thacker. I inquired on the ninth floor for the first file and then took it down to the office I'd commandeered. I lay both letters out on the desk and sat down to appraise them.

They were both on printed stationery. Both were hand-written using fountain pens, which was evident in the fact that both notes were neatly written. It was much more difficult to control a dip pen. Droplets and sudden blobs were common. Fountain pens controlled the ink more reliably.

The handwriting on the second letter, the one written by the real Dr. Thacker, slanted to the left and was harder to read. The vowels were crushed together and the extenders jumped into the line above or the line below. The first letter featured a hand that was elegantly curled with perfectly formed letters and well-behaved extenders.

And then there was the grammar. The first letter contained only one error that I could find. The second, the one I knew for a fact was written by Dr. Thacker, contained an error in each sentence. That suggested whoever forged the first letter was well educated.

That struck me as a problem. The person most likely to have been behind the fraudulent claim, the first claim, was Jurgis Rudkin himself. But I doubted he could have written such a letter. Nor did I see a reason anyone else in the family could have done it for him. Which left the open question, who wrote that letter?

Not finding an answer and not wanting to get stuck correcting the reports of other Pinks, I slipped out and went home. Mother managed to hold her tongue until we sat down to a simple supper of chicken hash and biscuits.

"You left for work very late this morning, and then you arrived home early. Are you trying to lose your job now that you have a rich fiancée?"

"I've been given a case to work. I expect I'll be quite busy the next few days."

"What case?"

"You can talk to your friend Mr. Cuthbert about it if you don't believe me."

"I'm not asking because I don't believe you, I'm asking because I'm interested." She frowned. She always frowned whenever there was a hint that she might be in the wrong.

"If you must know, it's my first case which has come back again," I explained.

"The woman whose husband was burned to death in the kitchen?"

I didn't remember discussing it with her. I must have, but I couldn't place exactly when I might have.

"Yes, except of course that wasn't her husband."

"Then why has the case come back?"

"Another corpse has shown up, and it seems she claims *this* one is her husband."

"Is it?"

"I doubt it, but I haven't been able to establish it's another fraud."

"She sounds like quite an ingenious woman, though." I detected a note of admiration in her voice.

"How so?"

"I'd be hard pressed to find one corpse, no less two."

"I suppose that's true."

"Will you be giving up your job after you marry?" she asked.

"Eventually, I suppose. I do want to return to school to finish my studies. Someday."

Did I want that? It now seemed like such a circumspect life. As disastrous as capturing a burglar had turned out to be, it was exhilarating. There wasn't anything exhilarating about finishing my studies. But then, to be completely honest, my real hope for exhilaration would be provided by Hal, my soon-to-be brother-in-law.

I sipped my glass of water, then said, "Don't worry Mother, Edna and I will always make sure you're taken care of."

"I'm not worried about that in the least," she replied stiffly.

I considered her a moment, wondering if I really wanted the answer to the question I was about to ask.

"You never really had money problems, did you?"

"I most certainly did. I wouldn't lie to you."

"Exaggerate then. Have you exaggerated your financial problems?"

"Not at all. Things have simply taken a sharp turn in my favor."

She was lying. The way she turned her attention to the

last few bites of her dinner made that clear to me. There was no point in pressing the issue I could think of. My dinner was finished.

I said, "I hope your plotting has gotten you everything you want." Knowing, of course, that it hadn't. Then I retreated to my bedroom, where I stayed for the rest of the evening.

CHAPTER 20

The next morning, I rose early so that I wouldn't have to see Mother. I washed, dressed, ate a few slices of Boston brown bread spread thick with butter, and was out the door. Riding the Elevated, I tried to decide what to do first. I needed the photograph. I was sure that if I took it to the Rudkin neighbors I'd find someone—well, likely several someones—to say that it wasn't Mr. Rudkin. Because I doubted the photograph would have arrived at the Pinkerton office since the previous afternoon, I tried to come up with something else I could do on the case.

As the South Side of Chicago drifted by me, I tried to put together a theory. Mrs. Rudkin and, presumably, her living husband, had tried to make a fraudulent claim against Mr. Rudkin's life insurance policy. I didn't have to reach too far to understand the motive. I'd been to Packingtown, and if I were a resident, there wasn't much I wouldn't do to get out. And a thousand dollars could do that. With that money, the Rudkins could easily move to another city and search for better jobs.

Now I needed to ask myself some important questions:

Did the Rudkins make a plan and then kill a man to implement it? Or did some person nearby die and then, seeing an opportunity, they concocted a plan and set it in motion?

I thought back through my academic training. The Rudkins seemed to me to be impulsive criminals. The social pressures of their environment combined with the presentation of an opportunity caused them to commit fraud. I considered that a very possible, even probable theory. But more to the point, how did the first corpse provide them an opportunity? Was the corpse a neighbor who had unexpectedly died? Was he a relative? Perhaps an uncle or cousin who'd been living with them?

I wondered how much the daughter, Revka, knew. I had to assume she knew everything. Their home was too small for the girl not to have known about the plot. And she'd made two visits to the morgue with her mother. She must have known that her mother lied the first time. And most probably the second. Since her mother's answers were filtered through her, the girl knew everything. I realized it was unlikely her mother would betray herself, not with her daughter standing guard as it were. I would be better off getting the girl alone. Without her mother to protest, she'd be more likely to reveal what was truly happening.

As I got off the Elevated and walked the short distance to the Pinkerton office, I considered the second corpse. If the first act of fraud was sparked by the unexpected availability of a corpse, then the second fraud clearly was not. I could imagine a corpse suddenly becoming available to the Rudkins once, but not twice. Obviously, they went in search of a corpse for their second claim. The most logical way to obtain a corpse—without murder—would be to steal one from a funeral home or to rob a recently dug grave. That created some interesting possibilities.

First, I went to the eighth floor and checked my rabbit

hole to see if there was any sign of the photograph. There wasn't. All that sat on my unofficial desk were three reports with notes asking that I look them over. I ignored those and climbed the stairs to the ninth floor. Daisy sat just outside the waiting area. I gave her a friendly smile and asked if there were any packages for me.

"No, sir. Nothing has come."

"I'm expecting an important photograph. If it comes, will you send a boy to look for me?"

"Yes, sir."

"In the meantime, though, do you know where police headquarters is?"

She glanced at a sheet of paper she'd tucked into the blotter on her desk, ran her finger down a column, and said, "I think it's on Clark."

"That's very clever," I said, indicating the paper.

"Thank you. I get asked the same questions over and over."

"Yes, I suppose you would. Thank you." I smiled and was on my way.

Even though I had a pocket full of nickels and could have caught a turtleback down Fifth, the police station was only around seven or eight blocks away. I decided to walk. It was still before nine and many office workers were rushing to their offices. The air was thick with smoke from the coal furnaces that were taking the chill off cold offices; not that I noticed. It was much worse in winter. I was used to the hazy gray look of the city. In fact, it was only when the wind came in from the Lake and the smoke blew off, and there was suddenly a brilliant blue sky above us that I ever noticed how gray the city really was.

Clark had once been a street paved in wooden blocks, planks cut down to the size of bricks and laid end up. It was a charming way to pave a street. One that has faded over time, leaving us to slather the streets with tar and crushed stone. Last winter was particularly bad, and when spring came the streets were pocked with potholes that went all the way down to cobblestone and wood blocks. For a few short weeks, I relished the feeling that the Chicago of my childhood was still there just below the surface. But that morning I was unappreciative. Wooden blocks were simply a way of paving streets and had no meaning for me.

The station was three-story, red brick. On one side was a flat, empty lot and on the other, a church. The front of the station attempted to be imposing. The floors were taller than needed and there was a thick cornice at the top of the second floor. It wasn't imposing though, or at least not as imposing as stone would have been.

When I walked in, I saw that most of the first floor was one large room. At the front, a waiting area with benches and at the back, several desks—which I supposed were unassigned like the small offices of the rabbit warren. Between the desks and the waiting area was an elbow high counter where one could press a grievance. Strangely, the station was quiet. As though no one had committed a crime in a very long time. There was one forlorn looking boy handcuffed to a bench, but that was all.

Behind the counter stood a red-haired police sergeant wearing a dark blue uniform with a double set of brass buttons down the front of the jacket and a copper badge gleaming on his chest. He wasn't much older than I was, and the freckles scattered across his nose and cheeks made it possible to see the child he'd once been.

"I'm Lewis Wait. I'm with the Pinkerton Agency. I'd like to ask some questions about a case I'm working. And you are?"

"Sergeant Seamus Grady." He had the remnants of an

Irish brogue. "I can't say how much help I'll be, but you can ask your questions."

His eyes were a very deep blue that distracted me for a long moment. He watched me look at him, until his look turned questioning. I sputtered.

"Our client is Continental Surety & Safety. The case I'm working on is one in which a corpse identified as a policy holder turned out not to be a policy holder."

I stopped, wondering if I was even making sense.

I continued, "I'm trying to find out where the misidentified corpse might have come from. Would you have any idea if there have been any thefts from either undertakers or hospitals or graveyards?"

"You mean thefts of bodies?"

"Yes, exactly."

I must have been making sense, to my great relief. He sighed. From beneath the counter, he pulled out a ledger about five inches thick. He let it fall open on the counter and, wetting his index finger, began to turn pages. I stood there uncomfortably, trying not look at him anymore than I had to and aware that he was looking at me. That went on at least three minutes, a very long time, before he found anything.

"They're missing a cadaver at Rush Medical College."

"That's near the morgue and Cook County Hospital, isn't it?"

He shrugged. "It's on Harrison. South of here."

I nodded, before I asked, "When did the cadaver go missing?"

"Last week."

"That might be the one I'm looking for. Is there a description?"

"Late thirties, female, dark hair—"

"No, no. That's not the one I'm looking for. I'm looking for a male."

Instantly, my cheeks were burning. I felt exposed. 'I'm looking for a male.' I wondered at how I might have said that in a way that wasn't quite so…

Suppressing a smile, Grady went back to flipping pages.

"So, how is it? Being a Pink?"

"It's…" Having only been a Pinkerton for a few weeks I had trouble finding the right words. "It's… very interesting."

"Is it?" He glanced up at me suspiciously. "There's a rumor running around that one of you killed a burglar in cold blood. Lay in wait and just shot him."

I knew he must be talking about me, but I didn't want to tip my hand.

"That's not what was in the newspapers, is it?"

"Newspapers. You think the Pinkertons can't buy the kind of story they want."

Could they? Perhaps. But still, I couldn't let a remark like that go by. Even though I'd only been an agent for a few weeks I couldn't let an Irishman, no matter how handsome, disparage my employer.

"In point of fact, I'm the Pinkerton agent who shot a burglar. I didn't kill him, and I didn't do it in cold blood. He reached for my gun and it went off. Which, as I recall, is very nearly what was said in the newspaper."

They tended to replace "reached for my gun" with "attacked" but did that of their own volition. When he looked up at me there was newfound respect in his face. Whether it was because I'd shot a man though I'm sure I didn't seem the sort or because I shot a man and told the truth about it, I couldn't be sure.

"Thank you for that. It's good to know the truth." He turned a few more pages, and said, "I'm afraid I'm not finding what you're looking for."

That disappointed me. I thanked him and was about to

walk out of the police station, when he said, "There are other ways to get a dead body without stealing it."

"Yes, murder, I know."

"Other than that, I mean."

"What do you mean?"

"Bums, hobos, vagabonds. They don't have no place to live. The die on the street every week. We pick them up and cart them to the morgue. If someone was to get there before us. Well, we wouldn't know what we were missing now, would we?"

It was an interesting idea. There were certainly enough indigents in Packingtown to provide the occasional corpse lying about. All the Rudkins needed to do was know where to look. I looked Sergeant Grady right in the eye. His eyes as deep a blue as the evening sky. "Thank you. I think you just helped me a lot."

"My pleasure," he said.

And again, I blushed.

CHAPTER 21

Before I went back to the Pinkerton offices, I found a Weeghman lunchroom at Madison and Dearborn and spent two bits on a boiled ham sandwich. I skipped the cherry pie that came along with the sandwich, partly because there was nowhere to sit and I didn't want to juggle the plate, and partly because I had an inkling about the way I was to spend the afternoon. A full stomach was not a good idea.

When I walked out of the elevator and onto the ninth floor, Daisy looked up and saw me. She picked up an envelope and waved it at me. The photograph I'd been waiting for was there.

As she handed me the envelope, she said, "I think pictures like that are terrible."

"You looked inside the envelope?"

"Of course I did. Mr. Cuthbert doesn't hire anyone who isn't a least a little bit the snoop."

I decided not to make an issue of it and opened the envelope myself. Sliding the photograph out, I saw that it was the right one. The second Mr. Rudkin.

"My mother has a whole drawer of those. Just about every dead relative we've ever had. I told her if I die she's not to take any such photograph of me!"

"If you're dead, you would be hard-pressed to stop her."

I don't know why I bothered with the girl, other than the fact that I had no desire to take the photograph and show it around the Rudkin's neighborhood. In fact, my plan seemed futile, though I knew it wasn't.

Then, I had an interesting idea. I wouldn't go directly to the Rudkin's neighborhood after all. I'd go to Whiskey Row. If Sergeant Grady's idea was correct, the picture was of some drunk who'd died in the street rather than Mr. Rudkin. Going to Whiskey Row would kill two birds with one stone. I could confirm that the corpse was *not* Mr. Rudkin and, possibly, find out who it was.

Before I left the Loop, I found a barbershop and stopped in for a shave. I didn't need a shave. I'd been adeptly shaving myself for some years. I did, however, need fortification for my return to Packingtown. When the barber removed the towel warm from my face and reached for a bottle of Florida Water, I pulled a handkerchief out of my pants pocket and held it out to him.

"Would you mind wetting my handkerchief?"

"What for?"

"I'm on my way to somewhere rather unpleasant."

"What kind of unpleasant?" the barber asked. He was old enough to be my grandfather and could have used a heavy dose of Florida Water himself.

"Malodorous."

That earned me a nasty stare and a grumbled comment, "It were just a question."

Still, he shook some Florida Water onto the handkerchief for me. I folded it so the dampness was on the inside and put it back into my pocket. After I climbed out of the barber's chair, straightened my vest, and returned my hat to my head, I gave the barber two-bits for a ten-cent shave. My business was not his business, and I didn't mind teaching him that minding his business could earn him a tip.

I took the Elevated south and transferred to the Stock Yards branch at Indiana. This time, I got off at Swift because it would get me to Whiskey Row fastest. I walked down 43rd Street, passing the Swift employee entrance. The cattle were making a ruckus, probably because the Elevated had just passed, but I couldn't help but hear in their cries some knowledge of what was to come. I didn't hold that thought long though, the smell was as horrid as it had been on my previous visits, making my stomach flip before I reached Ashland.

The afternoon was turning warmer than I would have liked. I wore my summer suit over a cotton shirt and union suit, with the photograph of the second corpse in my inside jacket pocket. Still, I was sweating as I walked down 43rd to Ashland. Boys walked in front of me carrying large pillowing bags of what I guessed might be animal hair across the street and into a two-story brick building. I shuddered to think what they made in there from the bags of hair.

Turning onto Ashland, I found myself looking at two long rows of brick buildings with a dusty, dirt street between them. Concrete had been poured in front of some of the buildings, more a long slab than a sidewalk. Benches ran across the fronts of the buildings and then again at the edge of the concrete slabs. I imagined that the benches must fill up in the summer when no one wanted to be inside. But at that particular moment there were only a few dozen men sitting on them.

The men on the benches wore shirtsleeves and vests. Their heads topped with shabby hats. Cans of beer sat in their laps. Some were ruddy faced and clearly drunk, though it was late morning. They huddled in small groups speaking in a collection of languages: Slavic, Bohemian, heavily accented English. I walked over and showed them the photograph. That earned me several scowls and a couple of grumbles but no answers. I backed up and continued on.

Walking further down Ashland, I drew more interest than I would have liked. I made a quick decision and entered an establishment, which had FORTUNE BROTHERS SAMPLE ROOM painted on the window in gilt paint. Upon entry, I decided the Fortune Brothers were down on their luck. The floor was wooden and worn, with tables scattered around the room with mismatched chairs. There were fewer men sitting around them than there were outdoors. Possibly because the air was thick and smelled of sour beer and bad plumbing. Or possibly no plumbing. I couldn't tell if what I smelled came from an outhouse in the alley or a malfunctioning indoor lavatory.

The bar, if you could call it that, was a long plank set on three barrels. A heavyset barman in a long apron stood behind the plank. Behind him, on another long plank, sat five wooden casks of beer. Walking over, I smiled at the man. He looked at me as though that were the most unusual thing that had happened to him all week.

"Hello. I'm from the Pinkerton Detective Agency," I reached into my jacket pocket and took out the photograph. "I wonder if you know this gentleman?"

The barkeep glanced at the image.

"He's a dead man," he said. At first, I couldn't tell if he was Irish or just sullen. "Yup, I know him. He's dead."

I almost yelled out the word, "Good!" but fortunately kept my composure. "And do you know his name?"

"Everyone knows him. He's a right popular fellow. Likes to buy rounds of whiskey when he's flush."

"What's his name?" I asked, sure I was about to hear some Irish name beginning with an O.

"Rudkin. George. It's not really George, but he liked people to call him that. Thought it was more American."

"This is Jurgis Rudkin?" I asked because I was so sure it wasn't.

"That's it. Jurgis. Yup, that's him."

I was quiet, trying to think what to do next. It really was Mr. Rudkin. How did that change things? Having failed at her fraud, did Mrs. Rudkin kill her own husband for the insurance settlement? He was a tall man, though. He was stabbed. Could she have done it?

My first thought was no. It was an evil act. A woman as beautiful as she couldn't have. Even with my proclivities, I couldn't view such a lovely woman as criminal.

I must have been quiet for a long time, when the barkeep finally asked, "You want a glass of whiskey?"

"No, thank you. So Rudkin came here often?"

"Most days, yes."

"What about… what about after the fire at his home? Did he come in after that?"

"We all thought he was dead."

That made me wonder, "So, how long after the fire did Mr. Rudkin begin coming in again?"

"He was back seven, eight days ago. Yup, that was quite the night. Everyone bought *him* a drink. He was drunk as a lord."

"Yes, I can see that coming back from the dead might merit attention. Did he explain who the man was who burned to death in his kitchen?"

"Said it was a bum. Broke in and tried to burgle the place."

This was a similar story to the one Revka had given. I asked, "Mr. Rudkin had something worth stealing?"

The bartender shrugged. "A bum wouldn't know that. A

bum would think it worth doing for a few coins and a slab of bacon."

It was terrible to think of someone so destitute that he would steal from the Rudkins.

"Did he say how the bum got burned?"

Another shrug.

"And how his wife came to misidentify the body."

"You know how women are."

"Blind, stupid or just simply liars?"

He didn't like that. He snarled at me. "That's enough questions."

I forged on anyway, "Mr. Rudkin didn't come in for a couple of weeks? Did he say where he went?"

"You don't have much sense, do you?"

"Probably not."

That made him laugh. I didn't think about it at the time, but making people laugh was a way to get people to open up.

He said, "People come; people go. It's better not to ask."

"Were you working the day Mr. Rudkin was discovered dead? For the second time, I mean."

"I was."

"Can you give me directions to where the body was found?"

"At the end of the street next to Bubbly Creek. Can't miss it."

"Who found him?"

"Boys. They ran into Shanahan's. Told the barkeep what they saw and ran off. My guess is they emptied Rudkin's pockets and didn't want no coppers asking for the coins back."

Ignoring his speculation, I asked, "Why Shanahan's?"

"They have a telephone in the back. Only one on Whiskey Row. Everyone knows that."

For a long moment, I stood there. I still couldn't quite

believe the corpse was Jurgis Rudkin, and that was clouding my ability to think.

"Can you think of anything else I should know?"

"Yeah. Don't come around here at night. It wouldn't be safe for the likes of you."

"I don't know what you mean by that," I said taking more offense than I probably ought. "I'm a qualified Pinkerton agent. And I'll have you know I shot a man last week."

"That's exactly what I mean. You come in here talking like that and someone will knock your block off just to say they did. I'm half tempted myself."

I saw that he had a point.

"I may need to come back at night," I said, though I had every intention of avoiding it.

"Well, don't come looking like that then. Stop at the rag pickers and get an old suit. And a pork pie hat. That bowler ain't the kind of thing people see 'round here."

It wasn't a bowler; it was a Marquise. The brim was different, and I nearly said so, though quickly saw that I'd only make his point.

"Thank you for the advice," I said stiffly and walked out of the establishment.

After the barkeep's comments, I was particularly aware of the sidelong glances and outright stares I got as I walked north on Ashland toward Bubbly Creek. I didn't understand why he thought coming at night would be so much more dangerous than the daytime. The men sitting on the benches that lined the buildings didn't look to be friendly.

Keeping my eyes to the ground, I crossed the railroad tracks then made it to the Creek. Unbelievably, the stench in the air became worse. I remembered the Florida Water-soaked handkerchief in my pocket and pulled it out. Opening it, I pressed it against my face to breathe through.

The Chicago River was a marvel of engineering. Using a

series of locks and canals the direction of the river had been changed, and rather than flowing into Lake Michigan it flowed out, connecting somewhere faraway with the Mississippi. Bubbly Creek was a south-reaching branch that seemed to not flow in any direction at all. The water in front of me was thick, brown, more reminiscent of molasses than water. It wasn't bubbling at that moment, but it was easy to see how it might soon start. There was little vegetation on the shore. Few plants were hardy enough to survive whatever was in the river, making the banks little more than mud and sludge.

I got as close as I dared, having developed an instant horror of falling into the muck, and looked about to decide where one might leave a corpse. There were several possible locations. I had been expecting to find a location decorated with recent footprints, but the shore was too much like oozing sludge to hold footprints long. I was favoring a flat spot near the foundation of a brick building of mysterious purpose when I had an interesting thought.

Why leave the body on the banks of Bubbly Creek? Why not throw it all the way in? It might never be found in the offal. Whoever killed Jurgis Rudkin wanted the body to be found, which again suggested his wife since it would be difficult to collect the insurance without the body. But how did she port the body around? Did she kill him right there on the banks of Bubbly Creek? How would she have lured him here? And did *she* kill him? Or did someone kill him for her? *Could she have killed him?* I asked myself, thinking back to the knife wound I'd seen in Mr. Rudkin's chest. It seemed unlikely.

Still holding my handkerchief over my face, I stood thinking carefully about what I knew with certainty. Mrs. Rudkin wanted her claim paid. So much so she'd put it through twice with different dead husbands. It was difficult to walk around Packingtown and not see why a woman would want money. But Mrs. Rudkin seemed to want money more than the women around her. Why? Did she need it for something specific? Something so specific she was willing to kill her husband to get it? Or was it actually Mr. Rudkin who wanted money, at least originally. He must have been involved in the original fraud. Did he need money for something specific?

From our visit to the morgue, I knew the real Mr. Rudkin liked expensive clothing and sometimes had the money to spend on them. The barkeep said he liked to buy rounds of drinks "when he was flush." Wouldn't the barkeep have said he liked to buy drinks on payday if that were the only day of the week he was flush? There seemed to be a real implication that Mr. Rudkin had another source of funds. One that ebbed and flowed.

Without giving it much thought, I found myself walking back to Whiskey Row. I put my perfumed handkerchief back into my pocket. I was enough of an oddity without covering my face like a harem girl.

When I got in front of Shanahan's I stopped. They had a telephone. Why? At the time, telephones were not ubiquitous as they are now, few people had them. And virtually no one in Packingtown would have had one. *So why did Shanahan's?*

I walked in and found Shanahan's to be quite different from Fortune Brothers. There was a proper mahogany bar on one side of the room. Bottled liquor sat on the shelves and there were no wooden casks in sight. Round tables were scattered around the room. At each were several men, every bit as shabby as the ones outside but more animated, more alive. Dice and cards were being played at each table. Pennies, nickels and dimes were scattered around the tables in small stacks. At a table in the back corner sat a small man with a very large, protruding belly. Had you told me he'd just eaten a sheep he'd stolen from the yards I'd have believed you. Next to him sat the fabled telephone. That made him the most important man in the room.

I took the photograph of Mr. Rudkin out of my pocket and held it in front the little man. "Do you know him?"

"You see much sitting in corner," he said. His accent was thick but his English passable. I couldn't quite place where he was from.

"Did he gamble here?"

"No, no. Gambling is illegal."

Of course, there was irony in his saying that since everyone around me was engaged in the vice at that very moment.

"I'm a Pinkerton agent. I'm investigating an insurance claim. I have no authority to arrest anyone for gambling. You need not be guarded with me. Did Jurgis Rudkin gamble here?"

The man stared at me. I had the fleeting fear that his accent was Italian. There weren't a lot of Italians in Packingtown to my knowledge, but then he wasn't here to work in the yards. I wondered if he might be part of the Black Hand and a trickle of sweat ran down the back of my neck.

Then I wondered at the bar's Irish name. It might not be the Black Hand, but—

"He played cards," the man said.

"Did he owe money?"

"They all owe money. I am fond of them."

"Did he owe a lot of money? Enough to get him into trouble?"

"We do friendly business. No trouble."

"No one ever needs to be made an example of?"

"You read… dime novels, yes? Mr.—"

"Wait. Lewis Wait. And no, I don't read dime novels."

To be completely truthful, I should have said I don't *often* read them. There were, of course, times when a badly written, mildly ridiculous story was just what was called for, though it was best not to wave them in front of Mother. She considered them a waste of time.

"And you are?"

"Al Bratore."

That sounded Italian. I was wrong about the name of the bar. It might have been a ruse. Calling the bar Giuseppe's would have been a bit obvious. I tried again.

"How much exactly did Mr. Rudkin owe you, Mr. Bratore?"

"I am not bookkeeper. It was but pittance."

I didn't believe him.

CHAPTER 22

*W*hen I arrived back at the Pinkerton offices, I went directly to the ninth floor. It was late and people had begun to go home, but Mr. Cuthbert was still at his desk. I had devised a theory on the Elevated and wanted to share it with him as quickly as possible, as it had some bearing on the Rudkin claim.

"Ah, Lewis," he said, looking up from a report. "You haven't been spending much time on the eighth floor, have you?"

"No, I've been investigating the Rudkin claim."

I looked at him suspiciously. How did he know I hadn't been in the rabbit warren? As though reading my thoughts—or more likely the confusion on my face—he said, "The grammar in our reports has slumped during your absence."

"It seems that the second corpse actually is Jurgis Rudkin."

"Yes, I was afraid that might be the case."

"Really? Why is that?"

"It seemed unlikely that Mrs. Rudkin would attempt a

second fraud. Even the most ignorant immigrant would know that we'd be looking closely at the claim."

"I have a theory."

"Excellent. What is it?"

"It seems Mr. Rudkin was something of a rake. Drinking and gambling. I suspect he acquired debts of some size. Mr. and Mrs. Rudkin found a bum in their neighborhood who was quite possibly dead already. They burned him in their kitchen so that he was unrecognizable. They quite likely expected the entire building to burn, but the neighbors were able to put the fire out quickly. The point of their fraud was to collect the insurance money and pay off Mr. Rudkin's gambling debts. When he reappeared after the claim was denied, he was seen on Whiskey Row. His corpse showed some fading bruises, suggesting that he received a beating several days before his death. I think it likely he was threatened over his gambling debts and then killed because he couldn't pay them."

"That's an interesting theory. But then why would Mrs. Rudkin submit the second claim? She is at risk of drawing attention to herself in this way. Do you think that she now owes the gambling debts?"

"I suppose that's possible. I hadn't thought of it. Of course, she may also have submitted the claim because it's now… well, legitimate, I suppose."

"Very good work. Keep investigating."

That surprised me. I felt like I'd solved the case.

"In what direction, sir?"

"I think it's time you go to see Mrs. Rudkin and find out what she has to say about all this. We still need a reason to deny the claim." I blushed. I hadn't told Mr. Cuthbert that I'd already met Mrs. Rudkin. I didn't think it would be any more productive if I tried it again.

"Yes, but wouldn't it be simpler for Continental Surety & Safety to negotiate?" I asked. "We have enough information to convict the woman of fraud due to the first claim. They could agree not to prosecute if she drops the legitimate one."

"It may come to that. But we need to know more. And I'm not sure I agree that we have enough evidence to convict Mrs. Rudkin of fraud. Not yet. The only thing we know for certain is that Mrs. Rudkin identified the wrong man as her husband. A jury of twelve men might actually believe she was too flustered to recognize her husband's charred corpse. And if that's the case, we've lost."

"I should go back to investigating the first claim then?" I asked, attempting to focus my efforts.

"Keep asking questions about everything. In a case like this anything could be important. And it's often difficult to see what is and what isn't until you have all the facts."

Reluctantly, I returned to the little office I'd adopted and took the file Mr. Cuthbert had given me from the drawer where I'd left it. The new claim had the Rudkin's current address on it. I copied it onto a separate piece of paper and left the building. As I got onto the Elevated, I grudgingly realized the best course of action was to return to Packing-town that night rather than wait until morning. If I waited until morning the Rudkin family would be back at work. Though I knew where to find them, I didn't want to confront them again with so many of their coworkers around. I wanted to speak privately with Mrs. Rudkin and her daughter.

The address Mrs. Rudkin supplied was in the 4600s block of Gross Avenue. The apartment on Justine was in the 4700s block. Given the way Chicago was laid out, that meant they were likely close to each other. For the second time that day, I took the Elevated to Packers station. I checked my pocket watch to find that it was after six-thirty. Night would soon fall. In fact, the sky was already a deep, hazy gray with a lavender tint lining the horizon.

In stark contrast to my previous visit, when I came out of the Packers station I noticed there were few children on the street. I knew the yards ran twenty-fours a day, but I must have arrived near a shift change because adults, or at least older teenagers, were coming and going. Some with an energetic step, some slogging along. Most carried gray metal boxes filled with their dinner or empty, their lunch eaten hours before. The children I'd seen earlier must have retreated to their homes for the dinner hour.

I was fairly certain I was on 44th Street, which would correspond with 4400 south, and I needed to walk roughly two blocks further and then have to figure out whether I needed to walk east or west. There were no streetlights, not even gaslight. And while the yards themselves were completely electrified, many, or rather most of the homes I walked by were not. The soft light of candles and kerosene lamps began appearing in windows. When I'd gone two blocks, I stood for a moment and assayed the situation. The characters walking by me did not look like the type I'd want to stop and ask directions. Still, I had no choice.

Choosing the milder-looking strangers, I attempted to ask where Gross Avenue might be, but they either didn't speak English or weren't interested in talking to a man in a well-brushed suit and a clean collar. Finally, I gave up and decided the best way to start would be to go to the Rudkin's house on Justine and work out from there. Since the address appeared to be close, it was the only logical thing I could think of.

The gray of the wooden houses against the darkening gray of the sky and the faded dusty street all seemed suddenly monochrome, like a photograph. I had the odd sensation of not being where I was, but instead examining an image of where I was. At that hour, in that light, Packingtown barely seemed alive.

I was on the diagonal street I'd come down before. I barely remembered it though, so it was something of a surprise when I noticed the three-story red brick building with a pitched roof. It sat next to an open garbage dump, but inside it was brightly lit. The building was electrified. In Packingtown.

Of course, it must be a settlement house. One I was sure was connected to the University of Chicago. I'd heard of them. Quite extensively, in fact. The value of settlement houses was a frequent subject of debate in some of my classes. The people who ran the houses, usually wealthy older women of the sort my mother met at The Women's Temple, lived in them and interacted with the community, finding ways to help them better their meager existence. Some professors thought the coddling of the indigent to be a pointless exercise. They firmly believed poverty to be evidence of genetic inferiority and weak character, and that providing hope of a better lot to these people was in its own way cruel. Likened to the feeding of stray animals. Other professors, though, thought the settlement houses—and there were many of them across Chicago—were an important social experiment worthy of study.

Standing in front of the building, I saw there were two entrances from the street. The nearest door had a board next to it where notices were tacked, and a sort of porch lamp hung from a wrought iron brace reaching out over the street. Above the door was a glass transom with the number 4630 painted in gilt. The number Mrs. Rudkin had given as her address. That was when I realized I must be standing on Gross Avenue.

The smell was terrible. It wasn't just due to the nearby

garbage dump; there was the terrible smell coming from the yards a few blocks away. But, as it happened, I'd spent so much time the last day smelling bad things that I'd begun to barely notice.

I walked through the nearest entrance to find myself in a small foyer. To my right was a wide hallway leading down to another foyer by the second entrance. The hallway was well lit and the doors to most rooms were open. I walked down the hallway looking for someone to ask about the Rudkins. Why had they given this as their address? Were they staying in the building somewhere? I didn't think anyone was allowed to live in a settlement house except those who worked there. But did they have emergency quarters? The Rudkin's had been burned out, after all. Or were they simply using the settlement house as a temporary address?

I glanced through an open door and saw a group of about twelve young women engaged in a sewing class. It hadn't occurred to me before, but having walked around Packingtown, I could see that becoming a seamstress would be preferable to working in the slaughterhouse. Though I doubted it was as pleasant a life as the ones the typewritists in my office led.

A voice behind me said, "Can I help you?"

I turned and found myself staring at a rather tall young woman with absurdly short bangs laying high on her forehead, wide ruddy cheeks and a stern condemning expression. I couldn't imagine what I had done to make her dislike me so. I hadn't even opened my mouth.

"I'm looking for the Rudkin family. They gave this address."

"And who are you?"

Just before I spoke, I realized if I told the truth I was unlikely to be allowed to see the Rudkins, so I quickly made up a lie. "I'm Professor Josiah Everett. From the University. The Rudkin's have been involved in a study I'm working on."

"Have they?"

I couldn't help smiling. Her attitude told me she was well-acquainted with the family.

"Yes. The study involves the acquisition of language and examines that acquisition in multiple generations."

Of course, that wasn't Josiah's area at all, but it would take this woman at least twenty-four hours and possibly a trip to the University to determine that.

She frowned at me a good long time before she said, "Revka is the only member of the Rudkin family here at the moment. She's teaching a class just now."

"Do you happen to know where the family is living?" It seemed a good idea to ask. Given my past encounter, I doubted Revka would actually give me that information. "I told my aunt about their terrible fire. She wants to send a basket."

"They're staying somewhere in the Lithuanian section. I couldn't say exactly where. I think they're with relatives."

I smiled weakly and decided not to pursue the question, though I suspected this severe woman knew exactly where they were staying.

"May I say that the work you do here is simply marvelous," I said, unconsciously imitating Josiah's tone and timber.

"Caring for the poor is the Christian thing to do. There's no credit in doing the right thing."

I don't think I'd ever been so rebuked for paying a compliment.

"Can you direct me Revka's class?"

She hesitated, calculating how much trouble I'd be if she said no. Finally, "It's down the hall to your left."

"Thank you."

As I walked down the hallway, I could feel that she remained there watching me. I resolved not to turn and look back at her. When I reached the classroom, I found that it was an empty room with little beyond a blackboard and two dozen children's desks. At the desks were about fifteen people ranging from teenaged to middle-age. On the blackboard, written in a lovely cursive, was I AM REVKA RUDKIN and below that the letter G, one of the most difficult letters to write in cursive. It was written many times. The students were all bent over slips of paper, using pencils to write the letter again and again. Revka stood at the blackboard quietly demonstrating, again and again.

In that moment, I learned something I hadn't known before. It was Revka who'd written the doctor's note regarding the first dead Mr. Rudkin. She heard me step into the room and looked up. Glowering, she set down her piece of chalk.

She walked across the room to me, and hissed, "Why are you here? Are you going to pay us?"

"Step into the hallway, please."

Experience had taught me that it would be best to speak to her alone. I didn't fancy being chased out of the building by a mob of ragtag students. When we got into the hallway, Revka began to cough. I politely waited for her to stop, glancing down the hallway to see that the horrible woman I'd just met was still standing there.

"Will you pay the claim?" Revka asked, barely catching her breath.

"Tell me about your father?"

"What? What do you mean?"

"What kind of man was he?"

"Why does that matter? You need to pay us. What is so difficult about that?"

"Keep your voice down," I said. "If you get me thrown out of here, I guarantee you'll never see a dime."

I wasn't sure I could do that, but I doubted Continental Surety & Safety would pay before I finished my investigation.

I repeated, "Tell me what kind of man your father was."

"He was friendly. He was charming. He liked to have fun. Is that such a terrible thing?"

The look on her face said it was.

"He gambled," I suggested.

She shrugged in response. I imagined that a lot of men in Packingtown gambled. Though gambling was thoroughly frowned upon in my household, I could see that the less you had the more attractive gambling could become. It seemed somehow tied to hope.

"When he was lucky it was all very good. We didn't have to go to work. My brothers and I, we all got new shoes. New shoes. Like rich people."

"And when he was unlucky?"

"Then we went back to work. Then we went hungry. But now he is dead. We will always work, and we will always go hungry." She punctuated this with a heavy cough into her handkerchief.

"Your father had debts, didn't he? Gambling debts?"

She shrugged again as though it was an insignificant matter.

"How much did he owe?"

"Some."

"And now that debt has come to your mother?"

"They can't do that. It's not legal."

I wasn't sure whether a debt could be transferred to heirs or not. I did know that a man like Al Bratore was unlikely to worry about niceties like the law. If he thought he could get money from the Rudkins, he would get it.

"The man who was burned in your kitchen was just a bum off the street, wasn't he?"

Her eyes flashed but she kept her mouth shut.

"Your parents found him and then burned him in your kitchen. Was he already dead? Or did they kill him?"

"I don't know what you're talking about. I told you. We weren't at home."

"Your parents were trying to get money to pay your father's gambling debts."

"No. That is wrong." She pursed her lips. I could tell she was about to say something useful, but then she burst into another coughing fit.

"You wrote the doctor's note, didn't you? You could go to prison for that."

Honestly, I wasn't sure she'd go to prison, but I thought terrifying her would likely garner me more information.

Finally, she said, "It was him. Never her."

"But your mother helped him. She could be in trouble for that. You helped him."

"What could we do? We had to do what he said."

"I don't think the law will see it that way."

"Please, you have to help. We are innocent. It's not our fault."

"I can only help if you tell me everything."

"My little brother found the man. He died behind a house. Two blocks away. The children would go and look at him. When my father heard about the man, he had the idea. My mother did not want to do it. She fought with him. But finally, he made her go with him to get the man. I brought my brothers here. I read to them about Mrs. Tiggy-Winkle. My older brother did not like that much, so he read on his own. My younger brother can't read yet."

"Then what happened?"

"They came and told us that our house was on fire. I helped to put in the claim."

"Who killed your father, then?"

"I don't know. I wish I did." Her eyes swept the floor as she said this. I wondered if they might be called almond shaped. Did that mean she was likely to be lying? The shape of her eyes? What about her sharp cheek bones? Did they betray her?

"Then he might have been killed for gambling debts," I suggested.

Reluctantly, she said, "Yes. That might be true."

"Except that it's not true. You just said so."

"You said you'd help if I told you the truth, but you won't, will you? You're the liar!"

"You haven't told me the truth. You said your father wasn't killed for his gambling debts. And then you said he was. How do you know? Why was he killed?" I grabbed her by the arm and said, "Tell me. Tell me the truth."

She began coughing again. "Cali-for-nia," she managed to sputter and then continued to hack.

"What about California?"

"I'll thank you to leave." The social worker with the bangs had come down the hallway and now stood behind me.

"I just need to finish asking a few more questions. For my study."

"You're no professor. Who are you?"

"I'm investigating a double murder," I said, though it was a statement that stretched the truth quite thin. It also made the girl cough all the harder in protest.

"You don't look like a policeman."

So much for my ruse. "I'm a Pinkerton agent."

"If there's been a murder, then I suggest you send the police. They can question the girl."

Revka went pale when she said that. I doubted she'd want

to talk to the police. And I doubted it was a serious threat. As a social worker, she knew how corrupt and inept the Chicago police force was at the time. She also knew that even when they weren't corrupt and inept they spent scant time in Packingtown.

Still, I had little choice but to leave.

CHAPTER 23

On the train ride home I wondered what exactly Revka had meant by California. The state was an obvious possibility. But there was also California Avenue. The courthouse and county jail were both on California Avenue, so even though I rarely traveled that far west I often read about the doings there in the newspaper. Once or twice, I'd attempted to get into a gallery to witness one of the more interesting trials.

Therefore, she might have meant California Avenue. *Or the state of California. Or something else entirely.* And I had no idea how one word would lead to Mr. Rudkin's killer. Was he killed by someone from California? Or someone who went by a nickname that included the word? Someone named the California Kid perhaps. What did the word itself mean? What language was it even? Spanish? Cherokee perhaps? By the time I walked into our apartment I was thoroughly frustrated. I felt like Revka had given me the answer, but I didn't understand it.

In the morning, I woke and realized my investigation had come to a complete halt. There was nowhere left to turn. I needed to learn what Revka had meant by California, but I had no idea how to approach the girl again. I'd been run out of Swift when I talked to her mother there, so I doubted they'd tolerate my presence for more than a few minutes. And I certainly couldn't attempt to track her down again at the settlement house. I could attempt to find her at home—if knew where the Rudkins were living. But I didn't know where.

I puzzled over this as I ate my breakfast of oatmeal and sausage. Finally, I noticed Mother's attitude. She was polite but distracted.

"Were you at a lecture last night?"

"Steering committee."

"Trouble?"

"Certain factions are more militant than necessary. There is such a thing as decorum, after all." She frowned and ate a piece of toast. "How are things at the agency?"

"I've reached an impasse, I'm afraid. I suspected that the second Mr. Rudkin was killed over gambling debts, but I'm beginning to doubt that's true."

"And that makes a difference?"

"I'm not sure. Given that Mrs. Rudkin committed fraud when identifying the first corpse, the insurance company should not have to pay her. But if she's not convicted of the crime they might have to."

"She identified the wrong man. That seems cut-and-dried."

"She's a very pretty woman who doesn't speak English. It would be easy enough for her to claim not to have understood what she was doing."

"And you think the key to this is to understand the second corpse?"

"Yes. I do."

The Polish girl came out of the kitchen and set Mother's

breakfast in front of her. Then she poured us both coffees. When she left, I explained to Mother my problem with finding Revka Rudkin again.

"I could go to the settlement house for you."

"Good god Mother, no. The neighborhood... It's not a place for you."

"Nonsense. I could go to Packingtown. I've been to Whiskey Row before."

"You've been to Whiskey Row with a group of women. I couldn't allow you to go alone."

"*Allow* me? How many women should I bring with me, then? Five? Ten?"

I really wanted to end the conversation, so I reapplied myself to my breakfast. Mother ignored my shift of attention.

"What was the girl doing at the settlement house? Attempting to improve herself?"

"She was teaching a class. Penmanship. It was Revka who forged a letter from a Dr. Thacker attesting to his identification of the body. But it was on incorrect stationery and written in a different hand than the doctor's. A hand exactly like that which I saw on a blackboard last night."

"How does that help?" Mother asked.

"Well, it proves the family was all involved in the fraudulent claim. She said that her father made them do it."

"Men are such beasts."

"Don't be too hasty, Mother. It's still possible these two women killed the father."

She pursed her lips. She'd always resisted the idea of women being criminal.

"Somehow it connects to the word California."

"The reason for the fraud?"

"I don't know. I'm not sure what it means. It could be the street, it could be the state, it could be—"

"Obviously, it means the state. They want the money to escape there."

That seemed very plausible.

"Your theory then is that the mother and daughter killed the father to collect on the claim?" I asked.

"I suppose it is."

"And what of the insurance agent, Harcourt. He lied to me about knowing Mr. Rudkin during the investigation of the first claim."

"Then he must have been involved somehow."

"He'd have at least known the claim was a fraud," I admitted.

Mother reached out and put her hand over mine. Her face seemed to soften in a way I'd rarely seen. "Your father always spoke to me about his cases. You're so like him. I just knew you'd be good at this."

I wondered how true that was. My impulse was to demur, but I said, "Thank you, Mother."

"Now, if you change your mind, I'm happy to go to Packingtown."

I thought I detected a tinge of relief in her voice. I wondered for a moment if being as brave as she was could also be tedious. I certainly wanted to avoid bravery as much as possible.

"Mother, Mr. Cuthbert said something about father. That his death was tragic."

"It was tragic."

"And that he was brave. As though—"

"Your father was brave."

"I'm sure he was. But the way it was said—"

"There was a bank robbery in Joliet. The culprit was on the loose. In the best of times, it was a five-, six-hour buggy ride. But it wasn't the best of times, it was February. It took much longer in the cold. He was mildly ill before he left. And close to death when he returned. He shouldn't have gone. I shouldn't have let him." She sat very still for a moment then added, "He died. And then a week later, your brother."

"And you and I didn't get sick?"

"Oh no, dear, you and I were very ill. But we didn't die."

I left for the Pinkerton office a short while later. As it turned out, it was an uneventful day. After I checked in, I decided to walk over to Continental Surety & Safety. Harcourt was not in the office. I asked the matronly woman who seemed to run the place if she knew what his route was. If I had some idea where to find him in Packingtown, it might be worth a try. But she claimed to have no idea what his route was.

"If you want to find him, you best follow the skirts," she said, sharply. I certainly wouldn't be doing that.

"Might I leave him a note?"

Without a word she handed me a small pad and a pencil. On the top sheet, I wrote the word CALIFORNIA. Then I pulled the sheet off the pad and folded it.

Handing it all back to the woman, I said, "I'll return in the morning. Can you have him wait for me?"

"I can tell him. But he's not the sort of man who takes orders from a woman."

"What time do you expect him?"

"He's to be here at nine, but he's generally late."

"Then I shall be on time. Thank you."

When I returned to the rabbit warren, there was a note on my unofficial desk telling me Edna had once again stopped by. In the rabbit warren, there was an office at the front of the floor overlooking Fifth. That office had large windows and its own party line.

The office was claimed most often by an agent named Clayborne Knowles. He was thirty years my senior, wore his hair slick to his scalp, and seemed to have some trouble matching his ties to his suits. That afternoon when I popped my head into his office, he wore a brown suit, a white shirt, and a deep green tie. Seeing me in the doorway, he growled a greeting.

"I'm hoping I can impose on you a moment. I'd like to place a telephone call."

Knowles did something with banks—I wasn't sure what exactly because he never asked me to check his reports. But given the amount of respect he was given and the fact that he was allowed the most appealing office on the floor without any grousing suggested it was important.

"Is it business?"

"No, it's not." Honesty seemed the better policy.

He studied me for a moment, and said, "There's a pay telephone round the corner in the lobby of The Rookery."

"Yes, of course," I said. "I was only trying to save a few minutes. But you're right. I should walk over there to place my call."

I began to walk out of the office when he stopped me with, "How do you know Cuthbert?"

"I don't know him. He knew my father."

"Yeah? Who was your father?"

"He was a Pinkerton agent. He died of the flu when I was a child."

"What was his name?"

"Aloysius Wait."

He gave me an odd look, and I realized for the first time that, given the connection, I was probably viewed as Cuthbert's pet. I quickly wondered if this would be a benefit or a detriment. But then Knowles waved at the candlestick telephone on his desk, and said, "Go ahead."

Benefit. I picked up the earpiece and clicked the switch hook, waiting for the operator to come on the line.

"This is the operator."

"Yes, Operator, can I have Michigan 4810. Thank you."

"One moment."

I waited as the call was placed. When it was answered it was Paula on the end of the line. "Riggins' residence."

"Yes, hello, is Miss Riggins in?"

"Who wants to know?"

"Good morning, Paula. This is Mr. Wait."

"Miss Riggins isn't at home."

It should have occurred to me that she might not have returned home yet. There was no indication of when she visited the office, but it had to have been during my absence. She might have just been there.

"I see. Is Mr. Riggins at home?"

"One moment."

I suffered through an awkward minute waiting for Hal to come to the telephone. Knowles was reading through a report he was writing on security measures taken at Globe Savings Banks. I noted several grammatical errors that I decided it would be best not to mention.

"Hello?" Hal said coming on the line.

"Hal, it's Lewis."

"Well, hello, what a nice surprise."

"Edna stopped by and I'm calling to see what it was she wanted. Do you know?"

"I'm sure she wanted to invite you for dinner. And if she doesn't, I do." The telephone distorted his voice, making it seem small and far away, but the fact that he wanted me to come for dinner regardless of whether his sister wanted it…

"Can you be here at seven?"

"Yes, of course."

"See you then, my friend."

I hung up smiling. With a nod to Knowles, I returned to my office at the other end of the rabbit warren.

The rest of the day I stayed in and read over reports. The

reports came to me typed, so presumably the typewritists had at least improved the spelling. While the girls all seemed nice, there didn't seem to be any educational requirement for their positions other than the ability to operate a typewriter. The reports gave me a solid understanding of everything happening at the office. There were six investigations for Continental Surety & Safety underway, three of which were arson, two bank robbery investigations and, most interestingly, a team of Pinks guarding a wealthy woman who lived a few blocks north of Edna on Lake Shore Drive.

It seemed the woman thought a band of Indians had slipped into the city with the goal of scalping her. The report referred to the woman as "bats" once and "bonkers" twice. Checking the file, her family was paying for the protection. This probably protected her from herself more than anything else, and they might not appreciate their loved one being treated with anything but the utmost respect. I added a note on the report about the language and put it in the box I'd taken to dumping the finished reports in so the agents could find them when I wasn't there.

I left when my pocket watch showed it was nearly five. The day had been warmer than usual, and the Elevated was crowded and stuffy. I wasn't able to get one of the seats along the side and had to hold onto a strap that hung down from the ceiling. Most of the passengers were men, though there was a good sprinkling of what was called the "new woman." There was much discussion about what exactly a "new woman" was. Edna's boldness and willingness to flaunt social convention by flouncing around the city alone and smoking in the street put her in that category, but she was nothing like the women I rode the train with. These were women who in some way were trying to improve their prospects. They'd left farming communities because they didn't want to be farmer's wives. They lived alone or with each other in small apartments specifically designed for single people. Most hoped to marry up and gambled that by coming to the city they'd improved the likelihood of that. Still, that left them wondering how they should behave in situations like the Elevated. Some of the young women were clearly flirtatious. Hoping, one presumed, they'd meet some well-employed decent fellow. Others sat stiffly, hoping to discourage advances, fearful they might be seen as loose.

That led to an odd thought: What sort had Mother been? She'd met my father on a cable car. She definitely wanted to project the image that she was the prim, proper woman sitting with eyes averted, but was that true? When she was young, might she have been the flirtatious type? Did she stare at my father boldly when she first saw him, just as the girl part way down the car was staring at… me.

I looked away quickly. Interest from women was always discomforting. I feared my disinterest in them would give me away. But now I had a fiancée. I could stare boldly back at the young woman because I had a fiancée and had only to say so.

As I walked into the apartment I was thinking about my tuxedo, hoping it still fit well and that it didn't need to be aired out. I immediately heard voices and was surprised to see Mother sitting in the dining room with Josiah. They each had a cup of tea set in front of them.

"My God, what are you doing here?" I blurted.

"Your mother invited me for dinner."

I looked at Mother. She wasn't exactly smirking, but she was clearly pleased with herself. There was some game afoot, but I wasn't entirely sure what it was. Though she'd never said—and would likely never say—Edna had been meant as a cure to my friendship with Josiah. But now that she'd turned against Edna, and Josiah sat in my dining room. She must have decided he was the cure to my engagement to Edna.

Aside from my discomfort at being manipulated, Mother overestimated my somewhat cooled attachment to Josiah while underestimating my commitment to Edna. Or rather, my commitment to what I now saw as freedom.

"I'm so sorry, Josiah, but Mother didn't tell me she'd invited you. I'm expected for dinner with my fiancée and her brother. I've only come home to change."

"Fiancée? Goodness, I had no idea. I only saw you a few weeks ago. You didn't mention..." There was obvious hurt on his face, and I felt horrible about that.

"I hadn't actually met her yet."

"You're engaged to marry a woman you've only just met?" He looked at my mother as though she might somehow explain this.

"Yes, I suppose it has come about quickly," I said as evenly as possible. "I hadn't given that much thought."

"You hadn't given it much— We *are* talking about marriage, aren't we? Marriage is irrevocable."

"Yes, I suppose it is."

I was wounding him and knew it. I wished that we were having this conversation in private where I could be more forthcoming. Though, in all honestly, my relationship with Josiah had always been somewhat indirect.

"Lewis, if you're going to spend your life with Edna, surely she'd understand your need for friendship. Can't you telephone her and suggest another evening? Or better yet, invite her here. We have plenty of food and I'm sure Josiah would love to meet her."

I was on the spot. I had no intention of changing my plans. For a moment I was stumped, but then I turned it around on Mother. "Actually, we're meant to discuss our engagement party. Now that I think about, maybe we could have some sort of party here. That way Josiah and the rest of my friends could meet her. And your friends, of course, Mother."

Other than Josiah, I didn't have many friends to speak of. But Mother did. She had many friends. None of whom she'd want to introduce to Edna.

"I'll have to think about that," she said stiffly. I took that as a no.

"If you'll excuse me, I need to dress for dinner."

Standing up quickly, Josiah said my name and then just stood there dumbly.

"Yes?"

"I'm afraid I need to go," he said, staring at his toes. "I have a touch of lumbago and need stretch out on my bed."

He didn't seem to be in pain. Certainly, he'd gotten out of the chair spryly enough.

"I understand completely," I said, meaning it in several ways. "We'll do this another time."

"Yes," Mother said, her voice as pointed as a pair of scissors. "Try to have your fiancée give you a schedule so that we can plan ahead."

"If you'll excuse me. Goodbye Josiah."

Quickly, I retreated to my bedroom. I took my tuxedo out of the closet and hung it on the back of the door. Then I took off my jacket and waistcoat. I unbuttoned my collar and set it onto the dresser.

Without knocking, Mother entered my bedroom.

"Mother, really."

"I've made terrible mistakes, haven't I?" she said, quite abruptly.

"Whatever are you talking about?"

"When your friend Josiah came to dinner, I thought he was a bad influence. I thought it wise to separate you."

I was right. Her scheming had been just as I thought.

"Is that why you claimed to have financial difficulties?"

"Yes. And it's why I invited Edna to dinner. I had no idea she was so… unsuitable."

"Unsuitable to you, Mother. But not to me."

"You can't think marrying that girl is a good idea. You're doing it to spite me."

"No, Mother, I'm not."

My statement was unconvincing. But then, I thought it better to let her think I was doing it to spite her than it would be to tell her the truth.

"I forbid it."

"Mother, I'm not a child."

"No, that's true. You were a lovely child."

CHAPTER 24

$\mathcal{M}$y tuxedo smelled faintly of mothballs, so I walked the seven blocks to Michigan Avenue where I caught a streetcar up to the river, standing near the back entrance hoping to air myself out. Then I crossed the Rush Street Bridge and walked up Pine Avenue to East Lake Shore. The doorman told me I was expected. Once on the sixth floor, as I rang the doorbell I hoped I no longer smelled of the odorous pesticide.

When the maid let me into the foyer, Edna was waiting for me. When she saw the tuxedo, she exclaimed, "Look at you! All gussied up!" and then kissed me on the cheek.

"Oh my," I found myself saying.

"Darling, we have to get used to that. My family will be looking for some display of affection."

"Yes, of course… I'm sorry."

I leaned over and kissed her cheek. It was only then I made note of the fact she was much more casually dressed than I. She wore a very simple white cotton dress embroidered in pastel roses. "I am sorry. I assumed you always dressed for dinner."

"And we assumed you didn't," Hal said as he entered the foyer. "Come with me, we'll put you in something more comfortable."

Hal wore a pair of fawn-colored pants, a brown striped waistcoat, and a pale-yellow shirt. Jarringly, he also wore a blood red tie. I glanced at Edna, and she gave me an encouraging nod. Paula, in her dour black uniform, scowled behind her.

With a ridiculous amount of excitement, I followed Hal back through the dining room to his bedroom, which was just off the solarium. It was a large room with three big windows, a mahogany four-poster placed in the center, a bureau carved in a similar wood to one side, and in one corner a leather chair sitting next to a small bookcase beside a standing lamp with a stained-glass shade. There was a large closet with built in drawers that made the bureau seem superfluous. There was also a private bathroom. A luxury I could barely comprehend.

Looking at the bookcase, I asked Hal, "Do you know the writer, Walt Whitman?"

"Does he write adventures? Those are my favorites." He'd opened the closet door and pulled out a drawer or two.

"No. He's a poet. Your sister knows him. I thought you might…"

"You're disappointed in me." I was, but had been trying not to show it. "My tastes aren't very highbrow, I'm afraid. I do have a copy of *Fanny Hill*. Have you read that?"

"No." I hadn't read the book but knew enough about it to blush. It certainly wasn't highbrow.

"I'll have to loan it to you then." He smiled and winked at me after he said it.

"After the wedding," I said. I didn't fancy having the Polish girl find it in my room and turn it in to Mother.

"I'm pleased you're marrying Edna," he said, handing me a

pair of flannel slacks and a starched white shirt. "I've always wanted a brother."

"I thought you had a brother?"

"Not that sort of brother."

I had trouble swallowing for a moment. I think I knew what he meant, though to be honest I might not have. I busied myself taking off my white gloves.

"You'll want a collar."

"Yes, of course."

After he handed me the collar he began digging around again in a drawer. I took off the jacket, then the waistcoat. Then I began to remove the studs from my shirt. I had the mortifying thought that Hal was going to stay there the whole time I dressed. That was a problem. I was already in an embarrassing state, and if I took my clothes off in front of him—well, he'd see that for certain. My union suit was too thin to hide my condition.

At the same time, I could hardly ask him to leave his own bedroom. My shirt was open, but I was still quite covered when he turned around with a red silk tie in his hand. It was similar to the tie he wore. He set it onto the bed next to the shirt and slacks. I would never have worn such a bold tie, but I couldn't reject it. Not with him wearing an almost identical one.

I had hoped he'd leave the room now that I had everything I needed; instead, he made himself comfortable in the leather chair. I turned away from him and removed my shirt.

"Tell me about your friends."

"Oh, well, I've been a student for a long time. My friends are students. And professors."

"Is that the only way you make friends?"

I thought about that for a moment. Occasionally Mother and I might speak to someone at church, but I wouldn't say they were friends. And I certainly hadn't made any friends at the Pinkerton office. I wouldn't call Bankhead a friend, despite his willingness to make me his brother-in-law. How else would I make friends? Suddenly, I had the feeling he was talking about something else entirely.

"I suppose it is."

I kept my back to him as I took off my pants and hurriedly pulled on the pair he loaned me. They were dove gray, soft and at least four inches too long. He noticed how long the pants were and was quickly on his knees beneath me folding up the hems. Reflexively, I turned to him. The pants were loose, my union suit as well. There was nothing to restrict me and I'm afraid there was an embarrassing protrusion pointed directly at Hal's face. He saw it and smiled up at me.

Standing, he said, "Perhaps I should give you a moment alone."

There was a devilish smile on his face. I didn't want him to leave me alone. I wanted him to close the few feet between us and kiss me again. And then I wanted... I barely knew what. I'm sure my face was flushed as I said, "Thank you, yes, a moment alone."

Hal walked across the room. At the door he turned, and said, "Later on, I'm going to teach you how to make friends."

I had no idea what he meant.

Dressing quickly, I returned to the front parlor. Edna and Hal sat on opposite sofas sipping tall, red highballs. Paula stood stiffly by the wall. On a table next to her was a tray with several more drinks. I sat down next to Edna. I was tempted to sit next to Hal but, after her affectionate 'practice' greeting, I thought I should sit next to my fiancée.

Edna glanced over her shoulder at the maid. When she didn't move, Edna raised her eyebrows pointedly. Paula picked up the tray of drinks and brought it over.

"We're having gin slings tonight," Edna explained.

Taking one of the drinks off the tray, I noted that Paula was glaring again. I wondered if I'd made some terrible social blunder. The drink was candy sweet with a bitter aftertaste.

"We're fine, Paula. If you could check on dinner…" Edna said to the maid while smiling in a way that managed to be both dismissive and affectionate at once. The girl blushed and walked out of the room. Even before she was all the way through the dining room, Edna whispered, "She gets so jealous."

"The maid? Why would the maid get jealous?"

I tried for moment to imagine our Polish girl jealous and failed. The only emotion I'd ever seen her attach to Mother was confusion.

My question wasn't answered. Instead, Edna said, "I spoke to my father. He and my mother will be coming to Chicago for a weekend visit, soon I'm afraid. At the end of the week."

"Oh my. That is soon."

"We're planning a salon Sunday afternoon. To celebrate the engagement."

"Yes, of course."

"I hope Angelica will come. And, please, invite anyone else you'd like."

"I'm afraid I don't have a great many friends."

And probably one less after my mother's failed dinner with Josiah.

"Well, I'm sure we'll change that," Hal said.

I wondered what he might mean by that. His being my friend certainly increased the number I had. I hoped that's what he meant.

"Put something on the Victrola, Hal," Edna said.

Languidly, he got up and walked over to the Victrola, which stood just next to the entrance to the study. He put on a recording of "Alexander's Ragtime Band."

"Collins & Harlan," Hal said.

I vaguely knew who they were. I'd been to the Vaudeville but only a few times. Mother didn't approve, so the few times I'd been were when she was deeply involved with suffrage doings. There were periods when she'd be at The Women's Temple for long hours, and as a result not to concerned with my whereabouts.

Edna insisted we dance. I couldn't refuse. I assumed we'd be spending at least some of our time that Sunday dancing. When I stood up, though, she wanted to do something called the bunny hug. Mother had sent me to dance class—one of her attempts to tempt me with female flesh—so I knew the waltz and even the polka, but I had no idea how to bunny hug. Edna attempted to show me, but it was really just so much hopping about. Despite that, she seemed quite pleased with our attempts; she had Hal play the record three times. During our third attempt Paula came into the parlor and told us that dinner was served.

We shuffled into the dining room, and Edna said, "Aunt Minnie will love him, don't you think Hal?"

"Aunt Minnie loves anything in pants."

"No, she doesn't. Don't you remember how scandalized she was when I showed her that photograph of Sarah Bernhardt playing Hamlet in pants?"

"Those were tights. Tights are different from pants."

"Oh, that's right. Still," she said, as though she had a point.

"What about your friend Bertha Bellamy?" Hal asked. "Didn't she like to wear her brother's pants?"

"Only in private. How did you know about that? I thought it was a secret?"

"Don't you remember when Bertha and Elizabeth Winslow fell out? There was quite a lot of secret-telling."

"These are people in Detroit you're talking about?" I

asked, imagining their lives full of interesting people I might someday meet.

"Hal, we're being rude."

"No, not at all," I said. "I'm sure I'll meet your friends. Someday. I should try to—"

"These aren't people you'll meet," Hal said. "Bertha Bellamy is not allowed in my parents' home."

"She's not allowed in her own parents' home, for that matter," Edna added. "Some people are not very discrete."

It seemed an odd thing to say. I had the distinct feeling Edna was anything but discrete. Certainly, the look Hal gave her seemed to confirm that.

We began with Duchess soup, which, being little more than a cheese and vegetable broth was not as elegant as it sounded. It was overly salted, though I seemed to be the only one who noticed. Halfway through the soup, Edna suggested, "Lewis, darling, bring us up to date on your case."

Excitement bounced in her eyes, and I wondered if she'd really be all that happy with me if I ceased being a Pinkerton. As I told the story of my meeting with Revka Rudkin at the settlement house, she interrupted, saying, "Goodness, I just had a terrible thought. You studied sociology. That doesn't make you one of those awful do-gooders always meddling in the lives of the poor, does it?"

"My studies were more theoretical. Though it is always interesting to see theory in action."

Hal clucked, then said, "The only thing I can imagine worse than poverty would be finding myself set upon by well-to-do spinsters trying to drag me out of my comfortable gutter."

"They can be quite severe," I admitted, then continued, "At any rate, the girl didn't say much of interest until the very end of the interview. At which point she suggested that her father was killed because of California."

"California? The state?" Edna asked.

"I'm not sure. The girl was coughing so she wasn't very clear, and then the social worker forced me to leave before I could get the girl to explain."

"She obviously meant the state, didn't she?" Edna guessed.

"She could have meant the street. The courthouse is on California Avenue. Or she might have been talking about someone with the nickname California. Or some version of that."

"You mean, he was killed by someone named California Sam or some such?" Edna slurped her soup a little right after saying that. Taking up her napkin, she dabbed her lips.

"Yes, I suppose that's possible."

"It could be a ship," Hal suggested.

"A ship?" Edna said. "Named California?"

"Remember the Maine," he said, referring to the sinking of the U.S.S. Maine, which began the Spanish-American war.

"Is there a U.S.S. California?" I asked.

"I'm sure there is," Hal said. "If we see any sailors later, we'll ask them."

"Later?"

"Hal's taking you on an expedition," Edna explained. I had no idea what kind of expedition might have us encountering sailors.

"There's a naval base up above Highland Park. The boys come down on leave."

I know it sounds incredibly naïve, but at the time I couldn't for the life of me imagine why someone like Hal Riggins would meet a sailor on leave. Of course, the rest of that evening did much to correct that naiveté.

Halibut was served next. Conversation turned to the motordrome in Riverview. Hal was quite excited by the story. Apparently, they were racing motorcycles at seventy-five miles an hour when one of the riders collided with another rider and was instantly killed.

"You'll have to forgive us, Lewis. We're fascinated by anything ghoulish."

"You're forgiven."

The meat course was a very tender cut of beef wrapped in pastry. Edna talked about the salon she was planning in the broadest terms. There were also instructions about her parents.

"Do not mention income tax in front of Papa."

"I can't imagine why I would," I replied.

"You'd be surprised how often it can come up in conversation. And avoid any mention of Wilson and the horrid Democrats."

"Ask him to explain how lumber is made. That will keep him talking for a good half an hour," Hal said.

"When you meet Mama, she'll seem dimwitted. Don't be fooled. She only does it to make Papa look smarter than he is."

"Which explains most of her behavior," her brother added.

I was actually thankful for the beef. I carefully kept my mouth full so that I wouldn't be expected to join in this conversation. It wasn't that I had nothing to say about complete strangers, it was that their comments were shocking. As difficult as Mother could be I wouldn't air those challenges over the meat course.

A French-style custard was served for dessert with coffee. Edna had only taken a few bites when she said, "If you'll excuse me, I must attend to some lady business."

With a fleeting smile she was gone.

I looked at Hal and said, given past experience, "She's not coming back, is she?"

"Of course not. Finish your dessert. We're going to have our adventure."

"I'm afraid I'll have to borrow a hat. I don't think I can wear the top hat I came in."

Hal hopped up and left to get our hats. I finished my dessert and wondered what adventure was about to happen. He came back with two boaters: one had a red-and-black ribbon while the other's ribbon was all black. He handed me the one that was all black. And then we were off.

It was already dark, as it was well after ten. We walked west to State Street to catch a streetcar. I didn't know what we were doing. During dinner, Hal had made several allusions to making friends. Allusions that seemed not to surprise my fiancée in the least.

On the ride, I asked Hal about where he'd gone to college.

"Harvard. Papa thought I'd make the best contacts there."

"Did you?"

He just leered, suggesting all sorts of impropriety. I wondered why my own college career had been so lacking in impropriety. Was it my college or was it me? Or was it perhaps Hal? Was he simply better, or perhaps more confident at finding that impropriety?

Twenty-five minutes later, we got off the streetcar across from Carson Pirie Scott at Madison. The store was closed, of course, yet the streets still teemed with life. We crossed the State Street and stood in front of the entrance as Hal gave me a list of instructions.

"Don't go into any of the saloons no matter who invites you. Don't go into an alley with anyone. If you like the looks of someone, ask if they've got some place to go. Most of them will know where to take you. A hotel room, a room in a brothel—those are the safest. Anything else and it gets too risky."

I must have looked surprised by what he was saying, because he added, "You really are an innocent, aren't you?"

Before I could answer, he walked away.

"Uh… shouldn't I go with you?" I called after him as I took a few steps.

"Oh god no."

"How do I find you again?"

Over his shoulder he said, "Hopefully you won't want to."

And then he winked a goodbye.

Even though I was very familiar with this part of Chicago, I felt completely lost. First, I walked north and looked into the windows of The Boston Store, thinking *What on earth was he going on about?* Then I turned around and walked south again. *Was something supposed to happen? If so, what? And I did I want it to?* After Carson Pirie Scott it was The Palmer House, then the Orpheum Theater and Rothschild & Company. I kept my eyes busy looking at the different businesses. I must have looked like a tourist from out of town come to see the buildings. Or I would have if it weren't for the red tie.

Wandering up and down State Street nearly breathless, I passed all manner of businesses, saloons, nickelodeons, haberdashers, vaudeville theaters, department stores. I began to notice there were other red ties; in fact, many red ties. The men examined me closely, several said "Hello." I was terrified and thrilled at once, but I kept walking. Eyes straight ahead. Putting one foot in front of the other. *Was this what he was talking about? That men would want to talk to me? That men would want...*

A newsboy hawking the last of the evening editions on the corner of State and Adams took one look at me and slipped his index finger into his mouth and sucked on it in a very suggestive way. He couldn't have been twelve years old. I had no idea how he knew such a thing. In fact, looking back, I'm not sure I knew such a thing. Though I did have the good sense to blush when he made the gesture.

Turning west at Adams, I walked the block to Dearborn. I was still seeing red ties and smiles everywhere I looked. As promised, a sailor in whites said "Ahoy" to me. A thick lump in my throat stopped me from responding. *What did I want?* I really had no idea. At that point, I barely knew what was possible. I'd like to be kissed again. I might have liked to do what the newsboy had been suggesting, though I wasn't sure exactly how to go about negotiating that.

Brothel. Hal had said brothel. Well, I wasn't going into a brothel. That was absurd. It sounded like what he'd meant was men like me, criminals of my sort, would rent a room in a brothel. Together. And then… It was the 'and then' that was a bit terrifying. And me… a Pink who'd shot a man.

At the corner, I caught sight of a shock of red hair from beneath a gray cap, a young man in a green suit with a beige waistcoat and a red tie. He looked like a very tall, very hand-some leprechaun. And then I knew him, it was Sergeant Seamus Grady looking completely at ease.

A smile broke out on my face, there was someone I could speak to, someone I might… I began walking toward him. When he saw me, I was at most a hundred feet away, hoping he'd smile back at me. But he didn't. In fact, he looked distressed. Ever so subtly he shook his head.

I was crushed, to be honest, that he didn't want me. Didn't even want to *talk* to me. Say hello. Instead, he was warning me off so that I wouldn't even get close to him and interrupt whatever possibilities...

I turned and stepped closer to the buildings. I noticed a very tall, effete young man approaching Seamus. A dandy who looked particularly well off. Seamus smiled at him and leaned in to hear whatever the man had to say.

Turning the corner at Monroe, I was on my way back to

State Street when I heard a policeman's whistle behind me. Those around me in red ties moved away quickly. I, however, walked back toward Seamus. I wanted to see if he'd gotten into some kind of trouble.

I hadn't gone far when I could see that it was Seamus who *was* the trouble. He was putting a pair of handcuffs on the effete gentleman who'd spoken to him. Whatever the man had said was clearly enough to cause his arrest. There were two other police officers in blue jackets and tall derbies approaching.

Seamus caught my eye again; this time shook his head in a gesture that clearly meant 'get out of here.'

And so, I did.

$\mathcal{A}$s planned, I went directly to Continental Surety & Safety in the morning. I was there on time but, as I'd been told to expect, Harcourt was not. At nine-thirty he was still not there. It was becoming uncomfortable to sit there with the same matronly woman I'd spoken to the day before. I decided to leave, but before I did, I asked "I'm trying to find the Rudkin's. Do you have any documents that might include their most recent address?"

"You'd have to ask Mr. Harcourt."

"Who's not here. He must keep files on his clients. And he must know where the Rudkin's live, he collects their premium every week."

"People stop paying after a person dies. Why do you want to find them?"

"I need to ask them questions about Mr. Rudkin's death. And since I'm conducting this investigation at the request of your company, you ought to help me. You don't want to be mentioned negatively in my report."

With an angry huff, she got up and went over to a wooden filing cabinet. Her fingers moved along the files until she found the right one. Then she read off, "4630 South Gross Avenue."

"That's a settlement house. They don't live there."

"Well, I'm sorry. That's all there is in the file."

She returned to her desk while I fumed. Someone had to know where they lived. And then the woman answered a question I hadn't asked.

"He was here after you left yesterday. I gave him the note you left. He seemed very upset by it. What did it mean?"

"Did you look at it?"

"California. What does that mean?"

"I don't know. That's why I'm trying to find the Rudkin's address, to find out."

"They could be living somewhere on California Avenue. But it's a mighty long street."

"I'm aware of that," I said, bitterly.

"I'm sorry I'm not able to help," she said, almost sounding sincere. "Harcourt is a charmer, but he's also a rascal. I'd say he's up to something."

That was glaringly obvious. It was also obvious that the characterization didn't do me a bit of good since the man wasn't there. I said good-bye and left.

Back at the Pinkerton office, I settled into my little office and read through three or four reports that had been left for me. Unfortunately, the typewritists were missing a lot of grammar errors. I wondered if I shouldn't take a cue from Revka Rudkin and give them a class. I'd have to bring that up with Mr. Cuthbert. I was wondering whether I should invite my superior to my engagement party over the weekend, when one of the boys stuck his head into the office.

"Got a girl here to see you."

Assuming it was Edna again, I was about to admonish the boy. Edna was a lady *not* a girl. But then Revka Rudkin walked in. It wasn't normal to bring a visitor down to the rabbit warren, but after I took one look at her it was obvious why the rule had been broken.

The girl's eyes were blackened, her cheeks swollen, there were angry red marks on her neck and arms.

"Have a seat, Miss Rudkin." I looked at the boy, whose name I couldn't remember and said, "That will be all. Thank you."

After the boy left, I wondered for a moment if I should close the door. But no, that would be untoward. Best to leave it open.

"Did Harcourt do this to you?"

She said, "Yes," and I was devastated. I'd left him the note with the word CALIFORNIA, and, clearly, he beaten the girl because of it. The blame was mine. I should have found another way to entrap the man. I'd been careless, impulsive, and had not considered the ramifications of my actions. And now this poor girl was bruised and battered.

"Tell me everything."

Before she could, she began coughing again. I realized I was going to have to break this down into smaller bits. I also needed to get her water. I told the girl I'd be right back and bolted out of the office. I ran up the stairs to the ninth floor. Reaching reception, I asked Daisy, "Would you get a pitcher of water and a glass and then bring it downstairs? It's the third office from the elevator."

I spun around and dashed back to the stairs before she could answer. Terrified the girl would bolt, I was back in the office as fast as humanly possible. Flying into the room, I was relieved to see she was still there. I slowed down, trying to gain control of my breathing, and sat behind the desk.

"Let's start with the first claim. Your brother found a body..."

"Yes, Tadus. He is my younger brother. He is eight. He and his friends found the man's body behind a house."

As she began to speak, I saw that her front tooth had been broken diagonally. It looked painful.

"Do you know the man's name?"

"Ludwik. He was Polish. I don't know his last name. He heard voices, spoke to people who weren't there. He didn't live anywhere. People would always shoo him away."

"A hobo."

"Yes."

"February. He froze to death?"

She shrugged. "It was very cold."

"Your father decided that you should burn the house down with the man inside and then claim your father was dead. And he wanted to do this to pay his gambling debts?"

"No. No gambling debts. The rest is true, but my father didn't owe money. It's true that he gambled, but he was good at cards. And he was friendly; people liked him. They liked playing with him."

"Even when they lost?"

"Yes. Everyone liked him."

Daisy entered the office with a pitcher of water and a glass, as requested. She began to give them to me, but I nodded to indicate they were for the girl. Daisy poured a glass of water, and Revka took it.

"Thank you, Daisy."

When she left, I asked Revka, "You didn't need money then?"

"No, we needed money. My mother took me to a doctor. He said I should not live here. That I should live somewhere with better air. Like California. Or Arizona. We liked California better."

"I see," I said, understanding now what California meant. Though I wondered why it had upset Harcourt so much. "Your family planned to use the money to move to California where they'd reunite with your very much alive father?"

"Yes."

"How was Harcourt involved in this? Was he helping?"

"He came every week to get the insurance premium from my mother. He fell in love with her."

"And that would be why he helped them?"

She shook her head. "He worked out what my parents were doing before you did."

"Oh," I said, feeling put in my place. "And he wanted money?"

She shook her head again. "He wanted my mother."

As though in response to her own statement, she began to cough again. She took the glass of water and drank. I waited until she seemed to have stopped.

"You're saying Harcourt was in love with a woman he couldn't even speak to?"

Revka frowned at me. "No. He speaks Lithuanian. His parents are from Lithuania."

"But his name is Harcourt?"

She shook her head, yet again, saying, "His real name is Rolandas Horbach."

"Was your mother in love with him?"

"No. But they didn't know what to do. He promised he would get the money for us. That he would give my father half and take us out to California. My parents fought terribly about it, but if they didn't do what he wanted they would go to jail. That's what he told us."

"And then what happened?"

"You. You saw that Ludwik was not my father. Then we didn't know what would happen. We got jobs at Swift. My father came out of hiding and started playing cards again. He hoped to win enough money to leave."

"But Harcourt kept coming around."

"He wanted my mother to leave with him. She wouldn't

do it. She's not in love with him. She loved my father. And then my father was murdered."

"By Harcourt," I guessed.

"I think so, yes. He was there right away, telling my mother how she could submit another claim. Promising that he'd make sure it was paid."

I wondered how he planned to make good on that promise. Did he really think I'd fail at my assignment? I had to be honest. He likely thought exactly that.

She nodded. "He promised that when she got the money we'd all go to California. He promised to marry her."

"Did she say she would?"

"She didn't know what else to do. We need someone to take care of us. What was she supposed to do?"

"Harcourt beat you because you spoke to me?"

"I told you too much. You can put him in prison, can't you? You can keep him away from us?"

"I need you to write all of this down and sign it. We'll give it to our client, Continental Surety & Safety and they'll involve the police."

I took out several pieces of paper and a pencil and pushed them across the desk to her. I added, "If you write it out, I can have one of the typewriterists make a copy with carbons and then have you sign it."

"Is it hard?"

"Is what hard?"

"To be a typewriter-ist?

Amidst all of this, murder, fraud, violence, she'd noticed that the girls upstairs we neatly dressed and worked in a clean, comfortable location. Despite all that had happened to her, she was looking for a way to better herself.

"We'll ask when we go upstairs."

* * *

AFTER REVKA RUDKIN LEFT, I spent the rest of the afternoon writing my report. As I did, I had to think through whether everything I thought happened actually had. For instance, was her mother as innocent as Revka portrayed? Or was she much more involved? Now that I knew Revka didn't have to translate every word between Harcourt and her mother, there could be things, many things, the girl did not know.

The claim would be denied, of course. There was the problem of the fraudulent claim Mrs. Rudkin clearly participated in based on her daughter's statement. Then there was Harcourt's involvement in submitting both claims. That made it seem Mrs. Rudkin was involved in her husband's murder in some way. We might not be able to prove it in court, but it didn't matter. *Might* was likely enough to deny the claim. Once denied, Mrs. Rudkin had few options that didn't put her in legal jeopardy.

I felt bad for them all. Well, not Harcourt, obviously.

Why wouldn't a woman who lived in such a place be capable of killing her husband? Death was a daily event. In fact, death was the business of the entire neighborhood. Was it such a leap from casually, callously watching animal after animal die to watching a single man lose his one, small life?

CHAPTER 26

Midweek, I decided to go to Central Station. This time I took a streetcar down Fifth. I was worried that if I walked I'd have too much time to change my mind. When I walked into the police station, I immediately saw that I was in luck and Sergeant Seamus Grady was standing behind the front desk. I walked over and said, "Hello."

He looked quite dapper in his deep blue uniform. It was clean and neatly pressed. For a moment I wondered how men like Seamus Grady took care of their uniforms. Did he have a mother who did his laundry? Sisters? Did he give his clothes to a laundress? I'd grown up with girls who came in. I wasn't that sure how other people lived.

Seamus looked over his shoulder and said something to another copper sitting at a desk. Then he turned back to me, saying, "Follow me."

He opened a barrier, and I went behind the front desk. Then he led me down a hallway and into a small barren room with just a couple of chairs and a scarred wooden table. We sat down.

"You're not to go down there like that again."

"I beg your pardon. I came to say thank you."

"And *I'll* thank you not to go down there again. I hope you threw that red tie away."

"It wasn't mine," I said, though I was sure Hal wouldn't have minded if I had thrown it away. "Why do you care? If I do it again, you can arrest me."

"That would be the point, wouldn't it? I don't want to arrest you."

"You don't know me."

"I might like to know you, but if you get arrested, I won't be able to, will I? I can't cavort with criminals."

"Oh."

I wasn't sure if he was saying what I thought he was saying. He must be though. Cavort. He wanted to cavort with me? Still, I couldn't do much more than stare at him.

"What were you doing down there?"

"My friend brought me. My fiancée's brother."

"Fiancée? Was he playing a joke on you?"

I didn't know what to say to that. Had he been playing a joke on me? He'd certainly abandoned me quickly enough.

"No. It wasn't a joke. I'm… I was… that's my nature."

"Does your fiancée know?"

"She does. She has the same nature."

He nodded, then repeated, "You're not to go down there again. You need to find one bloke and stick to him."

Like I had any idea how to go about that.

"Do you have a good memory?"

"Yes, I think I do."

He gave me an address on Dearborn up near Bughouse Square. Then he said, "I live alone."

I sat there quietly for a moment, then asked, "If it's your nature too, how can you arrest men like yourself?"

"I wasn't given a choice, now, was I?" Then, after a pause

he said, "I only arrest the rich buggers. The rich never pay for their crimes, now do they?"

* * *

WHEN I RETURNED to the Pinkerton office, I was called in to see Mr. Cuthbert. Sitting down across from him, I noted his attention was firmly held by a letter that lay in front of him. The moment he looked up, I asked something that had been on my mind for some time.

"Sir, forgive my impertinence, but does Mr. Pinkerton not come to this office at all?"

"He spends a great deal of time in Hot Springs, Arkansas, taking the waters. Which doesn't mean he isn't actively involved in the agency. In fact, he's managed to procure many clients at the resort."

"I hope I wasn't rude to ask."

"You were right about the cup. It was given to Mr. Pinkerton by his dear wife Margaret. She passed a few years before the turn of the century."

That first test seemed like a very long time ago. I felt a bit ashamed, since I was being complimented on what I'd hoped was the wrong answer.

He continued, "I submitted your report to Continental Surety & Safety. They're very pleased, Lewis. We're very pleased. I've spoken to Mr. Pinkerton about you. You did excellent work."

"Thank you, sir. I assume the client has passed the information along to the police."

"Yes, about that. They've released Roland Harcourt from his position without references. They've decided that's all the action they'll be taking at this time."

"But he killed a man."

"The company feels that to pursue a conviction would

result in far too much publicity. They don't want it known that one of their insurance agents was involved in a fraud. That would not be good for business."

"You mean he's getting off scot-free?"

"I wouldn't go that far. He's unlikely to do well in life. He won't be working in an office, that's certain. I imagine he'll have to eke out a living gutting hogs."

"That hardly seems a fit punishment."

"I'm not sure he'd agree with you. I'm told he was quite upset when he was let go. In fact, you should know he made a number of threats against you."

"Me?"

"Well, you are the author of his demise."

"None of what happened was my fault."

"I doubt he sees it that way. You do still have your father's gun? The police didn't take it away from you when you shot the elevator boy?"

"They let me keep the gun."

"You might want to carry it with you for a while."

"You can't be serious."

"I'm very serious. As you say, he killed a man."

I left his office shaken. I'd been reading newspapers every day since I was twelve, so I knew how much they loved a scandal, and I could see that an insurance agent caught up in murder and insurance fraud would be front page news at least for a few days. More if they managed to get a photograph or even a sketch of Mrs. Rudkin. Though it might have been a practical decision, it still seemed terribly wrong. No one should get away with murder.

And then there was the daughter to consider. Harcourt had beaten her. He might do it again. I wondered if there was anything I could do about that, but I couldn't think of what. I hoped the fact that he was blaming me meant he wouldn't hurt her. And then I wondered if her mother might step in to protect her.

I was basically useless that afternoon. There were reports left on my desk and I tried to focus on grammar, but it did nothing but swim around the pages. Late in the afternoon, I wondered why I cared at all what happened to Harcourt.

What matter was justice to me? I was a criminal, in thought and intention if not in action. There were laws I was eager to break. So what did it matter if one terrible man killed another terrible man? What did it matter if an urchin, one who would likely condemn me in heartbeat, what did it matter if she suffered?

It mattered, though. It truly did.

That evening when I returned home, I sat down for dinner with Mother. It was a weeknight, so the Polish girl had already gone, leaving dinner on the stove. Mother popped through the swinging door with something in her hands that was clearly not dinner. She lay that morning's *Daily Tribune* in front of me.

It was folded in such a way that the society page was face up. She said, "There," pointing to a short paragraph near the edge of the page. I glanced at it. It was barely more than a sentence, "Mr. and Mrs. Harold Riggins of Detroit are visiting their daughter Edna of East Lake Shore Drive at the weekend to celebrate her engagement to Lewis Wait of Hyde Park."

"I'm shocked," I said. "I had no idea you read the society pages."

"Don't be foolish, Lewis. That girl has trapped you now."

"I doubt she's behind this. She has little interest in society. I imagine her mother placed the story. Which would mean her mother has trapped me now."

She sat down at the table and seemed to deflate. "I've lost, haven't I?"

"It's not a sporting event. It's a marriage."

"You really can be quite naïve."

That felt like a slap in the face. What on earth did she mean by that? Did she think marriage was some kind of competition, and that Edna was attempting to win something from me? No, she was wrong. If marriage was a sport, particularly the kind of marriage we planned, then it was a team sport. We were on the same side. We'd be competing with the world together, not with each other.

"Have you decided?" I asked.

"Decided what?"

"What illness I'm going to give as your excuse. Or do you a think a simple she's not feeling well will do?"

"After this announcement, I'll be attending."

"Oh."

"I hope that doesn't disappoint you."

"Of course I want you there." I waited a moment, hoping she'd go into the kitchen and bring our dinner out. She didn't budge. "There will likely be alcohol."

"Yes, I'm aware."

"And you'll be good about it?"

"I promise. No picket signs, no petitions, no delegation from The Women's Temple."

I had no idea whether to trust her.

CHAPTER 27

I had not expected a picnic. I was sure Edna said salon, which implied… well, not a picnic. When Mother and I arrived at the Riggins' apartment we discovered that was exactly what was planned. It wasn't a terrible idea; the afternoon *was* unseasonably warm. A soiree in Edna's dining room would have quickly turned humid and uncomfortable. Particularly if there were a lot of people. Still, no one was as excited about it as Edna.

As Mother and I waited for the door to be answered, she said, "I understand you're an adult and feel you needn't pay any attention to my suggestions. But for god's sake Lewis, stand up straight."

I pulled myself erect as the door was opened, not by Paula as I'd expect, but by Edna herself.

"There you are! This is all so exciting."

She took a step forward, stood on her toes, and kissed me on the cheek. Then she and my mother greeted each other stiffly. Behind Edna, lingering in the foyer, were her parents whom she quickly introduced.

Harold Riggins was a stout man well into his fifties. His

hair had long since fled the top of his head and his face seemed to be collapsing in on itself. None of which would have mattered if he'd been at all friendly. When Edna introduced Mother and I, the look on his face was exactly what you'd expect if he'd just bitten into a rotten, wormy apple. In fact, I suspected he'd have been happier doing that than meeting us.

Next to him was Mrs. Riggins, whose first name was Florence though she didn't suggest we use it. She was remarkably thin, which made it seem as though her black satin dress was likely to slide off. The dress was a bit mannish, looking like a suit despite her white blouse having a number of lacy flounces. Atop her head she wore two large feathers, one black and one white.

She seemed a bit friendlier than her husband, saying to Mother, "Edna tells me you met at The Women's Temple and that you're interested in suffrage. Don't mention suffrage to Harold. It angers him so much he's likely to burst a blood vessel."

"I am standing here, Florence."

"Yes dear, do you want to discuss suffrage?"

"I do not." He was so adamant I thought the words might injure one of us.

"It's just as I said. I'm merely paving the way for you. Isn't life easier when the way is paved?"

During the exchange I wondered why we were all in the foyer. It was certainly large enough, but there was an entire apartment. That's when Edna surprised us with the idea of a picnic.

"It's such a lovely day, I can't think of anything better than sitting in the grass, looking at the lake, and having our lunch."

Of course, she could see the lake from at least six of her windows, but I'd already learned that once Edna had an idea it was difficult to separate her from it. Across the street from their building there was a narrow park with a few fledgling trees and benches. The lawn was growing in nicely and looked lush on the warm day.

And then Paula and a woman I took to be the cook, were standing in the foyer holding large, heavy picnic baskets.

"It looks like we're ready," Edna said. "Shall we?"

We left the apartment, the seven of us, already a party.

"Is this everyone?" my mother asked.

"Oh no, I don't think so," Edna said. "It's still early. I've instructed the doorman to direct our guests across to the park."

"And Hal?" I asked.

"Don't worry, he'll be along." Then she leaned in close and leaned close to whisper, "I'm sorry. I'm afraid it's going to be quite the crowd. Mama monopolized the telephone for hours yesterday. She's invited friends of friends, bare acquaintances, business associates of my father and relatives—third cousins, if you can imagine."

"Oh my."

"Yes, oh my. Hal and his friends are bringing down a few card tables and the champagne, of course."

I glanced at Mother; she had to have heard every word. Her face was rigid. I hoped she'd be reasonable. She'd promised to be reasonable. No one could force *her* to drink wine. At least, I hoped not.

Once we were in the park, Edna flitted about choosing a spot. As promised, Hal and two handsome young men arrived with folding card tables and the cases of champagne. I wasn't sure, but I thought I recognized one of the young men from our trip to State Street. I tried to smile at Hal, but he was preoccupied with his friends as they set up the tables.

An already faded young man and a bland woman arrived, and Mrs. Riggins pulled me over to meet them. This was the other brother, Henry; the one who'd inherit the family business as his brother was an invert. The way he sneered at me suggested he had some idea what was truly happening here. The woman with him was his fiancée, Vivian. Though she rested a hand on his arm, the two seemed completely disconnected.

Tablecloths were spread onto the card tables, food was placed—sandwiches, jellied meats, tiny cakes and fruits—while a rug with cushions was laid out on the grass.

"This is so exotic," Vivian said in a sharp, annoying voice. Henry already seemed practiced in ignoring her.

Across the street, I began noticing well-dressed couples walking into Edna's building and then walking back out again. The guests. Most of whom I was forced to meet as soon as they crossed the street to the park, their names offered and immediately forgotten.

I'm afraid much of the party is a distant swirl of faces glimpsed and impressions fogged by time. I remember there being music. A phonograph had appeared. The kind with a crank, not the electrified kind. In deference to Mother I turned down the champagne, but as I recall the food was good. And there was a point when I was sitting on one of the cushions with my mother and Edna.

Edna asked, "Angelica, did you read the *Sunday Tribune* this morning?"

I was instantly appalled. I had read it and I knew exactly why she'd asked. There was a cartoon on the front page about kindliness. One of the panels depicted a barkeep who was kind compared to a panel of a wealthy man of 'immaculate' character who was anything but kind. Thus challenging the truth of our viewpoints—and in particular those of my mother.

Was this a glimpse of my future? Would Edna needle my

mother every time they met? I sincerely hoped that would not be true.

"Of course I read the newspaper," Mother said tersely. "I read it every morning," Then with decided sparkle in her eye, she added, "I assume you're referring to the article about the woman shot by her husband who was mad with drink."

Turning to me, she added, "A friend had telephoned to warn her. She was still on the call when she was shot."

Mrs. Riggins, who must have been with us too, said, "Edna, you shouldn't talk about such things. A young lady restricts herself to polite topics. It is a lovely day, don't you think?"

"It's a bit windy," Edna said, probably a reaction to the way the feathers on her mother's head were fluttering. "This was a terrible idea."

Honestly, I didn't know whether she meant the picnic or the party in general. We reassured her it, the picnic was not a terrible idea and the party continued. There was much talk about the weather. The differing charms of Chicago and Detroit. The question of which was better put to rest, when it was decided both were preferable to any city in the East.

I remember standing at a table with Edna and her parents. My mother was off chatting with Mr. Cuthbert, whom she'd invited without my knowledge. Not that I minded, although outside of the Pinkerton office I had little idea what to say to him.

"What are these?" Mr. Riggins asked.

"They're paper plates, Papa."

"Paper… I've never heard of such a thing."

"They've been making them for years."

"Why would I know anything about paper plates? Your mother and I aren't given to picnics."

Edna flushed angrily.

I leaned forward reaching for a deviled egg, and as I put it on my paper plate, Mrs. Riggins gasped, "Oh my goodness. Is that a gun? You've brought a gun to your own engagement party?"

"I have. I'm sorry if it frightens you."

"Lewis shot a man just a few weeks ago. Didn't I tell you?"

"No, you did not," her father said. I wondered if he made any sounds that weren't disapproving.

"You're not planning to shoot someone this afternoon, are you?" Mrs. Riggins said, going back to placing a delicate sandwich onto her plate.

"I never *plan* to shoot people," I said. Immediately, unnerved that I'd made it sound like I often shot people.

"Well, I suppose that's encouraging," Mrs. Riggins said.

At some point—it might have been before we ate, I'm not certain—I attempted a moment alone with Mr. Riggins.

"I'm told you're a Pinkerton man," he growled.

"Yes, sir."

"Good work crushing the strikes. Shame Congress put an end to that."

"Yes, sir."

I wasn't sure how I got credit for something that happened twenty years before. Taking a deep breath, I jumped in.

"I did ask Edna if I should ask your permission before I proposed." Of course, that wasn't exactly a truthful statement. She had been the one to do the proposing and it had been done without my mother's approval. "She thought it would be old-fashioned."

He stood silently for a moment. "You're marrying my daughter for her money."

"That's not true, sir."

"It had better be true. There's no other reason for you to marry her. She's nearly a spinster and... Well, I'm assuming you know the rest."

That placed me an awkward spot. I obviously couldn't acknowledge the truth nor could I convincingly espouse my love for her.

"I think you underestimate your daughter's charms."

"After the wedding I'll be settling a large sum of money on you. There are caveats. You're not to live in Detroit. And you're to make sure Edna does not make a public scandal. And you're not to allow her control of the money."

"I understand your terms," I said. I knew that I wasn't exactly agreeing to them, only seeming to. His terms conflicted with Edna's terms. At some point, I'd have to resolve the conflict.

I wondered what he might do if and when I broke one or all of the caveats. He wouldn't be able to demand the money back, so I failed to see what power he'd have over us. But then, he didn't seem like the kind of man to allow himself to be powerless.

It was later, much later I think, when the party guests had turned into a noisy crowd and the sun was easing itself into the west, when the women arrived singing a hymn of some sort. There was far too much noise to determine exactly what it was they were singing, but they were loud enough to draw attention. There were about a dozen of them, dressed completely in white carrying picket signs with messages like PURITY IS OUR MOTTO and VOTE DRY! and LESS BEER MORE CHEER.

Nearby, I heard Mrs. Riggins saying, "How ridiculous. No one here is drinking beer."

I was tempted to search out my mother and strangle her. Then there was a sudden shriek. I turned and at first didn't see anything. But then I noticed a number of people also turning in the direction of the shriek. They stepped aside and a man broke through, something shiny flashed in his hand. It was Harcourt, disheveled, red-faced and clearly drunken, even at a distance you could see that. He swayed toward me, the flash in his hand a knife. Quite probably the one he killed Rudkin with.

"You ruined my life!"

"Harcourt, think about what you're doing."

He kept on; he was mere feet from me. I could smell the sickly sweet smell of alcohol. He was steeped in it. Another step, and then I had the presence of mind to reach into my coat and pull out the Colt. This time I brought it out without a hitch, having practiced taking it out of the holster.

I thought to warn Harcourt, but now he was close enough to stick me. He raised the knife to do just that, and I fired. Despite the fact that there was a shower of blood everywhere, he took another step closer. He was almost on me.

I backed away, as quickly as I could, but he stepped forward again. I fired a second time; this time I caught him dead center in his chest. He fell to the ground dead. There seemed a long moment when everything was silent—except that can't be true. I can't imagine silence that day, but that's what I remember. Silence.

Mrs. Riggins had been standing quite close when the shots were fired. We might have been chatting awkwardly, I don't remember. I do remember her screaming after I shot Harcourt. She was covered in a spray of his blood. The severity of her black-and-white ensemble ruined in red.

Mr. Cuthbert took charge, taking the gun away from me, and I was grateful for his assistance. Someone was sent back to the Riggins' apartment building to ask the doorman to telephone the police. They arrived a short time later. An ambulance appeared, though I believe it was to bring the body to the coroner. Before Harcourt was taken away, I was brought to the police station, the thirty-fifth precinct I think. It was all different then, the divisions and the precincts, and since that time I've visited so many of the stations they blend together.

I was at home by the evening, quite late. It must have been too late to place a telephone call, because I know I didn't speak to any of the Riggins' that night. And Mother and I... Well, when I came in she had a light supper prepared for me and then suggested we continue to read aloud from a book we were reading.

Henry James, I recall.

CHAPTER 28

Justice is a quiet beast. If you manage to lure it from its lair, do not make sudden moves, keep your voice low, and if it raises up and stands on its hind legs know that you've not found justice. You have instead trapped revenge or retribution or even punishment. They have similar markings and are easily mistaken for justice. No, justice is quiet. It will eat from your palm and sit with you next to a fire. And when you doze off it will slip away not to be seen again for a very long time.

Of course, I didn't understand that then. I was simply happy to be alive. There were stories in the papers: *The Tribune, The Inter Ocean, The Examiner.* All featured headlines of the society picnic that turned deadly. Once again, my colleagues teased me about my violent nature. Bankhead sought me out the Tuesday afternoon when I returned to the office, having spent most of that Monday explaining myself to the police.

"You really are bucking for promotion, ain't you?"

"The man was attempting kill me."

He shrugged. "Killing two birds with one stone. Smart."

"Is there something I can do for you?"

I suppose he was trying to be friendly, but I didn't like the bend of the conversation.

"Ask for me," he said simply.

"I beg your pardon."

"When you get an assignment. You know you're gonna get the best ones. Clients'll read about you in the papers. They're gonna ask for you. And you're already Cuthbert's favorite. You're going places. I want you to take me along."

"I don't know that any of that is true." And then I said again, the thing I'd been saying for more than forty-eight hours. "I had no choice. He was going to kill me."

I didn't feel particularly good about it. I wondered, quite frequently in fact, if there hadn't been something I could have done or said that might have prevented the man's death. If there had been a few more moments, could I have talked him out of it? Or should I have shot him in the foot? I doubted I was that good a shot. I might have ended up stabbed if I tried that. But then, it hadn't even crossed my mind at the time. I wanted him dead. And so I shot him in the chest.

"Yes, of course," I said, finally. "Should the need for assistance arise, I will ask for you."

He nodded, and then said, "There's a gentleman upstairs waiting to see you."

"Why didn't you— Did he give his name?"

"Riggins, he said. Tried to give me a card. Like I couldn't remember his name."

"All right. Thank you."

Bankhead left and I took a moment to prepare myself. Edna's father was upstairs. I could only imagine what he wanted. I had to assume he wanted me to break our engagement. Well, I wouldn't agree to that. Having met her parents,

I understood why she wanted to be independent of them and I was pleased to assist her.

When I reached the ninth floor, I found not Mr. Riggins but Hal sitting in a chair in front of the typewritists, all of whom were eyeing the handsome gentleman. A rush of feeling spread through my chest. He'd come to see me out of concern. It meant a great deal.

He wore a fawn-colored suit with a cream waistcoat, a spotless collar and a lavender tie. In one hand, he held a straw boater—the one he'd worn on State Street—and in the other a package wrapped in newspaper.

"Thank you so much for coming," I said. I wanted to reach out and touch him, but that would not have been appropriate. A handshake perhaps, but he didn't extend a hand, possibly because they were full.

"Could we talk privately?"

I suppose I could have taken him down to the rabbit warren, but the shabbiness of the entire floor seemed deflating. I could have invited him into the office Mr. Cuthbert shared with Mr. Pinkerton, but I was not that presumptuous.

"Perhaps a stroll around the block?"

"Perfect."

I called for the elevator, relieved that I'd had the presence of mind to bring my hat. Assuming it had been the older Mr. Riggins, I'd thought we'd be leaving the building. On the ride down, we were silent in deference to the operator. Walking out onto Fifth Avenue, we were able to relax a bit. We could talk without anyone listening.

"I'm so glad you've come."

"I know this is terribly unfair, but my father has laid the blame for the shooting incident at your door."

"Yes?"

I didn't understand what he meant. Displeasing her

parents had seemed part of Edna's plan for our engagement. It satisfied her father's demands while also dashing his hopes.

"Father has decided to settle Edna's portion on her regardless of whether she marries."

"Oh. Well, good for her."

"Which means your engagement is over."

I have to say it stung quite a lot more than it should have. It was to be an unromantic marriage, of course. And I wasn't especially interested in the allowance. But I would have enjoyed the comradery. We three inverts, as it were. For the most part, our trip to State Street had disabused me of romantic notions where Hal was concerned. I would have liked him as a friend, though. And I would have liked Edna as my friend. I thought she *was* my friend.

"I have to ask, was that the plan all along?"

"Don't be ridiculous. Edna can't have known you'd shoot a man."

"Yes, but she did know I was not appropriate. I pointed it out."

"She was more than willing to marry you, Lewis. The fact that you offended my father's sensibilities? That was a bonus. She believed he'd have accepted you… if you hadn't shot a man quite so publicly."

"I would have been more marriageable if I'd have let the villain stab me?"

"In my father's eyes, perhaps. He's not at all modern."

By that point we'd reached the corner of Lasalle and Madison. I'd stopped and was staring into the window of Francis C. Brown Western Passenger Agent. He offered tickets for various cruise lines. At that moment, I would have enjoyed buying a ticket to some place very far away.

"Edna couldn't have come herself?"

"You know what she's like. She's hates saying good-bye."

"What if I don't want to say good-bye?"

In those years, a broken engagement was grounds for a lawsuit. Breach of promise. It wasn't uncommon, particularly when people like the Riggins were involved. It would have been disastrous, of course. Had the actual terms of our contract come to light we'd have both been ruined.

"I know you're going to be a good sport about all this," Hal said. It sounded a bit too much like a threat. Then he said, "I've brought you this." He held out the package wrapped in newspaper.

"What is it?"

"Your tuxedo. You left it."

"Of course," I said, taking the package. "I didn't bring your clothes. I can bring them to you another time."

"They're not important. I can assure you."

"Does this mean we're not even going to be friends?"

"Edna has written you a check. A gift for your friendship. I told her you wouldn't accept it."

I wouldn't. But how could he know that? Shaking my head, I stood there thinking I'd seen this man at most five times. Despite the fact that he'd kissed me once, I didn't know him. Why did it feel so terrible that I was losing his friendship?

"Are your parents still here?" I asked, thinking that things might be different once they left, once Edna and Hal had time to think about their own lives again.

"We're going back the day after tomorrow."

"The four of you?" I'd completely discounted his brother. But then it seemed the family did as well.

"Edna's staying here. I'm to be engaged. Well, married shortly. A family friend. She finds herself in a predicament."

"Another white marriage?"

"You'd be surprised at how often they occur."

"What's in it for you?"

"A child to call my own. The right sort of scandal. And a rather large dowry."

"You're letting your father win."

"Men like my father always win. The challenge is in how well you lose."

Impulsively, I decided not to lose. I looked him straight in the eye, and said, "Now that I think about it, I will take that check. Why not?"

Hal retrieved an envelope from his jacket pocket. Handing it to me, he looked disappointed. I wondered if this was how rich people kept so much of their money, relying on the goodness of others not to take it when offered.

Cooly, he said "Good-bye," and walked away. Before walking back to the Pinkerton offices, I tossed my old tuxedo into a trash bin at the corner. And then, instead of going upstairs, I opened the envelope and looked inside. There was no note, no calling card, no good-bye, nothing but a check for two thousand five hundred dollars. Nearly three years' salary. Enough for me to quit the Pinkertons and return to school. Enough to live the life with Josiah I'd hoped to live before my mother's interference.

The check was drawn on American Trust & Savings Bank. They had a building at Monroe and Clark. Just two blocks from the Pinkerton offices. I walked over to find an attractive brick building only a few years old, standing twenty stories or so.

In the lobby, I found a teller and cashed the check. I immediately opened an account and deposited one thousand five hundred dollars at three percent. I put the remaining thousand dollars back into the envelope and slipped it into my jacket pocket.

After that, I took the Elevated back to Packingtown. The days were noticeably getting longer, and it was still bright though it was nearing five o'clock. I got off at the stop for

Swift and made my way down the stairs to the street, into the building and then climbed to the third floor. I scanned the tables looking for the Rudkins. It took only a few moments to find them. The matron got in front of me and tried to stop me.

"Don't, I'm not here to make a scene. This will only take a moment."

"No, you get out."

But Revka had seen me and come over. There was a bit of awe in her face. I'd killed her tormenter, after all. She told the matron, "It is okay. I am fine."

Grudgingly the woman walked away.

"You killed him," Revka said.

"It was self-defense."

"Thank you."

Her bruises were still pronounced, possibly even worse than when I'd last seen her. I took the envelope out of my pocket and gave it to her. She opened it.

"They paid the claim?"

"Yes," I lied. "They've paid the claim. Your father's dead. Your mother didn't kill him. They had to. You can go to California now."

"Thank you."

I nodded and walked away, hoping that I'd never have to visit Packingtown again.

Forty-five minutes later, after taking three different Elevated lines, I stood in front of 1100 North Dearborn Avenue. It was a twenty-story, limestone and red brick apartment building. I'd read about buildings like it in the *Tribune*. They were designed for the young people, particularly women, who were moving into the city from rural areas to become salesclerks, office boys, typewritists and all sort of things. The apartments, according to what I'd read, were one room affairs with small kitchens and bathrooms.

When I entered, I discovered the lobby was much smaller than I'd anticipated. It was covered in dark wood paneling. As you entered, there was a window for a doorman. Its shade was pulled down, so I imagined he was only there during the daytime. I passed a small reception area with two horsehair sofas on my way to two sleek elevators, both appeared to be in use.

I looked for the stairway and hurried up three flights. The apartment number was 312. Easy to remember. I walked down the long hallway and found it near the back of the building.

I took a deep breath and knocked. Just moments later, Seamus Grady opened the door. He wore a collarless shirt open at the throat, suspenders and flannel slacks. He was barefoot.

"I hope this is all right," I said.

"I wouldn't have given you my address if it weren't."

He stepped back and I walked into the apartment. As expected, it was one room with two narrow windows, a breakfast area with built in cupboards and a rudimentary kitchen, beyond that a large closet and a bathroom.

Seamus had very little furniture. A small table and chairs in the breakfast area. Two secondhand armchairs in the living room with a pretty floor lamp between them. And little else.

I wondered where he slept, but before I could ask, I surprised myself by stepping forward to kiss him. He put his hands up and held my face. His kiss was gentle, curious, patient. It was not as dramatic as kissing Hal, but then it occurred to me I might have been the one who'd been dramatic. This kiss was calm, soft, even kind. But then he stepped back, terrifying me.

"Did I do something wrong?"

He nearly laughed. "No, you haven't done anything

wrong. But you smell bad. Rank."

"Oh dear. I'm sorry, I've just come from Packingtown. I had an important errand to run."

"Well, I'm glad you fit me into your busy schedule," he said, smiling to let me know he was teasing me. "You should probably take your clothes off. We'll open the window in the kitchen and put them on the back of a chair to air out."

He made it sound very practical. I slipped off my jacket, and he took it from me. Put it on the back of a kitchen chair. Opened the window.

"What kind of errand would you need to run in Packingtown?"

"I had to deliver some money to a family there. An insurance claim."

"An insurance company paying a claim in Packingtown? I don't believe it." He slipped my vest over my shoulders and took it away. "Does it have to do with the corpse you were looking for?"

"It does," I said, then as I took my shirt off, I explained a bit about the case. It all sounded a bit ridiculous. Finally, I confessed, "You're right. The insurance company wouldn't pay the claim. The money came from me."

He eyed me up and down, asking, "How much money?"

"A thousand dollars."

"Take your pants off and tell me how you came by a thousand dollars to give away. Did you steal it?"

"I did not." I said, holding up my pants which I'd undone, completely forgetting about my shoes.

"I'm glad of that," he said, then bent on one knee to untie my shoes and slip them off. "Now tell me how you came by the money."

I explained the situation with Edna, forgetting that I'd already told him a bit of it. I was standing there in my union suit, socks and garters. He put my shoes near the door and my pants by the window. He was standing in front of me by the time I got to the picnic.

"That was you? You shot *another* man? And this one *died*?"

My cheeks were hot. I knew I was blushing. I was very nearly poking out of my union suit, as I had a few days before with Hal. This felt different, though. When Seamus noticed, he reached out and took me in his hand. I gasped.

"I did. I mean, he did. Yes. I shot him dead."

"You wouldn't shoot me, would you?" he asked.

I shook my head, barely able to think. I gathered myself, and asked, "'You said I should find one bloke and stick to him.' You meant... you... didn't you? I should stick to you."

"Would you like that?"

"I think I might. One thing though... You don't have a bed."

"Of course, I have a bed."

He stepped away from me, which was both a relief and an agony. He pushed the large closet door, and it spun around. There was a bed hanging from the door. He reached up and unhooked it so he could bring it down to the floor. He came back over to me. Kissing me, he pulled me down onto the bed.

It was surprisingly sturdy.

HISTORICAL NOTE

I began writing *The Pink* in 2013. Like much of my work it's historical, though unlike my other books it takes place well outside my own lifetime. Most of the research for the book was done on the Internet and my sources are too numerous to specifically mention. Image galleries aided with the fashion described, period maps with contemporary street names, and newspapers with current events. I specifically remember consulting a guidebook to Packingtown. I searched but could not find this again. There is a Packingtown Museum in Chicago (www.packingtownmuseum.org) should you be interested in more information about the variety of experience people had there. Another important document was the program for the Armory Show, as well as photos available online, which visited Chicago in the spring of 1913. In case you're familiar with the exhibit and feel the characters' visit too short, you'll note that the exhibit at The Art Institute was much smaller than the exhibit shown in New York.

When writing historically about any kind of queerness, an author must decide how much a character is aware of, communication at the time being much slower than it is today. As an example, Edward Carpenter's *The Intermediate Sex* was published in 1908, five years before the events in the novel. While Carpenter was known to the Bloomsbury set in England and socialized with E.M. Forster, I doubted his work was widely known in the Chicago of the period. There could have been a copy or two floating around the University of Chicago, and I debated including it in my story, but ultimately, I wanted Lewis' journey to be more personal than academic.

Offline, I consulted *The Encyclopedia of Chicago*, which includes a great deal of general information; *The Chicago "L"*, which give the history of the elevated of the period; and St. Sukie de la Crois' *Chicago Whispers*, which inspired the scenes of cruising in red ties on State Street.

As to the Pinkertons, they are most famous for their strike-breaking activities which happened in the late 19th century and again in the 1930s. During the period depicted the Chicago office would have been handling the more traditional detective work I've utilized in this book.

I hope you've enjoyed the story of Lewis Wait.

Year of the Rat

A Mean Season

The Happy Month

A Week Away

IN THE WYANDOT COUNTY SERIES

The Less Than Spectacular Times of Henry Milch

A Fabulously Unfabulous Summer for Henry Milch

The Fall and Rise of Henry Milch

A Winter of Discontent for Henry Milch

OTHER BOOKS

The Perils of Praline

Desert Run

Full Release

The Ghost Slept Over

My Favorite Uncle

Femme

Praline Goes to Washington

Aunt Belle's Time Travel & Collectibles

Masc

Never Rest

Code Name: Liberty

Fathers of the Bride

Sentenced to Christmas

ABOUT THE AUTHOR

Marshall Thornton writes several popular mystery series, most notably the *Boystown Mysteries* and the *Pinx Video Mysteries*. He has won the Lambda Award for Gay Mystery three times. His books *Femme* and *Code Name Liberty* were Lambda finalists for Best Gay Romance. Other books include *My Favorite Uncle*, *The Ghost Slept Over* and *Fathers of the Bride*. He holds an MFA in Screenwriting from UCLA.